# REPRISAL

AN EYE FOR AN EYE, A TOOTH FOR A TOOTH...

MARK DAVID ABBOTT

Copyright © 2020 by Mark David Abbott

All rights reserved.

No part of this book may be reproduced in any form or by any electronic or mechanical means, including information storage and retrieval systems, without written permission from the author, except for the use of brief quotations in a book review.

*For Coral*
*Who provided the beautiful space in which this book was written.*

## DO YOU WANT ADVANCE NOTICE OF THE NEXT ADVENTURE?

The next book is currently being written, but if you sign up for my VIP newsletter I will let you know as soon as it is released.

Your email will be kept 100% private and you can unsubscribe at any time.

If you are interested, please join here:

**www.markdavidabbott.com**
(No Spam. Ever.)

# 1

John leaned forward, reached for his glass, wiped the condensation from the bottom on the paper napkin, then sat back and took a long pull of his Botanist and tonic, licking his lips. Delicious. The hotel made it well, especially after he had expressed his preference for an orange garnish. Ashok, the Indian bartender, didn't even have to be asked now, preparing John's drink as soon as he saw him. With a contented sigh, John placed the glass back on the table.

After the incident in the Oman desert, he and Adriana had taken time out, high in the cool air of Jebel Shams, spending the days walking together along the mountain paths and reconnecting. John told her everything—about his time in India, the murder of his wife Charlotte, and his subsequent revenge. He explained how he got his money and what he had gone through in Hong Kong. Holding nothing back, it was a relief—he felt free, the burden of guilt and secrecy falling away like a snake shedding its skin to be born anew. Adriana listened, asking a question here and there, but never judging. When he finished, feeling years younger and somehow kilos lighter, he waited nervously for her response but needn't have worried. She wrapped her arms around him, gazed into his eyes, and told him she loved him with all her heart and would never leave him. He breathed a sigh of relief and melted into her embrace. In a way, the attack by the men sent by Surya Patil had been a blessing, opening up pathways of communication and breaking down any last remaining barriers between John and Adriana.

After four days, they missed the sea and headed back down to the coast, booking themselves into a beautiful resort just south of old Muscat town, where they lazed on the beach, content in each other's company.

John closed his eyes, the warm rays of the Arabian sun caressing his skin, filling him with well-being. For the first time in a very long time, he felt truly happy.

A drop of water fell on his face and blinking his eyes open, he looked up at the cloudless sky in puzzlement. Not a sign of rain in the vast blue expanse above him. He frowned. In fact, in Oman, it never rained at this time of year.

He shrugged and closed his eyes again, luxuriating in the sun's warmth and the buzz from the gin and tonic.

Again, drops of water fell on him, this time on his face and chest. Hearing a giggle, he opened his eyes, raising his head to see Adriana grinning at him from the poolside, her head just above the pool edge, resting her chin on her arms. Her hair was slicked back behind her, her face and arms deeply tanned, and her eyes were twinkling with mischief, the gold flecks in her hazel eyes sparkling in the sun.

"*Habibi*," she winked.

"It was you!"

Adriana beckoned him over, "Come in."

John smiled, his heart swelling with affection, and shook his head.

Adriana pouted, pulling the corners of her mouth down, then grinned and pushed herself back from the edge of the pool, swimming across to the ladder and climbing out. John studied her over the rim of his Ray-Bans, watching the water stream off her lithe, tanned body as she climbed out of the pool. She reached up and smoothed her long black hair away from her face with both hands, flicking off the excess water. John watched the play of sunlight over her skin, the gentle definition in her arms, the swell of her breasts as she lowered her arms and walked toward him. There weren't many other guests by the pool, but they were all looking at her.

"Pass me a towel?"

John reached over and tossed the blue and white striped hotel towel. Catching it with ease, she wiped herself dry. John shifted on his sun lounger, uncomfortably aware of the visible effect the tall slim woman in the black bikini was having on his body. He sat forward, lips parted, and removed his sunglasses.

"Shall we go back to the room and freshen up?" He followed the suggestion with a wink.

"Mr. Hayes! It's only four in the afternoon!"

John shrugged and smiled.

Adriana leaned forward and reached for his hand, pulling him up off the sun lounger.

"An excellent idea, *habibi*," she murmured in his ear, her lips brushing his earlobe, sending shivers down his back.

## 2

There was a knock on the door, it cracked open a little, and Venkatesh, the servant, popped his head around the door. "Sir?"

"Get out!" roared Surya Patil, throwing his glass at the door. The glass shattered, spreading glass, whisky, and ice across the door and wall.

He stood up and paced toward the window, looking out as the lights came on across the sprawling metropolis, signaling the end of the day.

It had been two weeks since he had answered the call, the video call from that bastard Englishman—the living, bastard Englishman. What had gone wrong? The mercenaries had come highly recommended, and when he met Bogdan, the man seemed capable. He was ex-French Foreign Legion for God's sake! How the hell had John Hayes survived?

And what was worse, Hayes now knew Surya Patil had sent the men after him.

Surya thought back to that call. He had been shocked to see John Hayes looking back at him from the phone screen, but when Hayes had threatened him, the shock had changed to anger,... followed by an overwhelming feeling of dread.

Powerless to discover what had happened and unable to contact Bogdan, he had packed his bags and fled Dubai for the safety of his home in Bangalore. Since coming back, Surya hadn't been able to settle, making excuses for not attending government business, sleeping badly, and seeking solace in bottles of whisky. But enough, was enough!

Leaning against the window frame, he stared out at the darkening sky. A pair of fruit bats, their wingspan over a meter across, flapped lazily across his line of sight, but he didn't notice, his mind whirring away.

What was he doing, cowering alone in his study? He was Surya Patil, leader of the Progressive People's Alliance and one of the most powerful men in Karnataka State. Taking a deep breath, he straightened, thrusting out his fleshy jaw. He would not live like this. He was in control, and no man would get the better of him. There was no way that bloody foreigner could enter the state without Surya Patil finding out—nothing happened in this state without him knowing. He had connections everywhere. The police were under his control... and so was the criminal underbelly.

Surya turned, walked to the sideboard, picked up a fresh glass, and poured himself another large whisky, foregoing the ice this time. Knocking it back in one mouthful, his eyes watered as the spirit burned his throat, then poured himself another.

"Venky!" he bellowed, using the diminutive of his servant's name. Enough self-pity, it was time to act.

The door cracked open, and a nervous-looking Venkatesh looked inside. "Sir?"

"Clean up this mess,"—Surya nodded toward the broken glass and liquid on the floor—"and bring me my phone."

# 3

Detective Inspector Rajiv Sampath tugged down on his uniform tunic, adjusted the buttons, then tapped gently on the door with the knuckles of his right hand.

"Enter."

Rajiv opened the door, walked in, noticing three of his colleagues already in the room, and nodded at the man sitting at the large wooden desk taking up the rear of the office.

"Sir."

"You're late."

"Yes, Sir, sorry, Sir. I was out when the call came in. I came as soon as I could."

Senior Police Inspector Basavraj Muniappa scowled and opened a manila file on his otherwise empty desk.

Rajiv nodded and smiled at the other men standing with him, raising a questioning eyebrow, but the others just shrugged. Rajiv looked back at his boss. It must be serious to have called all the department heads in at the same time.

S.P.I. Muniappa made a show of looking through the file before closing it and leaning back in his chair. Steepling his fingers over his large belly, he studied them one by one over the rims of his gold-framed reading glasses, the angle of his head multiplying his chins.

"I've called you all here today because we've received notice of a possible threat to a senior politician's life. It's serious and credible."

The men looked at each other, waiting for their boss to continue.

"I want you all to be on alert, I want increased patrols, and I want two men posted outside his house."

"Who is it, Sir?" Rajiv asked.

Muniappa fixed his gaze on Rajiv. "Our esteemed minister, Surya Patil*ji*."

Rajiv raised an eyebrow. Esteemed?

"I have put in a request to Delhi for Z class security, but until that comes through, the responsibility is on us," Muniappa continued. "Understood?"

"Yes, Sir." The men answered in unison.

"Good. Now, sort it out among yourselves how to handle it. I don't need to remind you how supportive Patil*ji* has been of the police force, and given that his home is within our station's limits, we must take special care."

Muniappa turned to the constable, standing to attention beside him and nodded. The constable stepped forward and from another manila folder, passed a photo and a sheet of paper to each of the officers in turn.

"This is the man we are looking for. The details are all there." Muniappa stabbed a fat finger at his own file. "Patil*ji* has received a threat to his life from this man."

Rajiv looked down at the photograph pinned to the fact sheet in his hand, and his heart sank.

"I've notified our colleagues in the C.I.S.F., and they are keeping watch at the airport. Patil*ji* believes this man to be very dangerous and resourceful. So, all of you be alert."

All except Rajiv replied, "Yes, Sir."

Muniappa turned to stare at Rajiv. "Understood?"

Rajiv didn't hear him, instead still staring at the photo in his hand—John Hayes. What the hell was going on?

"Rajiv!"

Rajiv snapped out of it and looked up. "Sir?"

"Do you understand?"

"Yes, Sir."

Muniappa nodded. "Stay behind, I want a word." He looked at the others. "The rest of you can go."

"Sir." Rajiv's colleagues stood to attention then as one turned for the door, beating a hasty retreat, leaving Rajiv standing alone in front of the desk. No one enjoyed being the focus of the senior inspector's attention.

Muniappa waited until the door closed, his eyes on Rajiv. Once the door clicked shut, he stood and walked around the desk, stopping in front of him, his face just inches away. Rajiv could feel his breath on his face, the smell of stale spice and unbrushed teeth irritating his nose.

"I know you recognize this man. I know the history. I don't want any screw-ups. Do you understand me?"

"Yes, Sir."

"You're doing a good job here, Rajiv, and if you handle this properly... who knows?" Muniappa shrugged. "There could be a promotion in it for you."

"Thank you, Sir."

"But if there are any mistakes..."

"Yes, Sir. I understand, Sir."

"Good." Muniappa nodded toward the door.

Rajiv set his mouth in a mirthless smile, turned on his

heel, and left the room. He returned to his office and slumped back in the chair, the photo of John on the desk in front of him. Shaking his head, he let out a long exhalation. What the hell was John up to now?

# 4

John lay, staring at the ceiling, Adriana's head resting on his arm, her leg draped over his as she dozed, drained after their lovemaking. The early evening light filtered through the sheer curtains as he ran his fingertips down her back. He felt her stir, then her head moved, smiling as her soft, moist lips nuzzled his cheeks.

"You were snoring."

Adriana raised herself up onto her forearms and looked down into his eyes, grinning. "I didn't hear a thing."

John smiled wider and raised his head up to kiss her. "I love you."

"Then why are you sad?" she asked, tilting her head to one side and tracing the line of his top lip with her fingertip.

John sighed and looked away. He didn't want the past to intrude on their small moment of bliss, but it had to be dealt with, eventually. He gazed back at her, studying her face, her tanned skin with the sprinkling of sun freckles across her nose. Looking into her eyes, he marveled again at the play of light in the hazel and gold of her irises, even in the low light.

"I don't want this to end, but I have to deal with what

happened in the desert and make sure it doesn't happen again."

Adriana's face grew solemn, and she drew her lips together. She looked down at his chest, her finger tracing a path from the base of his throat, down and across his chest, then up to his shoulder.

John waited for her response, watching the myriad of emotions playing across her face.

She looked up. "I know." She shivered and rolled over, pulling the sheet up to her chin and gazed up at the ceiling. "When?"

John sat up, swung his legs off the bed, looking across the room. He reached down for the swimming trunks he had discarded on the floor and pulled them on, then paced across the room to the window. Pulling the curtain aside, he stared out across the deep blue of the Gulf of Oman. In the distance, a fishing trawler made its way back to port, a trail of sea gulls flying behind it. Pink tinged a solitary cloud in the sky as the sun descended toward the horizon.

John turned his head and looked back over his shoulder at Adriana, who was sitting up.

"I think the sooner, the better." He turned fully to face her. "I want to begin the next phase of our lives together without the threat of someone coming to hunt me down." He looked down at the floor, sighed, then raised his head, his eyes moist. "I want to spend the rest of my life with you, Adriana, knowing we are safe and can grow old together."

"You've still not said when."

"I don't know." John shrugged and let out a long breath of air. "I'll need to plan, make some calls, but... I think by the end of the week?"

"How will you do it?"

John walked across the room and dragged a chair close

to the bed. He sat down, leaned forward, and took her hand in his, stroking the back with his thumb.

"I don't know. I still have to figure it out." He raised her hand to his lips and kissed her fingers.

Adriana watched, a tear forming in the corner of her eye. "It..." Her voice caught, and she looked away. "It will be dangerous?"

John looked up, noticing the emotion in her voice, her hand still held to his lips. He nodded and watched the tear trickle out of her eye and roll down the side of her face.

"Promise me you'll come back?"

John nodded.

"Say it."

"I promise," John murmured as he looked directly into her eyes.

Adriana forced a smile, then laid back, and with her free hand, she pulled back the bedsheet.

"Then come back to bed. There's no time to waste."

John gazed down at her, and despite the emotion, the sadness, the fear of losing her, he smiled.

## 5

John stopped, bent double, his hands on his knees as he sucked air into his lungs, his thighs trembling. Straightening up, he shook the tension from his legs. Behind him, a trail of footprints on the otherwise untouched surface of the beach glistened in the early morning sun. He had just finished his tenth sprint, and his legs were finished. Once his breath returned to normal, he lowered himself to the sand and did a max set of press-ups until he could no longer raise himself off the sand, his arms and chest quivering.

John prided himself in maintaining a reasonable level of fitness but had upped his activity in the past week. He still hadn't worked out what he would do with Surya Patil but wanted to be physically ready. Standing, he walked over to where he had left his flip-flops and water bottle in the sand and sat down. Taking a long swig of water, he gazed out across the glass-like surface of the bay. It was still cool, but beads of sweat ran down his face. Grabbing the hem of his t-shirt, he mopped them away and thought about what lay ahead. Visualizing a map of India in his mind's eye, he pondered how to get into the country without alerting the authorities. He was sure Surya Patil, with his political connections, would have alerted authorities to be on the lookout for him, so he couldn't fly directly into Bangalore, the security in the airport second to none. The minute he presented his passport, alarm bells would ring, and the next thing John knew, he would find himself in a prison cell... or worse. He could try flying into another city, but it was still risky. That left arriving in India by sea or land. John didn't like the sea route, it would take too long, but overland didn't give him many options either.

He couldn't go via Pakistan, the two countries coexisting in a constant state of tension with border controls among the tightest in the world. China was similar, and as a foreigner, he wouldn't be allowed anywhere near the border on the Chinese side. That left Bangladesh, Bhutan, or Nepal. John took another sip from the bottle and watched as a black-and-white oystercatcher alighted at the water's edge and strutted along the beach, its head bobbing up and down as it searched for food.

Bangladesh would be difficult, India patrolling the border constantly to prevent illegal immigration from the country. Bhutan was possible, but if John remembered correctly from when he and Charlotte had planned a trip, visas were restricted for foreign passport holders, and itineraries had to be specified in advance.

Which only left Nepal. It was an easy country to get into, used to many foreign visitors, and shared an open border with India. In fact, Indians had visa-free entry to Nepal and could drive in and out with ease.

He screwed the top back on the water bottle and stood up.

Yes, that was how he would do it, and he already knew

someone who could help him.

# 6

Thapa checked the timer beside the French Press; only twenty seconds left. He took a paper cup and a plastic lid from the shelf behind the counter and set them down. The timer beeped, and Thapa slowly pressed the plunger, his experienced eye observing the color of the coffee. Satisfied, he poured it into the cup, popped on the lid, placed a stirrer and a sachet of brown sugar on the counter, and called out, "French Press, Single Origin, takeaway for Jacob."

A tall westerner in a business suit looked up from his phone, then walked toward the counter. "Thank you." He picked up the cup, slipped the phone into his jacket pocket, scooped up the stirrer and sugar in his spare hand, then pushed his way out the door.

Thapa grinned and looked over at Celia, who was busy at the espresso machine.

"People are always in a hurry in Hong Kong. What happened to sitting down and spending time, enjoying a nicely brewed cup of coffee?"

"Why are you complaining?" Celia replied as she frothed a jug of milk. "It's good for business."

"That's true." Thapa shrugged as his phone vibrated under the counter. He looked down and frowned. Not a dialing code he recognized. Wiping his hands on the cloth tucked into his apron, he picked up the phone.

"Hello?"

"Thapa?"

"John!" Thapa broke into a wide grin at the familiar voice. "How are you? Where are you? I don't recognize the number."

"I'm good, Thapa. I'm in Oman."

"Oman?"

"Yes, my friend, but tell me, how are you? How's the café going? Business good?"

Thapa looked around the cafe. The tables were full, and two customers were waiting at the counter for takeaway coffee.

"I can't complain, John. Business is booming."

"That's good."

Thapa could hear the smile in John's voice. John Hayes was a good man. Thapa had known him for almost three years now, first as a regular customer. But when John got into trouble, major trouble, Thapa, along with his father, Tejpal, had helped him out. The shared danger and consequent financial rewards had formed a bond between them. John later enlisted Thapa's help with rescuing the family in Bangladesh. He wondered if John was in trouble again. He seemed to have terrible luck.

"How's your dad doing?" John continued.

"He's well, John. I'll tell him you called."

"Thank you."

Thapa sensed a hesitancy from John's end, so he asked,

"Is something wrong, John?" He heard a sigh on the other end.

"Yes, Thapa, I'm going to need your help again."

Thapa pursed his lips and looked around the cafe, "Just give me a minute, John." He cupped his hand over the mouthpiece and called out to Celia, "I have to take this, Celia. Look after everything, will you?"

"Sure, boss."

Thapa stepped around the counter, pushed open the door, and stepped out onto the street, narrowly missing a group of Chinese tourists shuffling past, staring at their phones. He waited, then walked down the slope and stopped in an empty doorway three shops down. A passing taxi honked impatiently in the road, and covering his ear with one hand, he brought the phone up to the other.

"How can I help, John?"

# 7

"Have you got everything?"

Adriana checked her passport and boarding pass, then nodded. She looked up at John.

"Are you sure I can't come with you?"

John smiled and pulled her close. He kissed her forehead, then pulled her head to his shoulder.

"It's better I do this alone," he murmured as he stroked her hair.

Adriana pulled away and gazed up into his eyes, "Promise me, Mr. Hayes, you will be careful."

"I promise."

"I..." she gulped and looked away. Looking back, she said, "I don't want to lose you."

"You won't." John gave her a smile and squeezed her arms. "When is your interview?"

"Thursday."

"You'll do well." John nodded. "I'll be back before you know it, and you can tell me all about your new job."

Adriana smiled, but it didn't reach her eyes, which were

moist with tears. She swallowed again, not taking her eyes off John.

John turned his head and listened to the announcement over the airport intercom. "That's your flight. Last call." Leaning forward, he kissed her on the lips.

"I love you."

"I love you too, John. Be careful."

"I will." John guided her by the arm toward the gate. "And good luck with the interview. I know you'll rock it."

Adriana nodded, looked down at her boarding pass, then back at John.

"Come back soon."

John winked, struggling to control his emotions.

"Go, or you'll miss it."

Adriana turned and walked to the gate. John watched as she handed over her boarding pass, then walked toward the air-bridge before turning and waving. Forcing a smile, he waved back, then watched her disappear around the corner. He closed his eyes and exhaled slowly. He didn't want to be apart from her, but there was no way he could risk taking her to India. It was too dangerous. What he had to do, he had to do alone.

Opening his eyes, he glanced at his watch. Still an hour before his flight to Kathmandu. He walked over to the window and watched as the air-bridge disconnected from the plane, and the Emirates flight to Lisbon prepared for departure. He would be much more relaxed, knowing Adriana was safe in Lisbon while he was pursuing Surya Patil. Fortunately, the newspaper, Publico, had offered her a job, a job she had always wanted, after seeing her work on the human trafficking scandal in Thailand. John, although sad to be apart from her, was happy she would have something to occupy her mind while he was away.

As the plane pushed back, he turned and looked around Dubai's busy Terminal Three, bustling with travelers from all over the world. He joined the flow of people thronging the main thoroughfare and considered his next steps. Thapa had once again been very helpful and put John in touch with one of his uncles in Kathmandu, who promised to help. John hadn't spoken to him yet, but Thapa assured him his uncle would provide John with any assistance he needed. The first thing was to find a way across the border into India without alerting immigration officials or the police. John had researched and had a couple of ideas, but until he was on the ground in Nepal, he wouldn't know which ones would work.

Spying an optician's shop, he paused and looked in the window. An advertisement for colored contact lenses caught his eye and gave him an idea. He walked inside and bought two boxes of blue lenses, slipping them into his carry-on. He glanced again at his watch. Time for a quick drink in the lounge before the flight.

## 8

Detective Inspector Rajiv Sampath looked over the report from his men. He had doubled patrols in Shivnagar and stationed two constables outside Surya Patil's house in twelve-hour shifts. It was a long time to be standing outside his house, but Rajiv couldn't spare any more manpower. He was reluctant to divert resources away from the more important task of fighting crime just so a politician could sleep soundly at night. A politician who, if rumors were to be believed, deserved to be put away for corruption, instead of being protected by the police. Rajiv sighed and slid the report onto his desk. The sooner Delhi approved the Z Class security, the better. That would mean four NSG Commandos, known as "Black Cats" and another eighteen policemen. Then he could take his own men off the job, wash his hands of the responsibility, and go back to his real work.

He pushed his chair back, swiveled, and gazed out the window. A crow alighted on the branch of the Peepal tree and looked back at him, cocking its head from side to side before deciding it had better things to do and flying off.

Rajiv couldn't understand what was going on. Patil had reported a threat from John Hayes, but it made little sense. Rajiv had heard nothing from John for years and thought, after the death of his wife and John's departure from India, he would never hear about him again. Just one more unsolved case in the pile of files, rotting away in the back room of the station... until last month when Patil asked for his file.

The request had troubled Rajiv, and eventually, he sent a warning message to the last known email address he had for John. He liked John and deep down, felt John—if it had been John who carried out the vigilante style killings of Charlottes' alleged murderers—had done the right thing. Rajiv believed in the law, but sometimes, he couldn't enforce it—particularly, when men like Patil were involved. It frustrated Rajiv, causing many sleepless nights. It went against everything he believed in, everything he had trained for, but the reality was, John would never have got justice any other way.

Rajiv hadn't heard back, didn't know if John had received the email, or if anything had happened, but it was strange that a month later, Patil was warning of a threat from John. He hoped John was okay but was duty bound to carry out his job, and if that meant protecting Patil, he had to suck it up and continue. He swiveled back to face his desk and reached for a file from the ever-growing pile on his desk. Enough time had been wasted thinking about Patil. Time to get back to the real work of catching criminals.

## 9

The driver of the white S Class Mercedes honked as he sped down the street, then pulled up abruptly outside a large, four-story house, waiting for the gate to slide open. In the rear of the Mercedes, hidden behind black tinted windows, Surya Patil watched the police constable jump up from his plastic chair, fumble with his bamboo *lathi*, and stand to attention. Patil cursed under his breath and shook his head. He didn't understand how an overweight and sleepy policeman with a wooden stick could protect him. Delhi must approve his Z Class security soon and send him some Commandos to watch the house.

The Mercedes pulled inside as the gate slid to a close behind it, and Patil waited for the driver to open his door before getting out. The problem was, the new Government was cracking down on the abuse of ministerial privilege and cutting back on who was allowed the security. In Delhi, ministers still drove around in convoys with guards armed to the teeth, but they didn't think a minister in the southern state of Karnataka was so important. Patil clenched his jaw and looked over at the two men lounging beside the gate.

They noticed him looking in their direction and straightened up, trying to look alert. Patil shook his head in exasperation. When he asked the party for men who could handle themselves, they sent him these two thugs. Thugs who wanted to advance in the party but were too lazy to make any effort. They were big and rough and had a reputation for meting out rough justice at party rallies, but bullying poor, undernourished villagers was easy. Whether they could handle a man like John Hayes was another matter. Still, he sighed, it made him feel better to have a few more eyes watching the house, and if nothing else, these men were loyal. They had to be; they were unemployable anywhere else.

Surya walked inside the house, handed his bag to Venkatesh, kicked off his shoes, and slipped on a pair of house flip-flops.

"Venky, is Madam home?"

"*Ji*, Sir. In her room, Sir."

Patil sighed and rubbed his face. His relationship with his wife had been bad before Sunil's death, but now, it was non-existent. They slept in separate rooms and never spoke. She was barely home, preferring to be out spending his money in the fancy boutiques of Bangalore and Mumbai or abroad in Dubai and Singapore. When she was home, she holed up in her room, avoiding him completely. What happened to the young girl from the village he had fallen in love with?

"Bring me a drink. I'll be in my study."

"Yes, Sir."

"And Venkatesh."

"Sir?"

"Don't forget ice."

"Yes, Sir." The servant turned and scurried off to the kitchen.

Patil climbed the stairs to the first floor, paused outside the closed door to his wife's bedroom. He raised his hand as if to knock, then thought better of it and continued along the corridor to his study. Flopping down in the overstuffed leather armchair, he put his feet up on the footstool and closed his eyes. Sunil's death had been hard on both of them, but it wasn't his fault, and he couldn't understand why she seemed to hold him responsible.

There was a knock on the door, and Venkatesh walked in, carrying a silver tray with a cut crystal glass, an ice bucket, and an unopened bottle of Black Label.

"Shall I pour for you, Sir?"

"No, I'll do it. Leave me."

"Sir?"

"What is it?"

"Something to eat, Sir?"

"No, now get out and leave me alone."

Venkatesh nodded and backed away, slipping out the door quietly.

Patil reached forward, opened the bottle, and poured three fingers of whisky into the glass. He grabbed a handful of ice and dropped it in, then sat back in his chair, the glass resting on his stomach. It had been his first day back in the *Vidhan Sabha*, Karnataka's state legislature since he had returned from Dubai, and it had been a long but important one. There had been a lot of maneuvering, negotiating, and deal making to get his latest bill passed. Months of hard work, diplomacy, promises, and backroom deals to get it through, but now that it had passed, it promised to make him and his supporters a lot of money. He should celebrate, but he couldn't relax, the thought of the bloody foreigner threatening him constantly in his mind. Normally, he wouldn't worry—he was untouchable—but the man had somehow defeated two ex-French Foreign legionaries in Oman. He couldn't afford to underestimate him again.

Opening his eyes, he took a long drink of the whisky, holding it in his mouth, savoring it before swallowing. He felt the amber liquid warm his throat, spreading into his chest. Taking another sip, he felt the tension easing away.

He knew just what he needed to cheer him up. He would pay a visit to Maadhavi later.

## 10

The flight from Dubai to Kathmandu arrived just after midnight, and despite being only a little over four hours, John was happy to get off. It had been a long day, and the flight was full, so he was keen to stretch his legs. After disembarking, he completed the arrival card and joined the long, snaking queue of tourists applying for the Visa on Arrival. There were plenty of other foreigners among the Chinese and Indian tourists, so John was confident he wouldn't stand out, and sure enough, the Immigration Officer stamped his passport with a thirty-day visa without even looking up. Thirty days would be more than enough for what he had to do. John only had a carry-on, the bulk of his belongings left with Adriana, so he wasted no time exiting through the green channel and out into the arrivals hall. He scanned the line of waiting drivers for a sign with his name on it but couldn't see anything. Frowning, he checked his watch. Thapa had said his uncle would meet him at the airport. He checked again, then not seeing his name walked past the drivers into the main hall. He looked around and noticed a man staring at him. The man looked down at his phone, then slipped it into his pocket and approached John, his hand outstretched.

"Mr. John?"

"Yes."

The man smiled, his face lighting up in a big display of white teeth and laugh lines. "I am Tamang, Thapa's Uncle."

"Hello, Tamang." John shook his hand. Tamang was small, not much more than five foot six or seven, but he was stocky and broad shouldered, looked fit, and his handshake was firm with a strong grip. John instantly liked him.

"How did you recognize me?"

"Thapa sent me a photo." Tamang looked at the bag in John's hand. "No more luggage?"

John smiled. "I travel light."

"Okay." Tamang grinned again. "Please come, my car is waiting."

John followed him through the crowd to the exit door and into the night air. It was cool outside, but the air held the familiar smell of smoke and dust John had experienced in Indian cities. Tamang led him to a double-parked Toyota Hi-Ace, opened the passenger door for John, then walked around the front and climbed into the driver's seat.

A string of colored Buddhist prayer flags stretched the width of the windscreen, and in the middle of the dashboard, a brass statue of the goddess *Maa Kali*, a small garland of flowers wilting at her feet.

"Are you tired, Mr. John?"

"Please, just John, and yes, a little."

"Then don't worry, Mr... ah, John. My home is not far from here. About twenty minutes."

John smiled. "It's okay."

Tamang started the engine and pulled away from the

curb. Glancing over at John, he gestured toward the glove compartment.

"There is a local SIM card in there for you."

"Thank you, Tamang." John reached forward, opened the glove box, and removed it. "Please let me know any expenses, and I will cover them."

Tamang honked as a pack of stray dogs ran across in front of them.

"Don't worry. Thapa told me you have been very good to him, and I was to look after you. You are my guest... John."

"Thank you." John settled back in his seat, the packet containing the SIM resting in his lap, and gazed out the window as the streetscape rushed past. He and Charlotte had never made it up to Nepal during their time in India, but it felt so familiar—similar architecture and street scenes, but disparities too, little things like names and the script on the signboards. The cars were different, too, more Japanese cars among the Indian models on the road.

Traffic was light, and they pulled up outside Tamang's home in less than the twenty minutes he had originally indicated. John stepped out and looked around at the quiet, unremarkable suburban street. Two- and three-story homes lit by the amber glow of the streetlights lined each side, and a dog curled up in the middle of the road, raised its head, regarded them for a moment, then tucked its head back into its legs, and went back to sleep.

"Please come," Tamang led him across the small concrete front yard, past a battered Vespa and a row of potted begonias, and pushed open the front door. "Welcome to my home."

John stepped inside and looked around at a modest-sized living room, furnished with carved wooden chairs. A display cabinet sat against one wall, housing various knickknacks, and on another wooden cabinet sat a large television shrouded with a plastic cover.

Tamang watched John shyly and visibly relaxed when John smiled.

"You have a nice home, Tamang."

"Thank you, John. Are you hungry?" Tamang gestured toward the staircase. "I will wake my wife and ask her to prepare some food."

"No, no. Please don't disturb her. I ate on the plane. I'm happy to go to sleep. You must be tired as well?"

"Are you sure, John? No formalities."

John walked over and put a hand on Tamang's arm. "I'm sure, Tamang. Thank you." He smiled. "Now show me where I can sleep, and we'll get better acquainted in the morning."

## 11

John sat on the single bed, kicked off his boots, and sighed. He felt alone, already missing Adriana. They had spent so much time together recently, it felt strange she wasn't with him. Still, it couldn't be helped. There was no way he could involve her in what he would do next. He looked at his G-shock and made a quick mental calculation. It was just after nine p.m. in Lisbon. He took the phone from his bag and removed the cover. Taking out the Dubai SIM card, he swapped it for the Nepal SIM Tamang had given him and waited for a signal. Once connected, he dialed Adriana's number. It took a while to connect, then rang four times before she answered.

"Hi, John."

John smiled at the sound of her voice, and his eyes teared up.

"*Habibi*. How did you know it was me?"

"Who else will call me from a foreign number? You made it?"

"Yes. How was your flight?"

"Good. Comfortable. Yours?"

"It was okay. This is my number for a few days. You can call me anytime."

"Okay." There was silence for a moment. "I miss you."

John rubbed his face with his spare hand. "I miss you too, but it won't be long."

John heard a sniff, then she replied, "I hope so."

"When is your interview?" he asked although he already knew the answer.

"The day after tomorrow."

"And you're staying with your parents?"

"Yes, I'm heading there now."

John nodded, forgetting she couldn't see him. "That's good. They'll be pleased to see you."

"Yes."

There was silence again, the distance and the emotion making the conversation stilted and awkward.

"John?"

"Yes, my baby?"

"Be careful. I don't want to lose you."

John's chest ached, and he gulped. Composing himself, he replied, "Neither..." He swallowed to clear his throat, "Neither do I. Don't worry. I'll be with you in Lisbon before you know it."

"I hope so."

"I'll let you go now. It's very late here, and I want to start early. I love you."

"I love you too, John."

"Goodnight."

"Goodnight."

John ended the call, then wiped a stray tear from his cheek. Turning off the phone, he lay back on the bed and stared at the ceiling. He had a big task ahead of him, and it wouldn't be as easy as he made out to Adriana. He didn't know what he would do, but above all else, he had to make it back alive. Closing his eyes, he held a picture of Adriana smiling in his mind's eye, and within a minute, he was fast asleep.

## 12

Despite John's best intentions, it was after eight before he woke. Rubbing his eyes, he looked around, trying to remember where he was before realization struck him. Sliding off the bed, he looked down at the clothes he had slept in. He would need to do some shopping today. Walking through to the small, attached bathroom, he filled a bucket with hot water before stripping off. Squatting down beside it, he used a small plastic jug to pour hot water all over him and scrubbed away the smell and grime from the previous day's travel. Feeling refreshed, he changed into a fresh shirt and underwear, slipped back into his cargo pants, then stepped out into the hallway, making his way downstairs. The smell of spices mingling with incense filled his nostrils. Reaching the ground floor, he followed his nose into the dining room where Tamang was reading the newspaper.

Tamang looked up as John entered and greeted him with a big smile.

"Good morning, John. Did you sleep well?"

"I did, thank you." John returned his smile.

Tamang waved to the chair opposite him. "Please." He turned toward the open kitchen door. "Mira?"

A tiny lady, large gold hoop earrings framing a round happy face, her hair tied in a long black plait, appeared in the doorway.

"John, this is my wife, Mira."

John joined his hands together in front of his chest. "Namaste."

Mira smiled shyly and nodded, then retreated to the safety of her kitchen.

Pulling out a chair, he sat down as Tamang folded his newspaper and placed it to the side.

"You must be hungry."

John grinned. "I am. Something smells delicious."

Mira walked out and placed a bowl of potato soup and a plate of spiced chickpeas in the center of the table, and John's mouth watered. She returned with a plate of *puris*, the deep-fried unleavened bread eaten by both Nepalis and Indians.

"Please start, John." Tamang took a *puri* and started spooning the potato soup into a small bowl. "I'm also hungry, and Mira makes the best *puris* in Kathmandu."

Mira smiled, gave Tamang a playful slap on the shoulder, and said something in Nepali that made him chuckle.

John helped himself, his stomach growling at the sight and smell of the food. He hadn't realized how hungry he was. Breakfast was followed by a cup of hot, sweet, and milky *chai*. Finally full, John wiped his mouth with a paper napkin and pushed his chair back as Mira cleared the table.

He was keen to get started but wasn't sure how much he could ask of Tamang and had been wrestling through the whole meal about how to broach the subject. He needn't have worried.

Tamang wiped his fingers clean on a paper napkin and cleared his throat.

"Thapa told me you needed help? That you need to get into India undetected?"

"Yes." John breathed a sigh of relief. "Do you have any ideas?"

"I do." Tamang sat forward in his chair. "I've been giving it some thought since Thapa called me. One second." He stood up and left the room, returning a moment later with a folded map. Spreading it out on the now empty table, he pointed at a spot on the map.

"This is Kathmandu." He slid his finger down the map. "And here, Birgunj, where you would normally cross by road into India."

John nodded, moving around the table, so he could see clearly.

"The problem is everyone crossing here is checked. If you are Indian, it's no problem, but as a foreigner, you will have to go through the passport control."

"I prefer not to do that."

"Yes, I thought so." Tamang nodded and studied John's face for a moment. He pursed his lips and studied the map before continuing. "There are some other places where you could slip across the border, but as a foreigner, someone will notice you, and there is a risk they could report you. A small risk but a risk, nonetheless."

John frowned and chewed on his lip. He wasn't sure how far Surya Patil's tentacles reached, wasn't even sure he had access to Immigration officials, but he wasn't prepared to risk it. If he could get into India without being recorded, it made things easier, reducing his risk of detection.

"So, what do you suggest?"

Tamang slid his finger to the right. "Here."

John leaned forward and peered at the map.

"Sandakphu. Have you heard of it?"

John shook his head, still peering at the map.

"It's a very popular trekking route that crosses the border from Nepal to India. Many, many foreigners do this trek. If you cross here, you won't be noticed."

"But there must still be a border checkpoint?"

"There is." Tamang posted at a small town. "This point here at Pashupatinagar is the main crossing point from Nepal, but that too is monitored." Tamang slid his finger to the north. "But see here."

John leaned closer and looked at what appeared to be an empty area with a small road running through it.

"This is all jungle. You can cross here, near the village of Jaubari, avoid the checkpoint, and join the trekking path. You will already be in India. That's the Singalila National Park in India. Once you reach the end of the forest road, you'll be safe. The forestry officials will assume you are one of many tourists trekking in India."

"What do you think?"

"I like it," John replied, nodding slowly. "How do I get there from here?"

"You can go by road, but it will take over fourteen or fifteen hours. Or..." he pointed at another town. "You can fly here. Bhadrapur. It's only a fifty-minute flight. You can go there by road and cross the final part on foot."

"When are the flights? Every day?"

Tamang grinned. "Five times a day, John. Five times a day."

"Good." John straightened up. "That's how I'll do it. But first, I need to do some shopping."

## 13

"What do you mean you don't have the budget?" Surya Patil growled into the phone. "Every minor Bollywood star is driving around with commandos and armed police."

He heard a sigh on the other end of the phone.

"Surya*ji*, I'm sorry, my hands are tied."

"Your hands are tied! What rubbish. I'm a State Minister!" Surya shouted, his blood pressure rising. "I don't think I need to remind you where you came from. I helped you when you were nothing. Just because you're now home minister, doesn't mean you should forget the people who helped you on your way up."

"Surya*ji*, please calm down. I haven't forgotten you, but the instruction is coming from Delhi." The home minister paused and lowered his voice. "Look, I can't give you Z. No one is getting Z right now. The PM has an eye on the ratings, and there's been too much publicity about the so-called VIP culture. There's nothing I can do. But..."

"But what?" Surya gripped his phone with white knuckles.

"I can get you Y for now, then let's see in a couple of months when the media fuss dies down, we'll try to up it to Z."

Surya closed his eyes and tried to remember what Y Class Security was. If he remembered correctly, it was eleven personnel, including two black cat commandos.

"Surya*ji*, is that okay?"

Surya sighed and scratched his head, the grip on his phone relaxing. "I don't have a choice, do I?"

"It's not that bad, and I give you my word. When the climate is right, I'll approve an increase in security for you."

Surya wasn't listening. He was calculating. He could supplement the eleven armed guards with some of his own men. He nodded to himself. It would do. He was confident there was no way John Hayes could get through a cordon of armed guards. It was more a blow to his ego that the PM's flunkies in Delhi didn't think him important enough to award him the top level of security. Bloody cricketers and starlets were driving around in convoys, accompanied by commandos armed to the teeth, and he, Surya Patil, the Lion of Karnataka, wasn't important enough. He ground his teeth.

"Surya*ji*?"

Surya grunted, ended the call, throwing the phone down on his desk, and rubbed his throbbing temples. He had woken up in a good mood, Maadhavi's scent still lingering on his body, his loins still tingling from the previous night's activities, but the call had put paid to all that.

"Venkatesh," he bellowed.

He drummed his fingers on the desk as he waited.

"Sir?"

"Coffee!" he demanded without looking around. He

reached for the phone and scrolled through the address book. He needed to mobilize more men.

## 14

John stepped back quickly as a motorbike, heading the wrong way down the one-way street, narrowly missed running over his toes. He waited as Tamang locked the van and slipped the keys into his pocket, looking at John with a big grin.

"So, John, do you want real gear or fake?"

John looked down the street at the myriad stores and signs advertising trekking equipment, tattoos, massages, and cheap boarding houses. He shrugged and looked back at Tamang.

"I just need to look the part." He glanced down the street again. "How cold will it be?"

"At this time of the year, not too cold. You can get away with a fleece and an outer shell. Maybe a down jacket for the evening." Tamang looked down at John's feet. "You already have boots, but you'll need a pack and maybe a trekking pole. Some thermals if you are worried."

"That'll be enough. I don't plan to be at altitude for too long, and once I'm in India, it will be much warmer."

"Then follow me. My friend has a shop where you'll get everything, and he'll give you a good price."

John smiled and allowed himself to be led down the street, ignoring calls from shopkeepers and street vendors. He was glad he was with Tamang. The number and variety of goods available were overwhelming.

Five minutes later, John found himself in a tiny shop down a side street, lined floor to ceiling with down jackets, fleeces, sleeping bags, and everything else you could think of. There were items from all the major trekking brands, some seemingly genuine, some with their misspelled names, obviously not. Tamang explained to the shopkeeper what was needed, and after sizing John up with an experienced eye, the shopkeeper started pulling clothing down from the racks and shelves. John examined a down jacket emblazoned with the logo of a well-known mountaineering brand.

"Is this genuine or a copy?"

"It's a copy, John, but a good one," Tamang replied. "Half the price of the original but the same quality. This is a China copy." Tamang shrugged. "Probably from the same factory as the original."

"Amazing."

Fifteen minutes later, John and Tamang stepped onto the street, a backpack filled with trekking clothing slung over John's shoulder and a collapsible trekking pole in his hand.

"That was much cheaper than I thought."

"You're lucky you're with me, John," Tamang replied, his teeth flashing in a wide grin. "Most tourists would pay double what you paid, even after haggling."

"Thank you, Tamang." John patted him on the shoulder. "I appreciate your help."

John spied a pharmacist across the street. "One minute, Tamang. There's something else I need."

John crossed the street and entered the shop.

"Yes, Sir?"

"Do you have hair color?"

"Yes, Sir, this way, please."

John examined the colors available, picked up a couple of packets, and after paying, joined Tamang outside on the road.

"Just one more thing, Tamang. I need to find a money changer."

"What currency do you need? You can get Nepali Rupees from any ATM."

"No, I need to carry a lot of cash. Rupees will be too bulky. Do you know anyone who can give me U.S. dollars?"

Tamang grinned. "Follow me."

## 15

Rajiv's phone buzzed on the desk, and glancing at the screen, he frowned. A Dubai number. He thought fast. Who did he know in Dubai? No one. Unless...

Picking up the phone, he stood and walked over to the door to his office, glancing down the corridor before closing the door. Walking back to his desk, he answered the phone and raised it to his ear.

"Hello?"

"Rajiv, my friend."

"J..." Rajiv recognized the voice but stopped himself from completing the name. "How are you?"

"I'm well, thank you." There was a pause on the other end. "I wanted to thank you for the head's up last month."

"Hmmm. Was it needed?"

"It was, unfortunately."

Rajiv said nothing, waiting for John to continue.

"Are you in the office?"

Rajiv glanced toward the door. "Yes."

"Okay."

Rajiv heard John breathing on the other end of the line.

"What's the weather like there?"

Rajiv frowned and thought for a moment, not sure what he meant.

"Ah... it's fine but... something tells me a storm is on the way." He sighed. "What have you done?"

"Nothing yet," John replied. "I'm sending you something. It will explain everything."

"Okay." Rajiv chewed his lip. "I'm sorry, but you know I can't help you."

"I know." There was silence. "I just wanted to say hello to an old friend and... give you some information that might help you understand things."

"That's kind of you, but..." Rajiv rubbed his face. "There's nothing more I can say."

"I know."

Rajiv listened to the silence at the end of the phone, a million thoughts racing through his mind.

"I don't know what the future holds, but... be careful."

"I will."

The line went dead, then a moment later, a message arrived from the same number.

Rajiv opened it and looked at the screen. It was a photo of a news clipping from the Times of Oman. Rajiv enlarged the screen and read the headline. *Man invades desert camp and kidnaps tourist.*

Rajiv frowned and read on. Thirty seconds later, he slumped back in his chair and dropped the phone on his desk. Swiveling around, he stared unseeingly out the window.

"Shit."

# 16

John removed the back of the phone and popped the Dubai SIM out into his hand, replacing it with the Nepalese SIM. Maybe he was paranoid, but he didn't trust anyone and wasn't willing to give clues about his current location. Rajiv was a good man, but he was still a policeman, and John had no way of knowing what side of the fence Rajiv would end up on.

John waited while the phone booted up, then scrolled through to Adriana's number and pressed dial. He waited a few minutes and broke into a smile at the sound of her voice.

"Hi."

"Hi, John. Are you okay?"

"Yes, my baby. All good." He sat on the edge of the bed. "And you?"

He heard a sigh at the other end. "I'm good, but... I miss you, John. And I worry about you."

John bit his lip and nodded. "I know, but don't worry, it will all be over soon." He changed the subject, eager to keep her mind off things, "How are your parents?"

"Good. Happy to see me."

"That's good. What does it feel like to be home?"

"I had forgotten how much I miss the food here."

John chuckled. "You mean it's better than Thai food?"

"No... not better... different."

John smiled as he heard the tone of her voice lighten.

"You know what I mean. The food you grew up on still feels special."

John shook his head, "I grew up on English food. I have no idea what you mean." He heard a chuckle at the other end.

"That's a good point. When you come to Portugal, when... this is all over, I'll show you what you've been missing."

"I look forward to it." John paused, reluctant to get back to the serious business. "Hey, I'm going to be on the move for the next few days. I'm not sure when I'll be able to call again, but don't worry. I'm not doing anything dangerous. I'm just crossing over into India and will be in areas with no cell coverage."

"Okay." The line went silent for a while. "How are you doing that?"

"Don't worry, I have someone helping me. A friend. It's straightforward, but it will take some time."

"Okay."

Adriana didn't sound convinced, so John elaborated. "I'm walking across the border in a well-known hiking area. There's nothing to worry about. It's just, there will be no signal, so I didn't want you to worry."

"Okay, but John, be careful, and call me as soon as you can."

"I promise. And good luck with the interview tomorrow."

"Thank you."

"I love you, don't forget that."

"I love you too, John."

"I'll call you soon. Take care."

"Goodnight, John."

John ended the call and dropped the phone on the bed. He clenched and unclenched his fists, his eyes moist, then took a deep breath. Everything would be fine. The sooner he dealt with Patil, the sooner he would be sitting in one of Lisbon's cafes with the woman he loved. No sense in getting sentimental. He had to focus on the task at hand. Tomorrow would be an early start, and he needed to rest. Kicking off his shoes, he laid back on the bed, still fully clothed, and closed his eyes. Despite the underlying stress, he was asleep in minutes.

## 17

John stood at the curb, his newly purchased backpack on the footpath beside his feet, and held out his hand,

"Thank you, Tamang. I'm grateful for all your help."

"John, it was our pleasure." Tamang grasped John's hand in both of his and grinned. "Thapa told me you have been good to him, and that's enough for me."

"I'm not sure when I'll see you again, Tamang, but I'll never forget you." He pulled Tamang closer and embraced him, then let go and hoisted the backpack onto his shoulder.

"John, you have my number. If you need anything, please let me know."

"I will."

"Look..." Tamang looked down at his feet, searching for the words before continuing, "I don't know what you are doing, John. I don't want to know, but... be careful."

John clasped Tamang's shoulder with his right hand and

grinned. "Don't worry." He winked. "I'll send you a postcard."

He squeezed Tamang's shoulder, then turned and headed for the terminal entrance. Once inside, he looked back to see Tamang still standing at the curb beside his illegally parked van and raised his hand in a final goodbye before heading toward the check-in counter.

Check-in and boarding were fast, the flight only half full, the plane a small, twin-engine ATR with seating for about fifty passengers. The window seat beside John was empty, so he slid over to get a view of the Himalayas as the plane made its short forty-minute hop down to the town of Bhadrapur. As the plane made its final descent, John closed his eyes and rested his head back against the headrest, mentally running over the next steps in his plan.

Experience had taught him not to think too far ahead—the task would be daunting—so he just ran through the next few steps. He needed to find transport to take him into the mountains to the small trekking village of Jaubari. It was three and a half hours in the wrong direction, but hopefully, John could slip across the border near there undetected.

Jaubari lay on a major trekking route, straddling the border between India and Nepal and terminating at the Sandakphu Peak. It was popular among both Indian and Nepali trekkers and frequented by many foreign tourists as well. John was comfortable he would blend in, and Tamang had assured him the border was ill defined and very open. John had studied the route with Tamang and was confident of success. But one step at a time; no point in stressing about what might happen or about things not in his control.

His thoughts wandered to Adriana, and he smiled, the vision of her face filling him with warmth. He couldn't wait to see her again, but until the threat of Surya Patil was dealt with, he knew he would always be looking over his shoulder.

The seatbelt light chimed off, and he opened his eyes as the plane reached the terminal. He took a deep breath and stood, joining the other passengers in the aisle. Time to find that transport.

## 18

His pack secured on his back, John walked out of the terminal and immediately regretted wearing a fleece. Bhadrapur was at a lower elevation than Kathmandu and much warmer. He stopped, shrugged off the backpack, and removed his fleece, tucking it into the flap of the pack where he could retrieve it easily. He glanced around for the taxi queue and joined the line. The first two drivers turned him down, only wanting trips into town. Just before he asked the third driver, a man standing nearby asked him where he wanted to go.

John explained, and the man thought for a bit before naming a price. After two minutes of haggling, they agreed, and the man reached for John's backpack. John shook his head and smiled. He had no idea if the man was genuine or not, so he wasn't about to hand over the bag. Holding his money, phone, and passport, it would stay with him. The man shrugged, gestured for him to follow, and led him across the road into the carpark. He walked back a few rows before stopping beside a battered Maruti 800, a tiny Indian made hatchback that looked about twenty years old.

Climbing into the driver's side, he leaned across to open the passenger door for John. Reaching through, John unlocked the rear door and dropped his pack on the rear seat before climbing in beside the driver. The driver directed a quick prayer to the brass statue of Buddha glued to the dashboard before starting the engine. He grinned at John and asked, "Okay?"

John nodded and grinned back. His knees were up in his chest, the seat belt wasn't functioning, and he was pretty sure the tires on his side had no tread. Hopefully, the driver's side was better. If he made it through this journey, tackling Surya Patil in Bangalore would be a piece of cake.

# 19

Approximately four hours later, the car pulled into a village and stopped. John opened his eyes and glanced over at the driver. He had kept conversation to a minimum, wanting to remain as anonymous as possible, and despite the cramped interior and the lack of air conditioning, he had dropped off to sleep.

The driver smiled at him and said, "Jaubari."

John blinked the sleep from his eyes and looked around. They were on a single street, lined with concrete and stone houses under rusted corrugated tin roofs. Some were shabby and decrepit, others freshly painted with window boxes filled with flowering begonias. A Yak stood to one side, its tail flicking lazily side to side while on the doorstep of the closest house a long-haired dog, its white fur discolored with grime, dozed in the last patch of sun before nightfall.

John reached into his pocket, counted out the fare they had agreed on, and handed it over, adding a bit more, much to the driver's delight.

"Thank you, Sir, thank you." He jumped out of the car

and ran around to John's side, removing the backpack as John climbed out. Stretching his legs and his back, John shivered in the crisp air, the temperature much cooler than on the plains. Reaching for his backpack, he removed his fleece, quickly donning it before shaking the driver's hand.

"Thank you."

The taxi driver grinned, then climbed back into his car. John waited until the car had completed a three-point turn and headed back the way it had come before shouldering his backpack and setting off along the street. It was too late in the day to cross the border, so he needed a place to stay.

Three buildings along, he spotted a sign which simply said, "Trekkers Lodge." It looked as good as any, so he pushed open the door, bent down to enter the low doorway, and stepped inside. The interior was dark and smokey, the only light from some dirty skylights set in the roof and the warm glow of a cooking fire in the kitchen at one end. A couple of empty bench tables filled the rest of the room, and the walls were lined with shelves, piled high with an unusual mixture of trekking gear and pots and pans. A group of men sat near the fire, and as John entered, a young man stood and smiled.

"Welcome. Do you need a room?"

"Yes, please." John smiled back as he slipped his backpack off his shoulder. "Just for the night."

"Shared or single?"

"Single, please. It has a bathroom?"

"Yes, of course."

"Hot water?"

"We will bring you a bucket, Sir."

"Fine, thank you." John looked over at the other men who were watching with interest. They all appeared to be locals, with the tanned and weather-beaten faces of men who spent their life outdoors. He turned back to the young man. "How much is the room?"

"Six hundred rupees, Sir."

"Good, I'll take it."

The young man beamed. He grabbed a dog-eared notebook from where it rested on a pile of woolen socks and hats, which were presumably for sale, although it wasn't immediately obvious. Opening the book, he asked John to fill in his details. John took the pen and hesitated. He didn't want any written record of his movements, although judging by the state of the register, it looked unlikely to see the light of day. Paranoid? Maybe. He looked over at the young man, who had turned away and was rummaging through a drawer, and took a gamble, filling in a fake name, address, and passport number. Closing the book, he removed a wad of rupees from his pocket, counting out six notes and handing them to the man in exchange for the key he had found in the drawer.

The man opened the book and glanced at what John had written.

John tensed.

"Hello, William. I'm Tej." He waved toward the front door. "Go outside, turn right, and the rooms are at the bottom of the steps to the right."

"Thank you, Tej." John pocketed the key and picked up his pack. He turned for the door, hoping to leave before Tej asked for his passport, but he needn't have worried. Tej had already turned away to sit by the fire again. John exhaled the tension and walked outside to find his room.

The accommodation comprised several single rooms, running off a long corridor on the level below the kitchen. The walls were plywood, the floor bare concrete, and the door was secured by a flimsy hasp and padlock. John unlocked his room and stepped inside, bolting the door behind him. He dropped his pack on the double bed, which filled most of the tiny room, a window in the far wall providing views down the valley. At one end, a door opened into the bathroom. John pushed it open to see the toilet, the slatted wooden platform, and a plastic bucket that made up the bathing area. It was basic but clean. He unfolded the thick woolen comforter on the end of the bed, and spread it out, kicking off his boots, and sitting down before checking his watch. His stomach growled with hunger, but it was still too early to eat.

Removing the paper map Tamang had provided from his pack, he unfolded it, running his finger over it until he found Jaubari. He traced the route he would need to take the next morning, committing it to memory before folding it and putting it back in the pack. The route was straightforward, and judging by the lodge owner's lack of interest in his documentation, it should be easy to cross over into India. However, the thought didn't stop the pellet of nervousness from growing in his belly. He lay back on the bed and closed his eyes, but couldn't relax, thoughts racing through his head. After a few minutes, he gave up and sat upright, slipping his feet back into his boots, lacing them loosely, and stood. If his mind wouldn't rest, he may as well eat something.

John stepped outside, climbed the steps onto the street, and shivered. The temperature was dropping fast, and he debated returning to his room to add another layer, but hunger got the better of him. Pushing open the door to the lodge dining hall-cum-reception, he walked inside. It was busier than when he left, and John nodded at a group of trekkers occupying one of the tables. He glanced over at the other table and stiffened when he saw four men in the black uniforms of the Nepalese police, playing cards, but they paid him no attention. In front of each of them was a large bamboo mug, and judging by the glow on their faces and their laughter, the contents were alcoholic.

"William, the room is okay?"

John almost looked around to see who Tej was speaking to but caught himself in time.

"Very good, thank you, Tej. Can I get something to eat?"

"Of course. Fried noodles, rice?"

"Rice, please, and..."—John nodded toward the cops' table—"what's that?"

Tej's face widened in a grin. "*Tomba*! You will love it."

John looked around for a space as far from the cops as possible and sat down. He unzipped his fleece—the room warmed by the cooking fire—looking around. The trekkers ignored him, too involved in their own conversation, and the cops remained engrossed in their card game.

Tej reappeared and placed a bamboo mug in front of him. It was filled to the brim with some sort of grain, a thick, steel straw standing in the middle of it.

"You have to wait."

"Wait?" John asked.

"Yes, wait for at least ten minutes before drinking, and don't stir it."

John frowned, "What is it made of?"

"Don't worry, William." Tej smiled. "It's good for you. It is fermented..." He searched for the word in English. "Millet. It will make you feel warm inside."

"Okay." John nodded. "It's alcoholic?"

Tej grinned and slapped John on the shoulder. "You'll see." He walked back to the kitchen and said something to the men sitting in front of the fire. They all looked toward John and laughed.

John pulled the mug closer and noticed one of the policemen watching him. His breath caught until the policeman raised his own mug in acknowledgment and smiled. John nodded, exhaled, and smiled back. Reaching for an old copy of National Geographic, he pulled the rechargeable solar lamp closer and leafed through the magazine while he waited for his drink to be ready.

By the time John had finished reading about the Okavango Delta, Tej had placed a plate of fried rice in front of him together with a jar of round red chilis.

"Be careful with these, William. They are very spicy." He pointed toward the drink. "Have you tried it yet?"

John shook his head.

"Try it now. It's ready."

John leaned forward and took a sip through the straw as Tej looked on in eager anticipation. It was slightly sour and warm, and immediately, John felt a warmth spread through his body. He looked up.

"It's good, thank you."

"I told you. Let me know when you finish, and I will refill it with hot water."

"Thank you." John took another sip, then made a start on the fried rice, ignoring the jar of chilis. Ten minutes later, his plate was empty, and he was feeling a definite buzz from the *Tomba*. Tej walked over with a flask and poured hot water into the mug of grains.

"Wait another five minutes before drinking again."

John nodded and smiled, one eye on the policemen who had finished their card game and were standing. They looked fit and slightly menacing in their black para-military uniforms. Three of them walked toward the door while the fourth walked over to John's table.

John tensed, avoiding direct eye contact. He had a

genuine visa and was legally allowed in Nepal, but he wanted to avoid attention wherever possible. He reluctantly looked up when the policeman was standing directly in front of him.

The cop smiled. "Welcome to our town. I hope you are enjoying the *Tomba*?"

"Yes, thank you."

"Very good. If you need anything, please come and ask us. Our station is just up the street." He held out his hand.

John reached forward and shook it. "Thank you."

The cop let go of his hand and turned unsteadily toward the door, stopped, and looked back. John clenched his teeth. The cop raised a hand.

"Goodnight."

"Goodnight," John nodded and forced a smile as he watched the cop make his way out the door. He breathed a sigh of relief, reached for his drink, and took a long draw of the hot sour liquid. Ten minutes later, confident the police were back in the station, he left a handful of rupees on the table and stood. The room tilted, then righted itself, and John blinked his eyes rapidly. The drink was deceptively strong. He raised a hand in Tej's direction, then headed toward the door.

Stepping outside, he took a few deep breaths of the crisp cold air, zipped up his fleece, and looked up at the sky. A blanket of stars filled the dark space above him, and just above the horizon was the beginning of a new moon. The stars remained clear for a second, then started moving around. John shook his head. He had better get to bed before he fell over.

## 20

John woke early, the rays from the dawn sun streaming through the flimsy curtain onto the bed, bringing the promise of warmth after the cold night. John rubbed his face and peeled off the heavy blanket, sitting up. He felt surprisingly fresh with no trace of a hangover after the evening drinking *Tomba*. That stuff was great.

There was a light tap on the door. He slipped his feet into his unlaced boots and walked over to the door. Unbolting it, he looked out into the corridor, but there was no one there, just a red plastic bucket filled with hot water, the steam spiraling up into the cold air. John grinned and brought the bucket inside. Perfect timing.

Washed and dressed, he looked around the room one last time to make sure he had left nothing behind, then shouldered the backpack and left the room. He climbed the steps up to the road, the air still crisp, the vapor from his mouth visible with every breath, then entered the dining hall.

Tej was already busy over by the kitchen, acknowledging

John with a raised hand. Two other trekkers nodded a greeting, then went back to staring into their mugs of tea. John dumped his pack by the door and found a table by himself.

"Good morning, William." Tej appeared by his side and placed a flask on the table.

"Good morning." John nodded at the flask. "Coffee?"

"Tea."

"Oh..." John failed to hide his disappointment. "Ah... Can I get something to eat?"

"Of course, eggs? Omelet?"

"Thank you. An omelet will be perfect, Tej."

Tej smiled and returned to the kitchen area as John reached for the flask and poured some into a mug. Blowing on the top to cool it, he took a sip. He pulled a face and put the mug back on the table and pushed it away. He had never been a fan of tea, especially milky and sweet. John stood up, walked over to his backpack, and removed the map, then sat back down and spread it on the table. He had already committed the route to memory, he just wanted to make sure. The route was simple, most of the trekking route comprising a rough road which ran through thick rhododendron forest along the border between India and Nepal. Most trekkers started in India in the small town of Maneybhanjang and followed the road through a series of small settlements until they reached the peak of Sandakphu in Nepal. John would be walking in the opposite direction and hoped he wouldn't attract too much attention.

John looked up as Tej walked over with a plate of omelets and pushed the map to one side to make space.

"Going to Sandakphu today?" Tej asked. "It's a good day for it."

"Yes," John lied. "Will I reach it by evening?"

"Easily, William." Tej glanced over at the other trekkers

then lowered his voice. "You look fit. It will be easy for you. Some of the other people who come here..." Tej shrugged.

John smiled and slid the plate closer.

"Do you have somewhere to stay in Sandakphu?" Tej continued.

"No, I haven't booked anything yet. Will it be a problem?"

"Then you stay at my friend's place, Everest Lodge. Ask for Batsa, tell him I sent you."

"Thank you, I will." John cut into the omelet and took a bite. "Mmmm, this is good."

Tej looked toward the door as another group of trekkers walked in, chatting noisily. He glanced back at John and smiled.

"Enjoy."

Twenty minutes later, breakfast finished, bill paid, and farewells given, John stepped out onto the road and looked up and down the street. The dirty white dog from the day before stretched and yawned, then lazily crossed the road, looking for the nearest patch of sun. High in the sky above, an eagle circled slowly as it climbed the updrafts. The street was quiet, the air still cool, but the cloudless sky above heralded the heat later in the day.

John adjusted the straps on his backpack, then pulled up a mental picture of his route. Left led up the trekking route toward Sandakphu Peak. He needed to go right into India. He took a step forward and stopped. Shit! From the doorway of another homestay further up the street stepped out a man in the now familiar black uniform of the Nepalese police, looking in John's direction. It was the friendly policeman from last night. John cursed under his breath, fixed a smile on his face, and raised his hand in greeting. He thought fast, then slipped off his pack and got down on one knee as if adjusting the laces on his boot. He didn't want the policeman to see him heading in the wrong direction. From the corner of his eye, he watched the policeman head up the street before disappearing between two buildings. John breathed out a sigh of relief, stood up, slipped the backpack back on, and headed toward the Indian border.

## 21

The route took John along a partially sealed road as it wound its way along the contours of the ridgeline. Sheep and yaks heavily grazed this area, and the grass was cropped short and burned brown by the sun. Further from the road, the slopes descended into a thick, green rhododendron jungle, the beginnings of the glorious blooms of red just starting to make their presence shown. In another month, the slopes would be blanketed in a canopy of red flowers. It felt good to be outside, breathing fresh, clean air. Still a little too early for trekkers to have reached his part of the route, he was alone in his thoughts, just the sound of birdsong from the grasslands and the occasional call of a bird of prey from its perch in the jungle. John crested a small rise and paused for breath, soaking in the beauty.

Across a series of valleys, he could see the Indian town of Darjeeling, famous for its teas, and beyond it, the peaks of Bhutan emerging from the clouds. He turned to his left and gazed at the sacred mountain of Kanchenjunga, far off in the Himalayan range, its series of five peaks glistening in the morning sun. Further behind it, he caught his first glimpse of Everest, just visible between wisps of clouds and blinked to make sure he wasn't imagining it. John moved to the edge of the track, slipped off his backpack, and sat down, content to drink in the glory of nature spread out before him. He was alone, with only the backpack and its contents, but at that moment, he needed nothing, all thoughts of the grim past and his uncertain future forgotten. He felt truly happy.

After a while, thoughts crept back into his head, and he remembered why he was there. Standing, he brushed off his pants, picked up his pack, and continued on his way.

Just under an hour later, still not seeing another human, a small wooden signpost in front of a cluster of untidy buildings announced he had reached the village of Tumling.

He was in India.

## 22

Rajiv stepped out of the police Bolero and walked across the road toward the line of white SUVs parked outside the palatial Shivnagar home of Surya Patil.

A group of uniformed policemen, perhaps eight or nine of them, filled the footpath, and two fit men in black combat uniforms stood separately to one side of the gate. At the sight of their boss approaching, Rajiv's two constables jumped up from the plastic chairs they had been lounging on and snapped to attention. Rajiv nodded and approached the two men in black.

"Detective Inspector Rajiv Sampath. Who's in charge here?"

One of the men stepped forward, smiled, and held out his hand. "Captain Ankit Sharma, Special Ranger Group Twelve."

"From Hyderabad?"

"That's right."

His handshake was strong, his forearm corded with muscles and tendons.

"This is my second-in-command, *Subedar* Rahul Ahuja."

"I'm happy to see you, Captain." Rajiv returned his smile as he shook the hand of the other commando. He gestured toward his two nervous constables. "My men don't have the experience to deal with something like this."

Captain Sharma followed the direction of his gesture and nodded. "Don't worry, we'll take it from here. My men are very capable. You can relax."

"Yes, I've worked with you guys before. I have every confidence in you." Rajiv turned to his constables. "Go back to the station, freshen up, and report to my office in half an hour."

"Sir." The two men visibly relaxed and rushed off before Rajiv could change his mind.

Turning back to the commando captain, he asked, "How many men do you have?"

"There are eleven of us. Three vehicles. A normal Y Class detail." Ankit paused and studied Rajiv's face. "How serious is the threat?"

"It's vague." Rajiv sighed and glanced down the street. "Mr. Patil claims his life is in danger. I'll send you the file, but we have little to work on..." Rajiv shrugged and looked back at the captain. "You know how it is. We can't ignore the requests of certain people."

"Say no more. It's not the first time for us. I'm sure it will all die down soon, and we'll be sent back home." He glanced toward the house. "What's he like to work with?"

Rajiv followed the direction of his gaze and thought carefully about his answer.

"Let's just say he's used to getting what he wants."

"The usual then." Ankit turned back to Rajiv, smiled, and held out his hand again. "Don't worry, Rajiv. We'll take it from here."

"Good luck." Rajiv shook his hand, smiled at the other commando, then walked back to his vehicle. Climbing in, he nodded to his driver and leaned his head back against his seat as the vehicle pulled away from the curb. He felt relieved—one less thing to worry about. Now, he and his men could go back to what they were trained for—solving crime instead of indulging the whims of powerful men... at least for a while.

## 23

A little over five hours later, John slipped off his pack, kicked off his boots, and breathed a sigh of relief. He was tired, dusty, and thirsty. From Tumling, he had hitched a ride down into Maneybhanjang with a local guide in his battered Series 1 Land Rover. The road followed the line of the Nepalese border, and it wasn't until John sat down on a local bus heading away from the border town of Maneybhanjang to Siliguri, he felt he could finally relax.

Tamang's plan had been a good one, no one paying John any attention, all assuming he was a regular trekker with all the necessary permits and visas. Despite that, the tension of the day's travel was draining, and he was looking forward to a hot bath and a good meal. In Siliguri, John had found a cheap hostel, shabby and run down, but they didn't ask questions, and when John had slipped the owner an extra five hundred rupees, he had forgotten the need to ask for identification.

Moving to the window, he moved the curtain aside and opened the latch. The sound of traffic honking poured in, and John screwed up his nose at the smell of diesel and dust. He quickly closed it and thought back to that moment on the hillside, breathing the pure air while gazing across at Kanchenjunga and the rest of the beautiful Himalayan range. He sighed. There would be plenty of time to relax when the job was done and Adriana safe.

He looked around the room at the peeling plaster on the walls, the spread of black mold on the ceiling, and the worn and tattered bedding on the narrow single bed. He felt a wave of self-pity rising up and pushed it down. There was no point in feeling sorry for himself. He had a beautiful woman waiting for him, a woman he could look forward to spending the rest of his life with. It wouldn't happen if he felt sorry for himself and failed to deal with the ever-present threat of Surya Patil.

If Patil could hunt him down and send paid assassins after him in Oman, there was no knowing where or when he could do it again. John didn't want to spend the rest of his life looking over his shoulder, always wondering if someone was coming. He had been in worse situations before. A night alone in a shitty hostel was nothing compared to what he had already experienced.

Looking at his G-Shock, he did a quick mental calculation. He knew what would raise his spirits. Rummaging through his backpack, he retrieved the phone and powered it on. He needed to hear Adriana's voice and tell her he had made it safely across the border.

## 24

The elegant woman in the emerald sari sighed and pushed her empty glass across the bar, nodding at the barman.

"Another one, please, Ramesh."

"Of course, Ma'am."

Maadhavi Rao checked the slim, rose gold Cartier on her wrist and ground her teeth together—not long now. She needed that drink. Ramesh placed a fresh martini in front of her, and she gave him a smile that didn't reach her eyes before picking up the glass. She took a sip and nodded with satisfaction. Ramesh fixed a good martini. It was her second of the evening, and she was starting to feel the buzz she craved—the buzz she would need to help her get through the night. She glanced around the bar. Apart from her, it was pretty quiet, being midweek and early evening. A table of foreign tourists sipped on their chilled pints of beer and discussed their day's shopping, and over in a corner, an Indian businessman huddled over a pile of papers with his Japanese clients.

Maadhavi reached for her glass again and thought back

to how she had ended up in her gilded cage. It had started well but, as with so many things in life, didn't end up as planned. Her parents had wanted her to get a degree, and she had, but her heart had been in acting. After honoring her parents' wishes for higher education, she had, much to her parents' dismay, taken acting classes, finally landing a small role in a Kannada film. She had loved it, and when she saw herself on the big screen, she knew she had found her calling. More roles followed, and her fame grew. She bought her parents a new car and moved them into a bigger house, and grudgingly over time, they had accepted her career. As her popularity grew, she was invited to appear at boutique openings and events, where she mixed with the high society and Who's Who of Bangalore.

It was at one of these events she had met Surya Patil.

The thought of him made her tense. She reached for her glass again, taking another big sip, then waved it in the air to get Ramesh's attention. He might as well prepare the next one. She would need it.

Surya had been all charm and graciousness at first—at least as much as he could. He wasn't a refined man, all his wealth and power not masking his village origins, but as a young actress, she had been excited to be in the presence of one of the most powerful politicians in the state. He had told her he was a big fan, had seen all her movies. He showered her with gifts, introducing her to other powerful people. Opportunities that had been closed to her before miraculously opened, and she was grateful. And he wanted nothing in return. She was happy and riding the crest of the wave.

Until that night...

Maadhavi drained her glass and took the fresh one from Ramesh. She took a sip, then breathed deeply. Her heart was beginning to race, canceling out the buzz from the martinis, and she needed to try to relax. Taking another sip, she placed the glass down on the bartop, and stared into the mirror at the back of the bar, almost not recognizing the woman looking back at her.

She still looked the same—had her looks, her hair beautifully coiffed, her makeup understated and elegant—but the woman looking back at her was not the young woman filled with dreams, excited about the future, and happy to be working in a career she had thought about since she was a young girl. There was sorrow in the eyes, the dark circles underneath them requiring more makeup as time went on. Her face looked drawn, the angles in her cheekbones becoming more pronounced. She didn't eat much these days, and of course, the drinking wasn't helping. She couldn't get through the days—the nights—without drinking. She took another sip of her martini. Each day it took more and more of the stuff to get the buzz she craved. She would need a few more before the night was over. A sparkle of light caught her eye, and she reached absentmindedly for the emerald earring dangling from her ear. He had bought it for her on that trip to Dubai—the trip where it all went wrong.

It was supposed to be one of the defining moments of her career—the main guest at the Sudarshan Film Awards. It was her first award, and she had been so eager to accept it and receive validation for the choices she had made. Her parents were so proud, inviting all their neighbors and friends to the house to watch the ceremony on television. She could never tell them what had happened afterward. She could never tell anyone.

## 25

The phone buzzed on the dashboard, and Rajiv reached forward, glancing at the screen. Frowning, he signaled to his driver to pull over.

"Manju, go for a walk."

The constable nodded and stepped out of the vehicle. Rajiv waited until the door closed, then answered the call.

"Hello."

"How are you, Rajiv?"

Rajiv couldn't help but smile at the familiar voice.

"I'm well."

"You read the article?"

Rajiv kept his eyes on the constable standing in front of the Bolero.

"I did." Rajiv remembered what he had read, how a foreign tourist had been kidnapped in a desert camp in Oman. "Your name wasn't mentioned, but I assume the woman means something to you; otherwise, you wouldn't have sent it."

"That's right. I was there. I saved her."

Rajiv chewed on his lip as he watched the constable

attempt to kick a passing stray dog. "You were lucky... but then you always have been."

"I don't consider what happened to Charlotte in Bangalore to be lucky," came the stern reply.

"Yes, of course." Rajiv shook his head and cursed himself for his mistake. He wouldn't wish the brutal gang rape and murder of John's wife on anyone. "I'm sorry... what I meant was..."

"I know."

Neither man spoke as they both dealt with their memories. The constable had wandered further up the road and was standing beside a handcart. The street vendor was frying something, but in the poor light of the streetlamps, Rajiv couldn't make out what it was.

John broke the silence first. "Can you guess who sent the men to kill me?"

Rajiv nodded slowly. "I've put two and two together. There's a man here in Bangalore who has recently increased his security."

"Really? Hmmm."

"Look." Rajiv glanced around the vehicle, then toward his driver again. "I shouldn't be having this conversation, but if you are planning to come here, my advice is don't. It's dangerous, there's a huge amount of security. There are alerts at the airport and the railway stations, and besides... I still have to do my job."

There was silence for a while, and Rajiv thought the line had disconnected.

"J..." he stopped himself from saying the name. "Are you there?"

"That bastard's son raped and killed my wife... and you guys did nothing."

Rajiv grimaced. He thought about protesting but knew

John was right.

"And now, the bastard himself sent not one but two assassins after me." John paused, and Rajiv could hear him breathing down the phone.

"I've found someone, Rajiv. I love her. I have a real chance of happiness again." John's voice rose, and Rajiv held the phone away from his ear a little. "But that bastard had her kidnapped and held hostage."

Rajiv heard John exhale. When he continued, his voice was quieter, much quieter, and Rajiv's brow furrowed as he strained to listen.

"I can never relax, knowing it could happen again. I have to deal with it."

Rajiv nodded slowly, forgetting John couldn't see him and gazed out the window. The street vendor was passing a bag of food to the constable.

"Are you there?"

"Yes, I'm here."

Rajiv sighed. "I'm happy you've found someone. You deserve to be happy."

There was silence for a moment.

"Thank you."

Rajiv rubbed his face with his left hand and took a deep breath.

"Be careful."

"I'm always careful."

"Yes, but..."

"Goodnight, Rajiv." The phone line went dead.

Rajiv stared out through the windscreen, turning the phone over and over in his hand, his mind conflicted. Tossing the phone onto the dashboard, he wound down the window and signaled to his driver to return. He watched the constable approach, a bag made of recycled newspaper in one hand, a half-eaten samosa in the other. The constable opened the driver's door.

"Go back and pay for it."

"But, Sir..."

"Pay for it," Rajiv growled and clenched his fists. It was a dirty world, but wherever possible, he wouldn't be a part of it.

## 26

The lead vehicle in the convoy of cars flashed its lights and barely slowed as the entrance barrier raised just in time for the convoy of vehicles to stream through and pull up outside the front entrance of the Vijaya Palace Hotel.

Three white SUVs, brimming with aerials, flanked the S Class Mercedes, and as the convoy stopped, the doors of the SUVs opened, and men poured out, most in police uniforms, all of them armed.

From inside the Mercedes, Surya Patil waited impatiently, his fingers drumming in irritation on his thigh as the men encircled the car. A commando dressed entirely in black, his face masked, a Heckler and Koch MP-5 cradled in one arm, tapped on the window, and gave him the thumbs up. Surya Patil stared at him, aware the man couldn't see inside through the black tint of the window. He waited for a moment longer than necessary—his little victory, his show of power, letting the men know who was the boss—then opened the door.

It hadn't taken long for the novelty to wear off. At first, it had been a great boost to his ego. Wherever he went, armed men surrounded him, his car followed by SUVs with flashing lights and sirens. It did wonders for clearing Bangalore's notorious traffic, but that was the only benefit. The constant presence of the men was wearing thin, and Surya found himself yearning for more privacy. He ground his teeth together as he stepped out of the car and straightened the jacket of his safari suit. The sooner that English bastard Hayes was dealt with, the better!

Surya strode toward the entrance of the hotel, leaving the commando to close the door of the Mercedes and follow after him. He waved away the hotel security, ignoring their gestures to enter through the metal detector. They should know who he was by now. Metal detectors and standard security measures were for the public, not for a man of his stature. The uniformed hotel doorman swung the entrance door wide open for Surya and his security, but Surya stopped and turned, eyeing the men surrounding him.

"Wait with the cars," he growled

"But, Sir, I'm supposed to accompany you at all times." The commando captain stepped forward. "How will we protect you?"

Surya raised his hand and glared at the man behind the black balaclava.

"I said, wait outside!"

"Sir..."

Surya stepped toward the Commando, their faces inches apart.

"I can have you transferred immediately," he threatened, and turned back toward the door, leaving the men standing in a semicircle outside.

Surya strode across the highly polished marble of the lobby, ignoring the general manager and his staff lined up in front of the reception desk to welcome him, and headed straight for the bar. Alone at last! He needed a drink and a couple of hours with Maadhavi.

## 27

It was after ten before a bone-weary Rajiv arrived home. He stepped inside, closing the front door quietly, and bent down to unlace his shoes, slipping them off, then padded across to the living room in his socks. The television was on, Aarthi asleep on the couch. Bending down, he placed a gentle kiss on her forehead. She woke with a start, blinked her eyes open, and smiled.

"Hi, *jaanu*."

"What time is it?" she asked.

"Late, why don't you go to bed?"

Aarthi stood up and shook her head.

"Have you eaten? Come."

She bustled into the kitchen, wiping the sleep from her eyes. Rajiv sat down at the small wooden table and leaned back against the wall, closing his eyes as familiar sounds carried from the kitchen—the cooking gas being lit, pots and pans moving around, plates being readied.

The events of the day passed before his eyes in fast forward until he reached the call from John. He frowned as he recalled the conversation. John Hayes was a good man, and although deep down, Rajiv knew John had taken the law into his own hands and taken revenge against his wife's killers, Rajiv respected him. He had broken the law, that was wrong, but in reality, Rajiv knew it hadn't been that simple. Rajiv hadn't been able to do his duty, his hands tied because of pressure from Surya Patil, and Surya's son and friends had got away scot free. Rajiv opened his eyes as Aarthi walked out and placed a plate of rice and sambar in front of him. He reached forward for her hand and smiled.

"Thank you."

Aarthi playfully pushed his hand away. "What thank you?"

"No, I mean it. You do so much for me, yet I'm never home." Rajiv stopped, his brow creased, and looked down at the plate.

Aarthi tilted her head to one side and looked at him quizzically. She pulled out a chair and sat down opposite Rajiv.

"What's the matter? A bad day?"

Rajiv looked up and smiled. Reaching for her hand again, he gave it a squeeze and sighed.

"Not really, just that..."

"You know you can tell me anything, Raju," Aarthi said, using the diminutive version of his name she used when they were alone together.

"I know." Rajiv smiled again, but his eyes were sad. "I won't trouble you. It's okay, really. I just need to make some tough decisions in the next few days, and right now, I don't know which direction to take." He slipped his hand free and rolled up his sleeves. "Anyway, it's not your problem. This smells delicious."

"Do you want some chutney?" Aarthi stood and moved toward the kitchen, stopping in the doorway to look back at

Rajiv. "Never forget Raju, I'm always here for you. You can always talk to me... and..."

Rajiv looked up.

"Wash your hands before you eat!"

Rajiv laughed, the worries of the day melting away. He pushed back his chair to wash his hands. Everything would be okay as long as he came home to Aarthi at the end of each day.

## 28

John woke early. He hadn't really slept, the bed hard, and the room full of blood thirsty mosquitos that feasted on him all night. If that hadn't been bad enough, the rush hour started early in Siliguri, and the noise from the traffic in the street outside ensured there was little chance of a lie in.

John lay on the bed for a while, mentally planning his steps for the next few days. The first thing he needed to sort out was transport. Bangalore was at the opposite end of the country, almost two thousand five hundred kilometers away. He couldn't fly, security too high at the airports, so he had two options, the train or by car. The more he thought about it, the more he was leaning toward getting a car. He would need good mobility once he reached Bangalore and wouldn't be able to move around by taxi or Uber for fear of being remembered. He would need his own vehicle. That opened up a fresh can of worms. John rubbed his face and pinched the bridge of his nose. He had cash but not enough to buy a car from a dealer, and besides, the last thing he wanted was his name on any registration documentation. He could steal one, but how would he do that? He had no idea how to hot-wire a car and had heard somewhere, you couldn't do that to a modern car because of the electronics.

Frustrated, he clenched his fists, banging them against the mattress, sending a cloud of dust into the air. His nostrils twitched and about to sneeze, he swung his legs off the bed and stood up, moving away from the dust motes floating above the bed. This whole thing was a stupid idea. Grinding his teeth, he walked over to the window, yanking aside the flimsy curtain that was doing a poor job of keeping the light and the noise out. He scowled at the endless stream of honking traffic flowing past the hostel as people began their day, staring unseeingly at the traffic, negative thoughts flowing through his head.

He should have planned things better. There was no way he would succeed. He would end up in an Indian prison or worse, dead. John gripped the window frame, his knuckles turning white. He clenched his jaw, then closed his eyes and took a deep breath, forcing the dark thoughts back where he had buried them. Exhaling, he relaxed his jaw, loosening his grip on the window frame. He could do it. He inhaled deeply again, feeling the tension leave his body.

Blinking his eyes open, he allowed his vision to roam across the cityscape, scanning the skyline. On the roof of the next building, a lady in a sari was pinning wet clothes to a wire strung across the roof. Further afield on one of the rooftops, two young boys attempted to launch a kite, but it appeared there wasn't enough wind, and they struggled to keep it in the air. Life was going on, and John needed to ensure his did too. His stomach growled. Perhaps if he ate something, his mood would improve. Just as he turned away from the window, something in the middle distance caught his eye, triggering a memory. He smiled slowly, an idea germinating. It might just be possible... but first, breakfast.

## 29

Breakfast improved his mood. After a plate of soft bread and spicy masala omelets, he felt better able to tackle the day. John stepped out of the hostel and found his bearings. Looking up at the building, he worked out where the window of his room was, then calculated where he needed to go. Ten minutes, a few wrong turns, and a couple of near misses with murderous drivers later, he stood in front of a pair of large, rusty, sheet-metal gates, secured by a chain. He peered between the gap in the gates into a yard filled with cars in various states of disassembly. The sound of hammering and grinding carried to him, and blue and white sparks from a welding machine flew into the air. This was the place he had spotted from his room.

John had remembered reading an article somewhere about the thriving trade in the North East of India in stolen vehicles. Vehicles were stripped down for parts, then smuggled across the borders into Myanmar and Nepal. He wondered if this was a place like that. There was only one way to find out.

He pushed one side of the gate, the slack in the chain, allowing just enough space for him to squeeze through sideways and step inside. A thin Alsatian, ribs showing through its fur, went berserk, barking and lunging on its chain. John stepped to one side to ensure he was out of reach. The sparks from the welding machine stopped, and a man squatting on the ground, a pair of dark plastic sunglasses his only eye protection, turned to see what had disturbed the dog. Slipping the sunglasses onto the top of his head, he shouted at the Alsatian and regarded John with a mixture of suspicion and puzzlement. John assumed few foreigners visited the workshop, so he smiled and holding both hands up to appear less threatening, walked toward the man who slowly got to his feet.

"Do you speak English?"

The man frowned and nodded slowly.

John stepped closer. "I want to buy a car."

"No sell." The man shook his head. "Go to showroom."

"No, I prefer not to." John gestured toward the cars in the yard. "I want a car like this."

The man shook his head again, so John reached into his pocket and pulled out a thick wad of dollars.

The man's right eye twitched, but he kept his face expressionless. He studied John, looking him up and down, then looked back at the roll of cash in John's hand. His gaze lifted over John's shoulder toward the gate.

"Wait."

He walked past John, shouted again at the Alsatian, swinging his foot at it, sending the dog scurrying away, then pulled the chain on the gate tight, making sure it was secure. Returning, he said, "Come," and led John toward a building at the rear of the yard.

John slipped the cash back into his pocket and looked around as he followed. Two men were removing a door from a relatively new Hyundai while another taped newspaper to the windows of a Toyota hatchback in preparation for painting.

Inside the building, the man gestured for John to sit, then seated himself behind a grimy desk covered in papers and engine parts.

"*Chai?*"

John glanced at the filthy glasses on the desk and raised a hand. "Thank you, but no. I just had some."

The man sat back in his chair and studied John.

"Who are you?"

John shrugged and pushed out his bottom lip.

"It doesn't matter who I am. I just need a car, and I can't buy one... officially."

The man's eyes narrowed as he nodded slowly.

"Who sent you here?"

"No one. I was walking around looking for..." John paused, thinking of the correct words. "A place like this."

The man said nothing, his forehead lined in a deep frown, studying John over his cluttered desk.

"I think you can help me. I need a car, cheap but reliable. I can pay, but... no papers."

The man held out a grimy hand, the nails black with grease and dirt. "How much?"

John eyed the man. He didn't want to tell him the truth; otherwise, the guy would take everything. He calculated what he might get a stolen car for.

"One *lakh*. A hundred thousand rupees." John thought he should start low but might be able to get something half decent for one hundred and fifty thousand rupees.

The man snorted and withdrew his hand. "No." Shaking his head, he countered, "Three *lakhs*."

They went back-and-forth for a couple of minutes before finally stalling on a price of just under two hundred thousand rupees. The man chewed on his lip, then sat forward.

"Okay. I help you." The man pushed his chair back and stood up. "Come."

He led John back out into the yard to a Hyundai hatchback. It looked brand new, the paint unmarked and glistening in the sun, but the newspaper taped to the windows suggested it wasn't the original coat of paint. John walked around it, checking the exterior and the tires. He paused at the front, noticing the Delhi number plates. They would stick out like a sore thumb down south in Bangalore. He looked up at the man who was watching him.

"What's your name?"

"Rakesh *Bhai*."

"Rakesh *Bhai,* I need Karnataka number plates," John requested. Karnataka was the state Bangalore was located in, and he would need the car to blend in.

"Five hundred rupees for different plates."

John gave Rakesh a withering look.

"But for you, friend, I give for free."

"Good." John moved to the driver's door and opened it looking inside, checking the interior. "She runs well?"

"Like new."

John sat inside and twisted the key dangling from the ignition, the car starting straight away. He gave the engine a rev, then checked the odometer. He had a long drive ahead and wanted to make sure the car would last. It had only done 45,000 kms, so was quite new. Satisfied, John switched off the engine and climbed out.

"I'll take it."

Rakesh *Bhai* grinned, exposing a row of yellowed teeth and held out his hand for the money.

"*Paisa.*"

## 30

Thirty minutes later, John dumped his backpack in the trunk and slammed it shut. He glanced at his watch. He had a long drive ahead of him. Bangalore was over twenty-five hundred kilometers to the south. John guessed, based on experience of India's variable road conditions, he would probably average around fifty kilometers an hour. Fifty hours of non-stop driving would destroy him. He would need to break it into manageable chunks, or he wouldn't be able to function once he reached Bangalore. John rubbed his face and ran his fingers through his hair. He was already tired after a poor night's sleep and wasn't looking forward to the next few days stuck in a car, but the longer he took, the longer he was away from Adriana. Sighing, he climbed into the car, started the engine, fixed his phone into the phone holder conveniently mounted on the dashboard, then with a quick glance at the direction arrow on the GPS, pulled out into the stream of traffic.

## 31

Surya Patil stepped out of the Mercedes as the gates to his compound closed behind it. His security detail fanned out around him, their eyes scanning the house and the windows of the neighboring houses.

"Sir, please let me check the house first," Captain Ankit requested, stepping between Surya and the front door.

Surya waved him away irritably. His temples were throbbing, the aftereffects of the bottle of whisky he had finished last night. This commando captain was getting on his nerves.

"It's my house, it's safe," he growled as he walked toward the door. "Stay outside."

"But, Sir."

Ignoring him, Surya opened the door and stepped inside, closing it abruptly in the captain's face. The previous night hadn't gone as planned. Maadhavi was becoming increasingly belligerent. He couldn't understand her problem. She lived in a suite in one of Bangalore's best hotels and received a generous allowance; he paid for everything. What did she expect? She could at least show some gratitude. She didn't even bother getting up to greet him in the morning, still asleep when he left... or at least pretending to be. He needed to teach her a lesson. He would cut off her allowance, then see how she felt.

Surya kicked off his shoes at the door as Venkatesh approached nervously.

"Sir..."

"Don't bother me now!" he growled.

"But, Sir..."

"Shut up and bring me coffee," he barked at the servant who scurried away quickly to the kitchen. Surya climbed the stairs, the pain in his temples increasing with the exertion. Walking past Malvika's room, he stopped, noticing the door was ajar.

"Malvika?" he called out. He probably should try to mend things with her. They hardly spoke these days—all the love of their younger days had withered away. She blamed him for losing their son, although it wasn't his fault. For some reason, she didn't see it that way and took it out on him.

There was no reply from inside. Frowning, he glanced at the chunky gold Rolex on his wrist. It was still too early for her to be up, she rarely rose until mid-morning... but her door was open? He gently eased the door open wider until he could see in. The bed was made, the curtains open, but no sign of her. He frowned and stepped inside, looking around. In fact, the room looked strangely bare. It was a moment before he realized why. Panic rising in his chest, he rushed to the en suite. All her toiletries and makeup were missing. Spinning around, he rushed to the walk-in wardrobe. Rows and rows of empty clothes hangers hung from the railings, and discarded shoe boxes covered the floor.

His heart sinking, he stepped back until his back hit the wall. She was gone, his Malvika—the girl he had first seen fetching water from the well in the village so many years ago, the girl he had built a life with, who had given birth to his son—had left him. Things had been bad between them for a while, but now... it was actually over. He slid to the floor, tears welling in his eyes, overwhelmed with a sense of devastating emptiness. Malvika, Malvika... He sobbed silently, his body shaking, his lips quivering. Tears ran down his cheeks, his body racked with silent sobs.

"Sir?" Venkatesh called from the hallway.

With great effort, he pulled himself together and pushed himself to his feet, wiping his face with the back of his hand. Gazing around the wardrobe, the sorrow ebbed away, replaced with growing anger. It was all because of that bastard Englishman. First, his son, now his wife.

"Sir?" he heard again.

He grasped his head with his hands, the pain in his temples almost unbearable as a fire kindled in the pit of his belly and rose, consuming him. He clenched his fists, threw his head back, and roared.

"Aaaaarrrrrrghhhhhhhhhh!"

From the hallway came the sound of a tray clattering on the floor, followed by rapidly departing footsteps.

## 32

Captain Ankit Sharma lifted the sling holding his Heckler and Koch MP-5 over his neck and leaned the weapon against the compound wall. He cricked his neck right to left, then stretched his back.

He hated doing VIP protection. The so-called VIPs had no respect for the men who were trying to save their lives. He would much rather be on counter-terrorism duty than protecting corrupt politicians, who, if the truth be known, often deserved to be attacked by disgruntled members of the public. Rubbing his face, he stifled a yawn and looked around. Half the team was guarding the gate and patrolling the perimeter of the house while the other men sat on the ground, leaning against the compound wall, exhausted, trying to catch some sleep. Ankit cursed and ground his teeth in frustration.

After escorting Surya Patil to the Vijaya Palace Hotel, they had sat outside in the vehicles, waiting for him to leave. The son of a bitch had stayed in the hotel the whole night, without the courtesy of telling the men to stand down. They couldn't carry on like this. He had to set some ground rules if they were to carry out their duties properly. Ankit signaled to one of the police officers.

"You, ahh... Rohit, see if you can rustle up some *chai* for the men."

"Sir."

Ankit watched Rohit rush off to the house. He hadn't worked with this particular team of policemen before, but from what he had seen over the last couple of days, they were okay. They knew what they were doing and responded well to his commands, but the reality was, they didn't have the specialized training he and his *Subedar* had, first in the army, then in the Special Ranger Group. How they would respond in an actual attack would remain to be seen, but they made up the numbers, and ninety-nine percent of the time were never actually needed, the threats to their VIP clients often more imagined than real.

He walked across the compound and stood beside his second-in-command.

"All okay?"

"Yes, sir, but the men are shattered."

"I know." Ankit shook his head in frustration. "Last night was ridiculous. If he was going to stay the night in a hotel, he should have advised us beforehand, so we could plan accordingly."

"The driver told me he keeps a mistress in the hotel."

"Well, that explains why he didn't want us to follow him in."

*Subedar* Rahul Ahuja grinned.

Both men turned as the front door opened and watched as Constable Rohit walked out, accompanied by Venkatesh, carrying a tray filled with steel tumblers and a flask. Both men took a tumbler each and took a sip as the other men gathered around.

"Well, I need to have a word with him. We can't have another night like last night if we are to protect him properly."

"Ahhh, Sir..." Constable Rohit spoke up.

"Yes?"

"I don't think now is a good time."

"Why?"

Rohit nodded toward Venkatesh. "He said the boss just found out his wife has left him."

## 33

John pulled onto the service road and turned into the forecourt of the petrol station. The tank was still a quarter full, but he didn't know when he would get a chance to fill up again, and he needed a break. Climbing out of the car, he shook his legs out and folded forward to touch his toes, feeling his spine pop and crack. He straightened up and steadied himself with a hand on the car roof as his vision blurred, and his legs felt weak. Frowning, he stretched his neck side to side and looked around. He needed caffeine and probably some sugar, but apart from the petrol station, there was nothing around—no shops or restaurants, just barren sunbaked fields and the highway with its stream of honking fume-belching traffic.

From the office, a boy stepped out and walked lazily to the pump. John smiled. He must have been only thirteen, but his swagger and the scowl on his face belonged to someone much older.

"Full tank, please."

The boy gave a curt nod and removed the nozzle from the pump while John popped open the filler cap.

"Zero." The boy jerked his head toward the meter. John looked over, confirmed it was zero, and nodded.

John rubbed the strain from his eyes and leaned back against the car as he watched the numbers on the meter tick over. He had been driving for three days, averaging seven hundred kilometers a day, and was exhausted. It wasn't easy driving, the lack of road discipline, the constant threat of wildlife, slow-moving and unlit vehicles, and villagers unexpectedly stepping out into traffic meant he could never relax. He had slept one night in the car and a night in a cheap roadside hostel with a hard bed and swarms of mosquitos. His stomach gurgled, and he looked around for a toilet. Something he had eaten two days ago hadn't agreed with him, and despite keeping his stomach light, he was still paying the price.

He felt tired and weak. Not for the first time, he questioned what he was doing and whether it was all worth it. Then he thought of Adriana and how her smile lit up his life. He wanted to spend the rest of his life with her, so he needed to make sure she was safe—that nothing from his past would come back to haunt them as it had done in Oman. It was definitely worth it. He had to push through the discomfort, the exhaustion, and the potential danger.

The pump clicked off, interrupting his thoughts, and the boy returned the nozzle to the pump stand. John glanced at the meter, then counted out a couple of thousand rupees and handed it over. The boy took them, licked a dirty oil stained finger, and flicked through the notes before stuffing them into his pocket.

"Bathroom *hai kya*?" John asked in Hindi. "Is there a bathroom?"

The boy nodded, waving a hand toward the rear of the office without a word or a smile.

"Thanks." John crossed the forecourt, passing a battered lorry painted in colorful messages and designs, parked to the side. In the shade of the lorry, its driver and his assistant squatted, a pot boiling on a portable stove in front of them. They stared idly at John as he walked past while a stray dog, ribs showing through its hide, watched from a safe distance, hoping for food scraps.

John rounded the back of the office and spotted the half-open door to the toilet. Screwing up his nose, he waved a fly away from his face and peered inside. It wasn't the worst he had used in the last three days, but it was bad. He sighed. He craved a decent bed, a clean bathroom, and twelve hours of uninterrupted sleep in an air-conditioned, mosquito-free room. He looked at his watch. It was early afternoon. John estimated it was another four to five hundred kilometers to Bangalore, so he wouldn't make it by nightfall. Unfortunately, it meant another night of bad sleep, but he didn't want to risk driving through the night. He took a deep breath, gritted his teeth, and entered the toilet.

Five minutes later, John stepped out into the bright sunshine and sucked in lungfuls of fresh air. Wiping his hands dry on his cargo pants, he blinked rapidly as his eyes adjusted to the light. His stomach growled again, and he wondered if he should go back inside although his stomach was definitely empty. Beads of sweat formed on his forehead as he steadied himself against the wall until his vision cleared. Glancing toward the lorry, he saw the men hadn't moved, still watching him with idle interest. He nodded in their direction, then frowned as the two men became four, then two again. He shook his head, blinked again, and started walking toward the car. He needed to finish this journey, get a good night's sleep... and maybe some antibiotics.

Nearing the car, he noticed a man squatting beside it, staring at him. John studied him as he got closer. He was thin, his skin burned black by the sun. His upper body was bare, as were his feet, a single strip of orange cloth wrapped around his waist, and tucked up between his legs. The tangled, matted mass of hair on his head was filled with gray, suggesting advanced age, but the skin on his face was young and supple, and his eyes were bright like a young child's. John had seen men like him before, ascetics who had renounced worldly belongings and wandered the country in search of God, inner peace, or just running away from responsibilities. John had no time for religion and doubted God even existed, but these men who lived their lives without possessions or even knowing where their next meal was coming from had always fascinated him.

John nodded and smiled at the man as he unlocked the car and opened the door.

"You are sick."

John stopped and turned around. The statement had been made in perfect, unaccented English. Studying the man closely, John blinked and shook his head. Was he hallucinating again? The man was still there, staring at John with his bright piercing eyes.

"I'm sorry?"

The ascetic pointed a long bony finger at John's stomach. "You are sick."

John frowned. He wasn't impressed. The man had seen him walk out of the toilet. He was a foreigner. It was an easy guess that his stomach was upset.

The man stood effortlessly, one moment squatting on the ground, the next standing upright as if there was no movement in between. He was tall, matching John in height but very thin, ribs showing through skin stretched tight across his bones. He stepped forward, and John took a step back, hitting the car behind him. The man looked intensely at John, his eyes boring holes into John's.

He reached out his right hand and placed his fingertips on John's stomach. John tried to speak, but his voice caught in his throat. The man's lips moved soundlessly, and John felt a warmth from the man's fingertips. He thought he felt a vibration, a tingling in his organs, but then it was gone. John narrowed his eyes, wondering what the man's con was. Would he sell him some medicine, or did he just want money? The man removed his hand but was still staring into John's eyes. John tried to look away but couldn't. The man's hand moved to his chest.

"You have pain here." The man smiled, exposing brilliant white teeth. "I can't fix that." He dropped his hand and took a step back. "There is more pain coming..." Turning, he bent down and picked up a long wooden staff from the ground. Looking back at John, he winked. "Everything will be okay. Always remember... breathe. *Jai Gurudev*."

John's frown deepened as he watched the man walk away through the shimmering heat haze rising off the petrol station forecourt. What was all that about? Breathe? Nonsense. Everyone breathed. John shrugged. Whatever it was, he wouldn't get closer to Bangalore by standing there, thinking about it. Climbing into the car, he started the engine and pulled out onto the highway.

## 34

John leaned on the cracked and stained sink and stared into the mirror. Ignoring the dark circles around his eyes and the sunken cheeks from three days without proper food, he turned his head, one side to the other, checking each angle. He had to admit, for a first time, he had done a good job. His hair was much lighter, almost blonde, and the beard he had been growing since he left Kathmandu was now reasonably thick, the patchy parts having filled out over the past two days. He frowned at the contrast of the darkness of his beard and his newly lightened hair and tilted his chin, examining it in the different light, then grinned. If Adriana could see him now, she would be horrified.

Throwing the empty packet of hair dye into the bin, he rinsed his hands, then reached over for the packet of colored contact lenses. With difficulty, he slipped the blue-tinted lenses over his eyeballs, then blinking the tears away, stood back to examine the result. Actually, Adriana would struggle to recognize him. It was amazing how subtle changes in hair and eye color could make so much difference. Satisfied, John cleared the bathroom of his toiletries and stepped back into the bedroom. Stowing the items in his backpack, he took one last look around the room to make sure he had left nothing behind.

His stomach gurgled, and he looked back toward the toilet. He wondered whether it was prudent to leave just yet, but his stomach quieted down. He was feeling better than the day before and thought back to the holy man he had met. Had he cured him? Or was it just time and the body's natural healing process? John shrugged. It didn't matter.

Picking up an almost empty plastic water bottle, he drained the contents, then shouldering the backpack, opened the door, peered out into the corridor, and satisfied there was no one there, stepped out. He left the key in the door lock and ignoring the lift, walked along to the stairwell, and jogged down two flights, exiting into the basement. He had paid in cash the night before, so he didn't need to check out and didn't want anyone to see his new look. Walking up the loading ramp into the bright morning sun, he paused for his eyes to adjust and looked out on the street. At the front of the hostel, a watchman sat, drinking *chai* from a paper cup while a boy swept the steps with a grass broom. John turned the other direction and walked briskly down the street and turned the corner. Crossing to where he had parked the car the night before, he threw his pack on the back seat, then climbed in and started the engine. He glanced at his watch. It was eight am, and he had only a hundred kilometers left before he reached Bangalore. Time to get going.

## 35

Surya Patil hadn't left the house for three days. He sat in the darkened room, the curtains closed, and stared at the wall. He and Malvika had been together for well over thirty years. She had been by his side through everything from the days as a junior member of the party to his climb to the top. She had supported him through thick and thin, been the pillar he leaned on, his sounding board. She had accompanied him on the campaign trail, visiting hundreds of villages in rural Karnataka, meeting farmers' wives and their children, and stood beside him on the dais during his speeches. She had always been there by his side.

There was a tap on the door, but he ignored it.

"Sir?"

He didn't budge, showing no sign of hearing anything. He sensed, rather than saw, the door open and heard a tray being slid inside, hitting the tray that had been left the night before. He ignored that too. He had no interest in food or drink.

The door clicked quietly shut, and he looked down at his

hands, turning them over in the dim light, looking at the palms and fingers. His right hand had a tremor he hadn't noticed before. Surya swallowed. Had his whole life been for nothing? His son was supposed to have taken over the political reins, but he had been a failure, interested only in partying and drinking, taking the wealth and power of his father for granted. He had been a constant disappointment, but... Surya forced back the tears... He had still been his son, his flesh and blood.

He was gone, his wife was gone. Surya had no one left. His thoughts turned again to Malvika. Images of happier times flashed before his eyes, although she hadn't been happy for a while. His son's death had ruined any chance of happiness they could have had together. She had retreated into a shell, barely communicating with him, often not even leaving her room when she was home. Surya closed his eyes and leaned his head back against the chair.

It wasn't his fault their son was taken, but she blamed him, and when they fought about it, she brought up other things, things she had been unhappy about for years, claiming their whole married life had been a sham. He leaned forward and dropped his face into his hands, his elbows resting on his knees. Yes, he had affairs, but what did she expect? He was a powerful man, young women threw themselves at him. It was a privilege that came with his status. But she would always be his wife, no one would ever hold that position. Besides, she had been richly rewarded—her bags, her designer saris, the trips to Singapore and Dubai. She never wanted for anything. He had taken her out of the village and transformed her life, yet she still complained about the way he treated her. He rubbed his face, his fingertips pressing into his forehead.

The ungrateful... He would cut her off, shut down all her

cards and accounts, then he would see how quickly she came running back. The thought made him feel a little better. He pushed himself up, stretching his back, his knees creaking as he stood. Yes, that's what he would do.

Surya shuffled across the darkened room to the window and pulled back the curtains, blinking rapidly as his eyes adjusted to the bright sunshine streaming in. As they adjusted, they picked up movement in the garden at the front of the house. He looked down, and his heart sank again as he saw the policemen and commandos moving about on the driveway. He had forgotten about them and that English bastard, John fucking Hayes!

## 36

It took four hours for John to drive the last one hundred kilometers into Bangalore. The traffic as he entered the city on the eastern side was appalling and slow-moving, taking him almost two hours just to cross the city from east to west. By the time John neared the suburb of Shivnagar, he was exhausted and irritable. Traffic in Bangalore had always been bad, but it seemed to have worsened since John had last been in the city, and the roads were in a terrible state.

John's first goal was to find somewhere to stay, somewhere close to Surya Patil's home in Shivnagar. He remembered a couple of small hotels in the nearby suburb of R. T. Nagar. Hopefully, they were still in business and would turn a blind eye to registration formalities if he slipped them enough cash.

As he neared the turnoff for R. T. Nagar, he hesitated—something Rajiv had said earlier, something about increased security. It was nagging away in the back of his mind, and he knew, despite being exhausted, he wouldn't rest until he knew more. Canceling the indicator, he drove straight on before taking the turn at Mekhri Circle. He sat at the signal for what seemed like ages, his fingers drumming a rhythm on the steering wheel until the lights changed, then turned right and took a left into Shivnagar. He didn't need to use the GPS, the layout of the suburb long ago etched into his brain. He followed the gridwork of streets past the large houses and fancy apartment buildings of politicians and captains of industry.

As he neared Patil's street, he could feel his heart racing, his knuckles turning white as he clenched the steering wheel. The memories of that terrible time years before came flooding back, the faces of Surya's son, Sunil, and his friends, looming before his eyes. John pulled over, switched off the engine, and closed his eyes, taking slow deep breaths. He thought he had dealt with the shock and trauma of his wife's brutal assault and the subsequent killings of the culprits, but the long-suppressed emotions were rising to the surface. He had to gain control, or he wouldn't be able to think clearly. He inhaled deeply through his nose, then exhaled slowly through his mouth, willing the negative emotions away. With each inhale, he visualized Adriana smiling back at him, and slowly his heart rate came back under control.

Opening his eyes, he looked at the street, shaded by the ancient flame of the forest trees, their trunks massive, their branches spreading from one side of the street to the other. The scene was calm and peaceful, nothing moving. A large black crow alit on the hood of the car and cocked its head quizzically as it stared through the windshield before hopping across the bonnet in two bounds and down onto the footpath. John took another deep breath, then started the engine before pulling out onto the road.

He took the next left onto Surya Patil's street and drove

slowly, his eyes recording everything he could see. Outside Surya's house was a line of white SUVs with darkened glass and numerous aerials. John frowned. As he neared the gate, he spotted two fit-looking, armed policemen, standing either side of the gate, and through the slightly open gate, he spotted another two uniformed men inside. He turned his head away as he drove past, but from the corner of his eye could see that apart from a cursory glance, the policemen were paying him little attention. He reached the end of the street and stopped, considering his next move. He indicated as if to turn right, then changed his mind. Making a U-turn, he turned back onto the street and pulled into a space on the same side of the road as Surya's house but with a clear view down the street to the gate.

All thoughts of rest had vanished; he was wound tightly like a spring. Despite what Rajiv had said, he had underestimated the amount of security protecting Surya Patil. These men didn't look like the usual sleepy old men who acted as security guards. They looked fit and alert, and the number of vehicles outside suggested many more men inside. He needed to observe, count how many men, and work out a way to access the house.

## 37

"All okay?"

"Yes, Sir."

Ankit checked his watch. "Stand half the team down and get them fed. You too."

"Sir." *Subedar* Ahuja turned away and started issuing commands while Ankit looked on. Satisfied with the arrangements, he walked down the side of the house, taking the narrow path between the house wall and the high wall of the neighboring compound. He rounded the back of the house, catching the single policeman stationed there by surprise. He jumped to his feet and stood to attention, but not before Ankit noticed the still smoking cigarette hidden in his cupped right hand.

"Get rid of that now," he growled.

"Sir." The policeman dropped the cigarette on the ground and stubbed it out. Judging by the pile of butts on the ground, it definitely wasn't his first. Ankit stepped close until his face was just inches away. The policeman averted his eyes.

"Look at me."

The policeman reluctantly made eye contact.

"When you are on duty, I want you alert at all times. Do you understand me?"

"Yes, Sir."

"If I catch you smoking once more, you will be off the job and back in your village before the day is over."

"Yes, Sir, sorry, Sir."

Ankit studied him for a moment longer, then stepped back. Without another word, he turned and headed back to the front of the house. To be honest, he couldn't blame the man. They hadn't moved from the house for three days, and the men were bored. At least they had a place to rest, away from the sun. Ankit had commandeered two of the rooms on the ground floor, but the hours were long and the duty arduous.

Not for the first time, Ankit questioned his choice of job. The training had been challenging and immensely enjoyable. He had extensive practice in firearms and hand-to-hand combat. He was strong and fit. But the anti-terrorist operations had never materialized. Instead, he had spent the better part of his career protecting VIPs and politicians from unknown threats—threats that never materialized. This looked like another one. It was wrong to wish something bad would happen, but he almost hoped for an opportunity to prove his ability, to prove his training hadn't been wasted. He crossed the front garden and slipped through the slightly ajar gate. The two men guarding the footpath snapped to attention.

"As you were."

"Sir."

He glanced up and down the street then turned back to the men. "Anything out of the ordinary?"

"No, Sir."

Ankit nodded. "Good." He glanced back inside again. He needed to be moving, to stretch his legs.

"I'm just going around the block. I'll be back in five minutes."

"Sir."

Ankit paused, adjusted his sling, so his weapon hung more comfortably, then turned left and walked up the footpath. The old watchman sitting outside the next house jumped up from his plastic chair as he approached. Ankit smiled and waved a hand.

"It's okay, Uncle. Please sit."

"*Ji*, Sir." He remained standing.

Ankit continued, stepping over a broken paving slab and glancing over the compound walls as he passed. Some of these homes were enormous, a far cry from the tiny farmhouse he and his two sisters had grown up in back in Jarkhand. Most of the houses were at least three stories and had two or three expensive European cars parked in the driveway. He shook his head. It was an unfair world. Most of his men came from poor, rural backgrounds and worked long hours for hardly any money, protecting people who spent more on dinner than his men earned in a month.

As he neared the end of the street, he sensed a movement inside a parked car, a white Hyundai. Its engine started, and it pulled out into the road. He looked closer, but the sun reflecting off the windshield meant he couldn't see inside. The car did a U-turn, and out of habit, he glanced at the number plates but only caught the first two letters and the first number before it turned around the corner. He shrugged; probably nothing.

## 38

John accelerated away from the turning, his heart racing. Fuck, fuck, fuck! He braked hard and took the next right, narrowly missing a car parked too close to the corner. Accelerating again, he climbed quickly though the gears. He glanced in the rearview mirror for signs of pursuit, but the road was clear behind him. Braking hard for the next junction, he turned left, a car honking in protest as he pulled out in front of it. He drove fast, taking three more random turns, all the while with one eye on the mirrors before finally slowing to a more reasonable pace. He relaxed his grip on the steering wheel and exhaled. That was close. Who was that guy? He wasn't the usual overweight, underpaid, lazy policeman. He was dressed in full black, like a SWAT Team member, with what looked like body armor and a serious looking automatic weapon slung over his shoulder. John narrowed his eyes as he searched his memory. It all happened so fast. Had the man seen him? Had he seen the number plates? John clenched his fist and banged on the steering wheel, inadvertently sounding the horn. Fuck, fuck! This wasn't like before when all he was dealing with were a bunch of drunk, entitled young men with no security. This was a whole other level.

John drove on blindly, his mind racing, paying no conscious attention to where he was going. He stopped at a red signal and sat there, considering his options. His heart was still racing, and he could feel acidic bile rising through his esophagus. He swallowed and willed himself to relax. Letting go of the steering wheel, he realized his hands where shaking.

Come on, John, you can't give up now. Think of Adriana. You can do it. You can see it through.

A honking behind him made him look up, and he realized the signal had changed. He slipped the car into gear and moved off, taking a left, finally recognizing where he was. Slowing his breathing, he reasoned with himself.

He had been in tough situations before. He had avenged his wife's death, dealt with Peter Croft in Hong Kong, broken up a human trafficking ring in Thailand, and killed a hired assassin in Oman. He could do it. He thumped the steering wheel with his fist. He was John motherfuckin' Hayes! He chuckled, the nervous tension finding a release, the chuckle turning into a laugh until he couldn't stop, his body shaking with laughter. Glancing to his right at the slow-moving traffic, he noticed the rickshaw wallah in the lane next to him, looking at him as if he was a madman. It made him laugh even more.

## 39

Five minutes later, the hysterical laughter had subsided, and a wave of exhaustion overcame him. He needed to find somewhere to sleep, to recharge his batteries, to plan his next move. John motherfuckin' Hayes—who was he kidding?

He could do it, though. He had to. If only for Adriana's future, their future together. That was enough motivation. He had to be careful... and lucky. He had been lucky before. He sighed. Unlucky too... He pushed that thought back down. No, he could do it. He needed a plan, but first, rest and a decent shower.

Heading north, back toward the outer ring road, just before the Hebbal flyover, he pulled into the service road, took the underpass, and turned into R. T. Nagar. Following the road through the houses, he took a right at the Sai Baba temple, driving on for about another kilometer until he found the hotel he was looking for. It was still in business—a clean, privately owned, three-star hotel. He would get a clean room and decent food there, providing they let him stay without

I.D. Indian law required all hotels to request identification from their guests, and so far, John had avoided it, but the places where he had stayed on the way down from Siliguri were more interested in money than complying with the law. Bangalore would be tougher, especially a better-quality hotel like this one, but John couldn't face another mosquito-ridden night in a filthy, low-grade hostel. He needed to rest if he was to function properly. He pulled into the forecourt and turned off the engine. Reaching over to the backpack lying on the rear seat, he removed a large wad of rupees and folded them over before stuffing them in the side pocket of his cargos. He stepped out and took a deep breath, summoning up a smile, then climbed the steps into the reception.

"Good afternoon, Sir."

"Hello." John returned the greeting and assessed the receptionist—a middle-aged man in a crumpled white shirt, his plain black tie not quite covering his top button. Good. John didn't want a young person trying to prove himself and make a career. A middle-aged man would be easier, hopefully jaded, resigned to a lack of advancement, with a family and commitments.

"How can I help you, Sir?"

"I would like a room, please. For about a week."

The man smiled. "Of course, Sir." He tapped on the keyboard. "We have a room available for you. Single or double bed, Sir?"

"Double, please." John had slept on enough single cots with rock hard mattresses the last few days.

The receptionist tapped a few more keys, then opened a drawer, and pulled out a key card. He placed it on a machine, stabbed at the keyboard again with his index finger, then placed the keycard on the counter.

"That will be three thousand rupees per night, including breakfast, Sir. Taxes will be extra."

"That's fine." John pulled out his roll of rupees and counted off enough for a week and placed it on the counter. "I'll pay in advance."

The man raised an eyebrow but reached over for the money, counting it out before placing it in the drawer below the counter.

"Of course, Sir. I will send a receipt up to your room." He placed a form and a pen on the counter in front of John. "I just need you to complete the registration and provide a copy of your passport."

John cursed inwardly and increased his smile, glancing at the man's name tag.

"Sunil,"—that was ironic—"I need your help." John looked around the reception, then leaned forward, lowering his voice. Sunil too leaned forward.

"You see, it's like this. I need to stay here... anonymously."

Sunil frowned and leaned back.

"I have been a bit naughty."

Sunil cocked his head and leaned forward again, curiosity getting the better of him.

"I have been seeing a lady and..." John looked around the reception again. He turned back to Sunil, who was leaning closer. "Well... she's married, and her husband found out."

Sunil broke into a grin.

John reached into his pocket, peeled off another couple of thousand from the roll of rupees, placing it on the counter, and winked at Sunil.

"It's not safe for me to go home, and I don't want him to know where I'm staying. Do you think you can help me?"

Sunil paused for a second, glanced up at the security camera in the corner, then slipped the registration form over the rupees. Beaming, he slid the key card toward John.

"Room 313, Sir. Please enjoy your stay."

John took the key, winked again, then turned away before Sunil could change his mind. Ignoring the lift, he took the stairs three floors up and found his room.

Opening the door, he walked in and bolted the door behind him. He kicked off his boots, collapsed on the bed, closing his eyes. Just before he drifted off to sleep, he remembered he had left his backpack in the car, but the pull of sleep was too much, and he passed out.

## 40

Rajiv stood to attention in front of S.P.I. Muniappa's desk, listening to his telephone conversation. Judging by his boss' responses, he was being given a hard time, and Rajiv didn't have to try hard to guess who was on the other line.

Muniappa placed the phone back on the desk and forgetting that Rajiv was there, let out a long breath, and rubbed his face with his hands.

Rajiv waited while Muniappa sat with his eyes closed, his forehead resting on his clasped hands.

"Sir?"

Munaippa looked up with a start as if remembering where he was, then scowled at Rajiv.

"That was Patil*ji*."

"Sir."

"He's not happy."

"Sir?"

"What's happening, Rajiv? You must have some leads on this..." He waved his hand as if trying to summon the name out of thin air. Rajiv didn't help him. "Uh... Hayes."

"Nothing, Sir."

Muniappa thumped the desk.

"What do you mean, nothing? I don't have to remind you, Rajiv, what this will mean for your career if something happens to Patil*ji* because of your negligence."

"No, Sir." Rajiv ground his teeth and fought to control his irritation. "Sir, there's been no record of Mr. Hayes entering the country via Bangalore Airport. In fact, we have enquired countrywide, and there is no record of him entering the country."

Muniappa just glared at Rajiv.

"Sir, have you considered this might all be a false alarm? Has Mr. Patil explained why this man is a threat to his life? He left India three, maybe four years ago. Why would he come back now?"

Muniappa raised his hand and pointed his finger at Rajiv.

"Now listen to me, Inspector Sampath. If Patil*ji* says there is a threat to his life, we must take it seriously. He is a good friend to the force, and I want to keep it that way. Do you understand?"

"Yes, Sir." Rajiv kept all emotion from his tone, his face expressionless, hiding the contempt he felt for the man in front of him.

"Now, get out of my office and bring me some results."

"Sir."

Rajiv turned and walked out of the office, making no attempt to close the door behind him. He marched back to his office, pulled the door shut, and threw his uniform cap on the desk. Closing his eyes, he counted to ten, then breathed out slowly. It didn't help. He opened the door and looked out.

"Manjunath," he barked.

The constable looked up with a start. "Sir."

Rajiv lowered his voice and forced a smile.

"Bring me some *chai*, please."

"Yes, Sir."

"Thank you." Rajiv turned and walked back to his desk. Sitting down, he swiveled his chair and gazed out the window, his arms crossed in front of his chest. A gentle breeze rippled through the leaves of the Peepal tree outside the window, and as Rajiv observed the movement of the leaves, his anger slowly subsided. This wasn't the first time his idiot boss had threatened him, and he was sure it wouldn't be the last.

Rajiv sighed, and his thoughts switched to John. What he had told Muniappa was the truth. There was no record John Hayes had crossed any border into India, but Rajiv didn't believe for a minute John couldn't enter the country without being picked up. He couldn't enter by air, India's airport security and immigration monitoring was world class, but if he entered by land, it was highly possible he wouldn't be spotted. Over fifteen thousand kilometers of land border was hard to monitor, and people came in and out all the time without being caught, but he wouldn't mention that to his boss.

It had been three or four days since he had received the call from John from an overseas number. Perhaps it was as he had suggested, all a false alarm, and John was still in Dubai. John was a resourceful guy, but would he really risk everything and come back to India? Put himself in danger unnecessarily? And if he did, what should Rajiv do? Rajiv had never proven what John had done, but Rajiv's duty was to uphold the law, and whatever the justification, if Rajiv caught John breaking the law this time, he would have to do his duty and put him behind bars. But... he would have to break the law first. He would not arrest him without reason. Rajiv sighed. He would cross that bridge when he came to it.

There was a tap on the door, and Rajiv turned around as his constable entered with his *chai*.

"Thank you, Manjunath."

"You're welcome, Sir. Will there be anything else?"

"No. Thank you." Rajiv took the cup and took a sip. "Oh, and Manjunath."

"Sir?"

"Less sugar next time."

## 41

Maadhavi toyed with the olive in her martini, twirling it around in her glass. The filming for a commercial she was booked for had been canceled, and the agency had been unable to give her a reason. Cancelation of filming wasn't unusual, it had happened before, but there was always a reason and a new date given. This time nothing. She frowned.

"Is everything okay, Ma'am?"

Maadhavi looked up and gave Ramesh, the bartender, a sad smile. "Yes, thank you, Ramesh. Just..." She sighed. "I just had a bad day."

"I'm sorry to hear that, Ma'am. I'm sure tomorrow will be better."

"I doubt that," Maadhavi muttered under her breath.

"Sorry, Ma'am?"

Maadhavi looked up again and smiled. "Thank you, Ramesh. I'm sure it will be."

She noticed Ramesh look nervously over her shoulder, and she glanced in the mirror behind the bar to see the figure of the hotel general manager approaching. The bartender moved away and busied himself, wiping the top of the already sparkling bartop. Maadhavi stared gloomily back into her drink until she felt a presence beside her. Turning, she summoned up another smile and greeted the G.M.

"Good evening, Anil. How are you?"

The G.M. gave a half smile, his eyes flicking to the barman and back. Lowering his voice, he leaned in. She resisted leaning back at the stale smell on his breath but raised an eyebrow in question.

"Maadhavi, Ma'am, might I have a word?"

"Of course. Is something the matter?"

The G.M. cleared his throat, glanced nervously around the bar, then continued in a low voice.

"Ma'am, I didn't want to have to come and tell you, but last month's bill hasn't been paid."

Maadhavi stiffened, her brow creased. "I'm sure it's just a banking error, Anil."

The G.M. wrung his hands together.

"Well, Ma'am, that's what I said. I'm sure it's just a clerical error somewhere, but you see..." he hesitated. "The accounts department has checked with the bank, and also with um... Sir's bank, and there is no error. The payment just hasn't been made. Of course, Maadhavi Ma'am, if it was just me, I wouldn't worry. You know I'm a big fan, and I am sure there is a very good reason, but the head office is putting a lot of pressure on me."

Maadhavi bit her lip and reached for her martini, took a large mouthful, and gulped it down before placing the glass gently on the bar. Turning on a big smile, she placed a hand on the G.M.'s arm, turning his face bright red.

"Anil, don't you worry. I will sort it out and make sure everything is paid."

The blushing G.M. smiled, "Of course, Ma'am," he gushed. "Thank you. If there is ever anything I can do, please don't hesitate."

Maadhavi smiled wider, looking directly into his eyes and keeping her hand on his arm longer than necessary.

"Anil, you have always looked after me. I will never forget it." She let go of his arm, and he stepped away, still blushing. He turned to the bartender.

"Ramesh, please make sure Ma'am is well cared for." He turned back to Maadhavi. "Another martini, Ma'am? On my account."

"Why, thank you, Anil, that's very kind of you."

The G. M. backed away slowly, bumped into the table behind him, then headed for the door as Maadhavi turned back to the bar. Picking up her glass, she knocked back the contents, then dumping the glass back on the bar, she clenched her fists. The bastard—it was all him, it had to be. First, the commercial being canceled, and now, the bill not being paid. Head office? Surya Patil was the head office. He owned the hotel! It was him, showing her his power—the impotent old fucker.

The barman set a fresh martini in front of her, and she picked it up immediately.

"Bring me another one Ramesh," she instructed just before she half emptied the glass in one mouthful, the liquid warming her throat as she drank. She felt a little calmer as the alcohol did its work. Placing the glass down, she drummed her long, manicured fingers on the bartop. The sooner she got away from him, the better, but she needed to keep him onside for just a little longer. Her parents' house was paid off, but she needed money for herself. She had been building her escape fund for a while and was so close to having the amount she needed—not long now. A few more jobs and she would have enough for an apartment overseas somewhere—maybe Dubai or even somewhere in Europe—and enough cash to tide her over for a while. But it wouldn't happen if Surya Patil canceled all her work. She took another sip of her drink and nodded a thank you to Ramesh as he set another martini in front of her.

It had been a mistake to fight with him the night before. She should have held her tongue, but it was getting harder and harder to pretend. Finishing her drink, she slid the empty glass away and reached for the next one. Just a little while longer, and she would be free.

## 42

John woke with a start. It was dark. Disoriented, he reached back into his brain, struggling to remember where he was. Sitting up, he looked around in the dim light filtering from the streetlights through the window. He looked down at his clothes. He was fully dressed, lying on top of the bed. Frowning, he gazed around the room until the synapses in his brain made the right connections, and he worked out where he was—Bangalore. Turning his wrist, he looked at the luminous face of his G-Shock—eight thirty p.m. He'd been out for almost nine hours. His stomach growled but with hunger this time. That was a good sign. Feeling better than he had in a week, he swung his legs off the bed and walked to the phone. Time to order room service and get himself freshened up.

An hour later, John turned off his headlights and slowly pulled over into an empty parking space at the end of Surya Patil's street. He wound down the window a quarter of the way and switched off the engine. Leaning back in his seat, he scanned the street ahead of him. There was little sign of human activity, most people inside having dinner. Even the ever-present street dogs were curled up in corners or under trees, dozing in the cooler evening air. The only movement came from outside Patil's gate. John could see the two police guards stationed there, one sitting on a plastic chair while the other paced back-and-forth, the glow of a cigarette in his hand. Along the curb, the three white SUVs reflected the yellowish light from the streetlamps. All was quiet. John settled back for a long wait, reflecting on how many times he had sat in the same spot, staking out the same house.

Last time, watching and waiting for Surya's son, Sunil, he had been a different person, driven by grief and a sense of injustice. Since then, he had changed so much and done things he could never have imagined when Charlotte was alive.

So, even though the stakes were higher, and he was up against a well-trained security team, he was confident he could find a solution. That morning, he'd had a scare, but now, after a decent sleep and a stomach full of food, he was confident he could achieve his goal.

The high-pitched whine of a mosquito distracted him from his thoughts, and he slapped at his neck. Turning the ignition key one click, he powered up the windows. It wouldn't help if he got malaria or dengue, but, he chuckled to himself, it was probably too late anyway, the number of times he had been chewed alive by mosquitos in those shitty hostels on the way down to Bangalore. John's thoughts wandered to Adriana.

*Are there mosquitos in Portugal? I wonder what she's doing right now?* He needed to phone her, tell her he had reached Bangalore safely, find out how her interview went.

Increased activity by Patil's gate caught his attention, and he straightened up in his seat. Peering through the dim light, he watched the two guards open the gate and a group of uniformed men walk out. They climbed into the SUVs, and John watched the lights flick on as they started the engines. The lead SUV pulled out into the middle of the road and waited as a white S Class Mercedes exited the gate. The lead SUV headed up the road, the Mercedes following, the two remaining SUVs falling in behind. John waited until the convoy turned the corner, then started the engine and followed them.

The red flashing lights strobed across the night sky, making the cars easy to follow even though it was dark, so John hung well back as traffic wasn't heavy. The convoy headed out of Shivnagar and onto Bellary Road, turning north toward Mehkri Circle. John adjusted his position in his seat, making himself comfortable. He was relaxed, now that he had something to do and was confident he wouldn't be spotted in the darkness. After Mekhri Circle, the convoy continued toward Sanjaynagar, then took a U-turn in the underpass, doubling back south before taking a left into R. T. Nagar. John frowned. He wondered where they were going. This was getting uncomfortably close to his hotel.

The convoy slowed, and John hung back as the train of vehicles pulled into the entrance of what looked like a large, expensive hotel. John waited until the vehicles were all inside, then cruised slowly past. He glanced across at the sign, "Vijaya Palace Hotel." It was new, not there when he was last in Bangalore and looked fancy. John continued on to the end of the street, then pulled over and parked, angling his rearview mirror so he could have a clear view of the hotel forecourt. Powering down the windows, he switched off the engine and watched.

The doors of the vehicles were open, and armed police milled around. John spotted the black uniform of the commando he had seen the day before, and there was another one with him, both with automatic weapons in their arms. Through the cordon of security, John glimpsed the figure of Surya Patil climb out of the Mercedes and head toward the front entrance, the men forming a ring around him, the commando leading the way. John chewed his lip. It wouldn't be easy to get to Patil with all these men around him. John continued watching as the group stopped at the front entrance, the commando having a discussion with Patil. Judging by Patil's body language, he wasn't happy. Serves him right. Patil pushed past the commando and disappeared inside, leaving the men standing around, looking at each other. What was going on?

After a discussion between the two commandos, John watched as the one who seemed in charge climbed into one of the SUVs. Most of the men followed him, the lights of two of the vehicles switched on and started moving toward the exit. John slid down in his seat, making himself invisible as the two white vehicles drove past. Slowly raising himself up, he watched them turn the corner, then looked back in the mirror at the hotel. One SUV remained with Patil's Mercedes, the other commando and two policemen standing beside it.

Another vehicle pulled up outside the entrance, and when its lights switched off, John could make out the yellow number plate indicating a taxi. Two Asian men in suits climbed out and walked inside the hotel. Surya's security paid them little attention as the taxi started up and pulled out.

John had an idea.

## 43

Ankit pinched the bridge of his nose and exhaled slowly as his Landcruiser pulled out of the hotel. He hated dealing with VIPs. They were full of themselves and treated him and his men like shit. They forgot Ankit and his team were there to protect them, to save their lives, ordering them around like they were second-rate citizens. At least this time, he got Surya Patil to commit that he would be in the hotel all night, so his men could rest. Ankit would come back and relieve Rahul in four hours.

Now that he had commandeered two of the ground-floor rooms in Mr. Patil's house, his men could roll out mattresses and get some sleep, instead of sleeping in the vehicles. It wasn't ideal, and Mr. Patil hadn't been happy at first, but a team that hadn't rested was no good at protecting anyone.

His thoughts wandered back to Mr. Patil as the two vehicles headed back to his house, the going slower without using the red lights to force their way through traffic. The rumors must be true that he had a mistress in the hotel. Ankit could think of no other explanation why he would spend the night there instead of in his own house. These powerful men were all the same, never content with a wife at home. Nearly all the men like him, who Ankit had protected over the years, had something going on in the background. Ankit sighed—because of them, he couldn't see his own wife and kids.

The convoy pulled up at a traffic light, and a girl of around ten years old tapped on the window. She had a bunch of flowers in her hand and smiled at him, hoping he would buy them from her. Underneath her matted hair and grimy, dirt stained face, she was pretty with bright, light-colored eyes and prominent cheekbones. If circumstances were different, she might have grown up to have her photos gracing the pages of fashion magazines. Instead, she was barefoot at the traffic lights and sleeping with her family under the flyover. Life was definitely unfair.

The signal changed, and his vehicle pulled forward, leaving the girl behind, the memory of her face imprinted on his mind.

## 44

John started the car, drove around the corner, and parked two hundred meters up the road. Getting out, he flagged down a rickshaw.

"Vijaya Palace Hotel."

The rickshaw wallah turned around and shook his head. "Sir, it's too close. I won't take you."

John reached into his pocket and removed a hundred rupee note. "I'll give you this."

The rickshaw wallah grinned, bobbed his head from side to side, and pulled out into the traffic. Two minutes later, John stepped out of the rickshaw and handed over the money.

"Thank you, Sir, thank you."

John glanced over at Patil's security, still standing outside, but they paid no interest to a guest arriving by rickshaw.

John placed his keys and wallet in the X-ray machine, walked through the metal detector, and smiled at the guard who returned his keys and wallet.

"Welcome to Vijaya Palace, Sir."

"Thank you."

Stepping through the open door, he walked into the lobby where an ornate flower arrangement towered above him, filling the lobby with a sweet fragrance. To the right, the concierge busied himself with some bags, and on the left, a marble reception counter took up the whole left side. John walked over and gave his best smile to the young female receptionist.

"Good evening, I want to get something to eat. Where are your restaurants?"

"Good evening Sir." The young lady beamed back. "Welcome to Vijaya Palace. We have a coffee shop downstairs, and on the tenth floor, we have two restaurants. Giovanni's is the Italian Restaurant, and we have an Indian Restaurant called Nawabi."

"Thank you, I will take a look."

"Sir, I recommend you try Nawabi. The biryani is delicious."

"Thank you for the tip." John winked at the girl, making her blush. "Tenth floor, you said?"

"Yes, Sir. Would you like me to show you?"

"It's okay, I'll find my way. Thank you, again."

"My pleasure, Sir."

John turned and made his way around the flower arrangement to the bank of lifts. He didn't think Patil would have come to the hotel to go to the coffee shop, so that left the Italian or the Indian. John didn't know what he would do once he found him, only that he had sent his security home, and it was too good an opportunity to pass up.

John pressed the button for the tenth floor and rode the lift up. On the tenth floor, the lift opened onto another lobby at the end of which stood two hotel staff behind a small counter. John approached with a smile.

"Good evening." He glanced to the left and spotted the entrance to the Italian restaurant. One of the staff, a young lady, peeled away from the desk.

"Do you have a reservation, Sir?"

John kept walking toward the door but slowed enough for her to catch up. He smiled at her and explained, "No, I don't. Can I look at the menu?"

"Of course, Sir." The young lady rushed ahead of him and held open the door.

John walked in and looked around, seeing one-half of the restaurant. A third of the tables were occupied, and he scanned them all but couldn't see Patil. The young lady passed him a menu, and he made a show of looking through it but scanned the tables again, then looked back at the young lady.

"What's on that side?" he gestured to the part of the restaurant he couldn't see.

"More of the restaurant, Sir."

John nodded and stepped forward, so he could look around the corner. Again, only some tables were filled, none of them occupied by Patil. He pretended again to look at the menu before closing it and handing it back to the waiting staff.

"Perhaps, I'll have Indian food instead."

"Of course, Sir, please follow me."

John followed the young lady out of the restaurant, across the lobby, and into the Indian restaurant. A tall man with a waxed mustache, dressed in a long tunic and a turban, held the door open for him. John nodded a thank you before stepping past him. This time, he could see the whole restaurant floor. It was noisy, and the smell of spices hung heavy in the air. Most of the tables were full, and the waiting staff bustled between them, ferrying plates of food from the kitchen to the tables. John felt a movement beside him and looked down to see a menu being held out by the young lady. He took it and leafed through it as he studied the diners at each table.

"Do you see anything you like?" asked a man's voice.

John turned with a start. "I'm sorry?"

The man in the turban was standing beside him. "Is there anything you would like to eat, Sir?" He gestured toward the menu in John's hand.

"Ah, no," John breathed out. "I mean not yet. I hear the biryani is good here."

"Yes, Sir. It's delicious."

John nodded, still scanning the restaurant. He couldn't see Patil anywhere.

"I think maybe I'll come tomorrow. I want to have something light tonight."

The turbaned man smiled. "Of course, Sir. Would you like me to make a reservation for you?"

"Ah, thank you, but I'll call once I know what time I'm coming. Thank you."

John returned the menu and turned to walk out of the restaurant. No sign of Patil in the restaurants. Where could he be? Surely, he wasn't staying in a room? That wouldn't make sense. He had a house nearby. John smiled again at the staff, manning the reception counter.

"I'll come tomorrow. Goodnight."

"Goodnight, Sir."

John stopped. "Oh, where are the toilets?"

One of the ladies gestured toward John's left. "Just to your left there, Sir."

"Thank you."

John walked over, hesitated a moment, then taking a deep breath, pushed open the door, and slowly walked in.

Patil wasn't at the urinals. John breathed out. He was sure he could handle Patil if it came to a physical confrontation, but that didn't make him any less nervous. John walked over to the three cubicles and pushed open the doors one by one—all empty. Damn.

John rode the lift down to the lobby, then took the flight of stairs down to the coffee shop on the lower mezzanine. An open kitchen took up the center of the room with a row of bain-maries and serving dishes laid out on the buffet counter. Walking around as if examining the buffet, he studied all the guests. He wasn't here either. John looked around for the toilets.

He wasn't in there either.

John slowly walked up the stairs. Where the hell could he be? Reaching the lobby, John paused and thought about his next move. He couldn't hang around the hotel indefinitely, and if Surya was in a room, there was no knowing when he would come out. A movement to John's right caught his eye. Two Japanese businessmen, both a little worse for wear, stumbled out of what appeared to be the hotel bar.

Aha!

## 45

Surya Patil stood at the window, looking out across the city lights, a glass of whisky in his hand. From the twenty-third floor, he could see across Bangalore, lights of all colors spread out before him as far as he could see. It was a view at its most beautiful at night, the traffic-clogged streets transformed into ribbons of white, red, and yellow lights. A city he exerted a lot of power over, a city he would truly control once he achieved his ultimate goal—Chief Minister of the State. Then the whole city would be his. It was no longer about the money; he had plenty. It was the power he would wield, the ability to bend men to his every whim and fancy. He nodded with satisfaction. It wouldn't be long now.

Taking a sip of his whisky, he held the amber liquid in his mouth for a time, then allowed it to slide sensuously down his throat and switched his attention to the interior of the suite reflected in the window. Through the open door of the bedroom, he could see Maadhavi in a yellow and gold sari, her back and one shoulder bare. Her long dark brown hair cascaded over the open back of her sari blouse as she sat at the mirror, brushing it slowly. She was a beautiful woman, and despite his anger with her, he felt arousal stirring in his body. She held a power over him, he would never admit to, and even though he had temporarily cut off her funds, it was only to teach her a lesson. He could never let her go.

He loved his wife, and it broke his heart she had walked out on him, but this was different. This was an obsession, one he had felt since he had first laid eyes on her years ago. Even then, he had desired her with his whole being and had made sure she would belong to him. It was expensive, providing her with a generous allowance and covering her credit card bills but nothing he couldn't handle. To have a woman like her—a woman half the country desired and swooned over whenever she appeared on the silver screen, a woman twenty years younger, with a body that made him weak at the knees—was worth every rupee he spent on her. But of course, he would never tell her that.

He took another long swallow of his whisky, then turned from the window and walked into the bedroom. Sitting on the edge of the bed, he watched her brush her hair. Meeting his eyes in the mirror, she placed the brush down on the vanity table, turning to face him.

His heart did a little jump as she looked at him, those big brown eyes, the full lips. Again, he felt a stirring in his groin. Shifting a little on the bed, he glared at her.

"Surya baby, I'm sorry we fought last time. I was tired, I had a long day." She formed her lips in a pout and batted her eyelids. "You know how it is, my *jaan*. Sometimes, the crowds are just too much."

Surya couldn't help it. He could feel his anger waning. It wasn't even anger. He could never be truly angry with her. It was more irritation, a need to show her he was the boss. A need to show her and indeed everyone else that he, Surya Patil, was still the King of the Jungle.

He drained the rest of the whisky and placed the empty glass on the bed as he watched her stand and walk toward him. His throat caught as she knelt down in front of him and rested her arms and her head on his lap.

"I'm sorry, my baby," she murmured.

Surya's heart melted, and he ran his fingers through her thick mane of hair. All was forgiven.

## 46

John stopped in the doorway and scanned the room. The bar was decorated like an English gentleman's club, all leather chairs and wood-paneled walls. It was empty apart from a young couple, whispering sweet nothings to each other in the corner and a lone middle-aged man sitting at the end of the bar, staring into his drink. A young barman in a white shirt and black waistcoat nodded a greeting to him from the bar, and John made his way over. If he couldn't find Surya, he may as well have a drink. He needed one and hadn't had a decent drink since the lounge in Dubai airport.

"Good evening, Sir."

John pulled out a stool. "Good evening."

"What can I get you, Sir?"

John's eyes ran over the lines of bottles behind the barman until he saw what he wanted. "I'll have a Botanist and tonic. Lots of ice, and a slice of orange, please."

"Yes, Sir."

The barman slid a silver bowl of peanuts in front of John, then reached for a glass.

"Ah, I don't want one of those..."

"Sir? We always serve in a highball."

"Yes, I'm sure, it's just that I prefer a copa." John smiled.

The barman looked puzzled.

"Do you have a burgundy glass?"

"Yes, Sir."

"Then please serve me in that. It stays cooler longer."

The bartender nodded and prepared the drink.

John popped some peanuts into his mouth and glanced at his watch, almost eleven.

"What time do you close?"

"Whenever the last person leaves, Sir," came the reply as he set John's gin and tonic down in front of him.

John took the glass, stirred it twice before removing the plastic cocktail stick, then took a sip, licking his lips as the barman looked on expectantly.

"Delicious, thank you." He needed it. It had been a tough week.

The barman smiled with relief and picked up a cloth and started polishing a glass.

"What's your name?"

"Ramesh, Sir."

"Ramesh, you make a very good gin and tonic."

"Thank you, Sir."

"What's with all the security guards outside the hotel?"

Ramesh glanced toward the door. "It's for one of the guests, Sir."

John pursed his lips and nodded slowly.

"Must be an important guest with all that security."

Ramesh gave a half smile and looked down at the glass he was polishing.

John sipped his drink and pretended to study the glass,

swirling the ice cubes around. He took another large drink, then set the glass down.

"I'll have another, Ramesh. It's been a long day."

"Yes, Sir."

"And fix one for yourself, Ramesh."

"Thank you, Sir."

John watched him fix the drink and thought about his next question. He drained the contents of his glass and pushed it away as Ramesh slid the fresh drink toward him.

"Does he stay in the hotel?"

"Who, Sir?"

"The man with the security."

"No, Sir, he..." Ramesh's eyes flicked toward the door, and he clammed up, picking up his polishing cloth and another glass.

John looked in the mirror. He could see no one in the reflection.

"Come on, Ramesh, you can tell me." John winked conspiratorially.

Ramesh paused his glass polishing, glanced toward the door, then leaned in toward John.

"He doesn't stay here, Sir." Ramesh paused, glancing at the door again before continuing. "His girlfriend stays here."

"Ah," John nodded, fixing a grin on his face. "Lucky man."

Ramesh leaned in again and lowered his voice. "She's an actress."

John raised an eyebrow. "Really? What's her name?"

"Sir, she's very famous in Bangalore. Have you heard of Maadhavi Rao?"

## 47

Three strong and well-made gin and tonics later, sleep was getting the better of John. He had a good buzz, and there was still no sign of Patil, so he decided to call it a night. He hadn't been able to get much more information out of Ramesh, apart from the fact Maadhavi Rao came to the bar regularly. He pushed back the bar stool, counted out some change, and slid it across the bar.

"Thank you, Ramesh." John smiled at the barman and reached out a hand. Ramesh took it with a grin. "I'll see you around."

"Certainly, Sir. Are you staying with us?"

"No, Ramesh, but I live nearby."

"Very good, Sir. Goodnight."

John walked into the lobby, keeping a ready eye for Patil, but there was no one around, apart from a solitary staff member on the reception who looked up and smiled. John pushed his way out the front door. The white Land Cruiser and the Mercedes were still parked outside, but the security guards weren't to be seen. John looked closer and saw the vehicle windows were all wound down, and the men were dozing inside the car, paying him no attention.

"Can I call you a taxi, Sir?" asked the doorman.

"No, thank you, I'll walk." He slipped a fifty rupee note into the doorman's hand, enough to keep him on good terms but not too much for him to stand out, and headed out the gate. It took only five minutes to get back to his car. The streets, even at that late hour, were still busy, scooters and motorbikes whizzing past him at great speed. The air had cooled considerably from the heat of the day, but dust and exhaust fumes still hung heavy in the air.

John drove slowly back to his hotel, bouncing ideas back-and-forth. The heightened security meant getting access to Patil would be a problem. However, if he could somehow get close to him whenever he visited the hotel, perhaps he could do something. He needed to find out more about this actress Patil was visiting.

Back in the room, he logged into the hotel wifi and googled Maadhavi Rao. After fifteen minutes, John sat back in his chair and scratched his head. He had found nothing particularly useful, the internet full of the usual gossip surrounding a film star. Interestingly, though, nothing about Surya Patil. John guessed Patil exercised his influence to keep that sort of thing out of the press.

After his research, John was no further ahead. At least he knew what she looked like. She was a very attractive woman, and he couldn't understand what she was doing with a fat slug like Patil. She must have her own money and wouldn't need his. Surely, power wasn't that attractive? John chewed his lip and thought it over. History was full of stories of powerful men surrounded by beautiful women. He guessed Patil was no different, but still... He sighed and rubbed his eyes, then checked his watch and did a mental calculation. Time to call Adriana, then turn in. Perhaps a good sleep would help him come up with a solution.

# 48

Detective Inspector Rajiv Sampath drummed his fingers on his lap as he waited for the traffic signal to change to green. The morning had been a busy one. Yet another early morning mugging had been reported on the grounds of G.K.V.K., the government agricultural university favored by morning walkers. Rajiv had interviewed the latest victim and talked to witnesses but didn't think he would have much luck catching anyone. The thief had five thousand acres of forest and farmland to hide in.

Rajiv stared out the windscreen as the traffic flowed past in the opposite lane. Why these women liked to go walking at six in the morning, wearing their gold jewelry, was beyond Rajiv. He understood there were traditions, requiring women to wear certain jewelry, the gold *mangalsutra* worn by married women, for example, but surely, common sense had to come into play? When you were out walking in a secluded area, who needed to know if you were married?

A car passing in the opposite direction caught Rajiv's

eye. It was driven by a westerner, which wasn't unusual these days in Bangalore, the city increasingly popular with expats and multinational companies, but there was something about this westerner that nagged at the back of his brain, although he couldn't put his finger on it. He shook it off and went back to thinking about the morning's case. He would increase patrols in the morning and have his men post notices at the entry points to G.K.V.K., warning of the danger of muggers, but there wasn't much more he could do. He watched the signal change from red to green, accompanied by a cacophony of horns as the impatient drivers around him itched to get moving. Perhaps he would make the rounds of known thieves in the area, put the squeeze on them. Someone might know something.

"Shit!"

"Sir?" Rajiv's driver looked over at him in puzzlement.

"Make a U-turn quick."

The driver swung the wheel over and stuck his arm out the window. Drivers honked in frustration at the obstruction as the police Bolero swung across into the opposite lane and headed back the other way.

Rajiv's forehead creased in a frown as he scanned the road ahead of him. It couldn't be, surely? The man had looked different, but it was a few years since he had seen him last. The hair color was different, but still, something was there.

The Bolero slowed as the traffic bogged down, and Rajiv clenched his fist in frustration.

"Put the lights on," he growled.

"Yes, Sir." The driver switched on the red and blue flashing lights, but they still made slow progress. The traffic in front tried to get out of the way, but there was little room for them to move. Rajiv scanned the vehicles ahead. It had been a white hatchback, small, a Suzuki or a Hyundai, both common cars in Bangalore. He wished he had taken note of the registration... or made the turn quicker. So many cars had passed since then. They continued forward, edging through the traffic, the driver using the horn whenever a car in front was too slow to get out of the way. Rajiv scanned every white hatchback they passed, looking for one with a foreign driver. They wound their way through the streets of R. T. Nagar, Rajiv getting ever more frustrated as he couldn't find the car he was looking for.

"Damn it," he exclaimed, his driver glancing at him from the corner of his eye, wondering what had got his boss so vexed.

"Pull over."

The Bolero pulled onto the side of the road as Rajiv stared out the windscreen at the traffic flowing past. He must have been mistaken, his mind playing tricks on him.

"Sir?" The driver cleared his throat. "What are we looking for?"

"A white hatchback."

"Yes, Sir," The driver frowned as a sea of white hatchbacks flowed past his window.

Rajiv shook his head. No sense in wasting time. He glanced over at his driver.

"Forget it, back to the station."

"Yes, Sir."

"No, wait!" Something had caught Rajiv's eye. He opened the door and climbed out, walking around in front of the Bolero. Holding up his hand, he stepped out into the traffic, crossing the road as the flow of traffic in both directions opened up and flowed around him, missing him by inches. Rajiv reached the other side and looked up at the building in front of him—Butterfly Suites, a small business hotel. Nothing out of the ordinary, like many that had cropped up around Bangalore, catering to traveling businessmen on a budget. What had caught his eye was the white car parked in the forecourt. He walked closer and mentally noted the number plates. The registration was from northern Karnataka, Hubli or Dharwad, maybe some other small rural town in the north of the state. Dust covered the car, the front of it peppered with insect splatter, indicating it had been driven a long way, but the registration could explain that.

He cupped his hands around his eyes and peered through the window glass. Nothing inside to give any clues about the owner.

Rajiv straightened up and looked at the entrance. He climbed the steps into the reception and pushed open the door. A middle-aged man at the reception glanced at his uniform and gave him a nervous smile.

"Good morning, Sir."

"Good morning." Rajiv nodded toward the front door. "Whose is the car outside?"

"Which one, Sir?"

"The white Hyundai?"

It was fleeting, but Rajiv spotted it—a brief twitch, gone as quickly as it appeared.

"I'm sorry, Sir, I don't know. I have just come on duty."

"Is that right?" Rajiv gave the receptionist a piercing stare, and the man looked down, unable to maintain eye contact.

"Show me your register."

"Yes, Sir." The man opened up a large book and slid it across the counter.

Rajiv stepped closer and ran his finger down the

columns of guest names—nothing. He chewed on his lip. Of course, John wouldn't use his real name.

Looking up, he fixed the receptionist with his stare.

"Are there any foreigners staying here?"

"No, Sir. I mean... I don't know, Sir."

Rajiv frowned, not taking his eyes off the man's face.

"You don't know..."

"No, Sir. I mean, I haven't seen anyone, but my colleagues may have booked someone in."

Rajiv nodded slowly. "If I find out you are lying..." He watched the man's throat move as he gulped. Rajiv reached into his pocket and pulled out a card. "This is my number,"—he looked at the man's name tag—"Sunil. If you see anything, I want you to call me."

The man nodded rapidly, his eyes blinking.

"Good." Rajiv turned slowly and walked out the door. Stepping down toward the parked car, he pulled out his phone and took a photo of the car's number plate. He would get one of his men to run the plates once he was back at the station. He walked toward the road and his Bolero, which had turned and was now waiting on the same side of the road. Rajiv opened the door, but before climbing in, he turned and looked back at the hotel. He looked up, scanning each window. Perhaps he was wrong, it could be nothing. It might not even have been the car he had seen, but... he had a feeling, and his gut seldom let him down.

## 49

"Hey."

"Hi," said the sleepy voice on the other end.

"Have I called too early?"

"No, baby. It's okay, it's... six thirty. I have to get up soon, anyway."

John smiled. Hearing Adriana's voice made everything okay.

"How's everything? How was the interview?"

"Very good. They asked me when I can start."

"That's fantastic. I'm so happy for you."

"Hmmm."

John frowned. "What's the matter?"

"But what about you? What will happen if I work here? Here in Lisbon."

John stood and paced around the room.

"Don't you worry about me." He ran his hand through his hair and smiled. "I can live anywhere... as long as it's with you."

"Do you promise?"

"Yes, of course. I've never been to Portugal. I hear it's beautiful."

"It is."

John heard the smile in her voice.

"How is your stomach? Last time we spoke, you weren't feeling too good."

"Good. Very good, actually." John subconsciously ran his hand over his stomach as he remembered his experience at the petrol station. "Huh."

"What?"

"Oh, nothing, it's just something happened a couple of days ago." He told Adriana about the *sadhu* he had met and how he had put his hand on his stomach.

"Do you think he cured you?"

John made a face and shrugged.

"I don't know. I was probably getting better, anyway." He scuffed the carpet with his toe. "It was just... a bit weird."

"Hmmm, well, at least you're better."

"Yes." He wouldn't tell her what else the *sadhu* had said.

"You are coming back to me, John? Promise me."

John chuckled and walked over to the window to let some air in. The room was getting stuffy.

"I promise. Nothing will keep me..."

John stiffened as he looked out. A white police Bolero was parked outside, the driver leaning against the hood, smoking.

"John?"

John stepped back from the window, his heart racing.

"John? Are you still there?"

"What? Ah, yes, sorry, I ah... just dropped something."

"Where are you now?" The note of concern was clear in Adriana's voice.

"I'm in Bangalore now. Everything is good."

John narrowed his eyes as he watched the driver suddenly straighten up and toss his unfinished cigarette into the road. He rushed around to the driver's door, opened it, and climbed in as a slim, smartly dressed police officer exited the hotel. John's fingers tightened around the phone as he watched the police officer stop in front of his car and take a photo of the number plate.

"Good, my baby. Please be careful."

The police officer walked toward the police vehicle and opened the door.

"John? John?"

John's breath caught in his throat as the officer turned and looked up at the hotel. John took two steps back from the window as his heart pounded. Rajiv!

"Baby, I'll have to call you back."

"What's the matter?"

John watched Rajiv climb into the Bolero, and it pulled out into the traffic.

"Ahh... nothing, I have to go. It's housekeeping. I'll call you tomorrow." John tossed the phone on the bed.

Shit, shit, shit. How the fuck had he found him?

## 50

Rajiv stared at the single sheet of paper on his desk—the report from the Road Transport Office. He read the text on the paper again, his forehead creased in a deep frown. The number plates on the late model white Hyundai hatchback belonged to a ten-year-old blue Suzuki Swift, registered in Belgaum, North Karnataka. That meant only one thing—the white Hyundai was stolen. Leaning back in his chair, he closed his eyes and took a deep breath. He needed to think clearly, examine the facts, and not jump to conclusions. He ran back over the sequence of events.

He had seen a westerner driving a white hatchback very similar to the stolen one outside the hotel, but he couldn't be sure if it was the same car. He searched his memory for the moment he had glimpsed the driver. It had been a westerner, that was definite, but it had been a fleeting glimpse, and despite his hunch, Rajiv was sure the man had fair hair, whereas John's was black. Rajiv opened his eyes and sat forward.

His job was to work with the facts. The car was stolen.

He needed to investigate that, but... if it was John? No, it couldn't possibly be. How would John enter Bangalore undetected and be in possession of a stolen car? Shaking his head, he pushed his chair back from the desk and stood. One thing at a time. Best not to let his imagination run wild. He picked up his uniform cap from the desk and left the office. As he walked out into the station carpark, his driver jumped up from his seat in the shade of a tree and ran to Rajiv's vehicle.

"Give me the keys."

"Sir?"

"Give me the keys," Rajiv growled.

The startled driver handed over the keys, and Rajiv climbed into the Bolero, started the engine, and pulled onto the road. It took twenty minutes to reach the hotel. Pulling into the forecourt, the white Hyundai wasn't there. Rajiv cursed under his breath and climbed out, jogging up the steps into the reception. The same man was at the counter, looking anxious when he saw Rajiv standing in front of him.

"Sir?"

Rajiv glared at him. "Where has the white Hyundai gone? The one that was parked outside."

The man shook his head, "I-I-I don't know."

Rajiv reached out, grabbing the man by his shirt collar, and pulled him over the counter until their faces were just inches apart.

"Listen to me,"—his eyes glanced down to the man's name tag and then back again—"Sunil. Don't play the fool with me. I know you know what I'm talking about. Which room is he staying in?"

Sunil gulped and shook his head.

Rajiv pulled his face even closer and twisted the collar tighter. Sunil's neck turned red.

"You can tell me, or I can get my men down here, and we will go through every room. The choice is yours. If we do that, this hotel will be closed down for days while we complete our investigation."

Beads of sweat began to form on Sunil's forehead.

"I'll ask you again. Which room is he in?"

"Room 313, Sir."

Rajiv relaxed his grip on Sunil's collar, and Sunil sagged back behind the counter and straightened his collar.

"Is he in?"

Sunil shook his head vigorously.

Rajiv held out his hand. "The key."

Sunil hurriedly processed another key card and handed it over to Rajiv, who took it and strode to the lift. He rode the lift to the third floor, checked the sign for the room numbers, then turned right, following the corridor until he stood outside Room 313. Stepping close to the door, he pressed his ear against it, listening, but there was no sound. He swiped the key card over the lock, and the light flashed from red to green. Rajiv pushed down on the handle and slowly, quietly pushed the door open, and stepped inside, closing the door behind him.

Looking around, he could see whoever had stayed there was gone, the unmade bed the only sign the room had been occupied. There was no luggage, nothing left on the bedside tables. Rajiv walked over and looked into the wastepaper bin—empty apart from an empty plastic water bottle. He rounded the bed and pushed open the door to the bathroom—again empty. A wet towel lay on the floor, but there was nothing else to indicate who the previous occupant was. Shit!

Rajiv walked back into the room, again running an experienced eye around the room, looking for clues. He dropped to his knees and looked under the bed and the writing desk. The room was clean. Getting to his feet, he adjusted his uniform shirt and walked over to the window. He looked down at his Bolero parked outside the entrance, approximately where he had parked earlier that day. Well, that's how he was spotted. The man must have seen him and was frightened off. But who is he? Could it be John? One thing was for sure. It was time to give Sunil a hard time and find out more.

## 51

John pulled onto the side of the road and switched the engine off, parking on a small country lane on the northern outskirts of Bangalore.

After seeing Detective Inspector Rajiv Sampath outside the hotel, he had flown into a panic. Whatever connection he had with Rajiv from before, he was still a policeman, and John had no idea which side of the law he would fall on. It was a risk John could not afford to take.

What John couldn't understand was how the hell Rajiv had known where he was. It made little sense. John hadn't used his name anywhere and had gone through all the trouble of sneaking across the border twenty-five hundred kilometers away. Yet within a couple of days of arriving in Bangalore, Rajiv was outside John's hotel. John screwed up his face and pounded the steering wheel. He needed to think, to regroup, assess the way forward. Opening the door, he stepped out into the lane—he thought best when he was moving. Usually, a run gave him the best ideas, but he couldn't do that now. John moved around to the front of the car and gazed out across the fields. A lone cow stared back at him, its jaw moving in rhythmic motion while a white egret perched on its hindquarters. John heard a shout and turned as two boys, riding pillion on a motorbike whizzed past, a hand raised in greeting.

Within five minutes of spotting Rajiv, John had stripped his room bare of any sign he had been there. Bundling all his possessions into his backpack, he had taken the stairs four flights down to the basement and slipped out the service exit, avoiding the need to pass the reception. Sunil hadn't even noticed him leaving until the car pulled out of the hotel forecourt, and by then, it was too late.

John turned, locked the car with a blip of the key fob, and walked into the field, the cow watching him pass. The ground was packed hard, the grass burned to nothing by the sun. John walked aimlessly, following a well-worn path along the edge of the field as it wound between patches of scrub and the occasional tree. A startled rabbit burst into action and streaked away from him while high overhead in the cloudless expanse of sky, a bird of prey screeched a call to its mate. It was an idyllic setting, completely at odds with the turmoil in John's head.

He couldn't fathom how Rajiv had found him. He had disguised himself, growing a beard and lightening his hair, had even changed his eye color with contact lenses. How would Rajiv have recognized him? Had the hotel staff informed him? But they didn't know who he was. Was it all an unfortunate coincidence? More importantly, what should he do now? There was no way he would give up, not after all this effort. Things wouldn't be easy, but then, nothing worthwhile doing ever was.

The more John walked, the more he calmed, and the clearer he began to think. He could worry about Rajiv all he wanted, but it wasn't going to help John achieve his goal. So, first things first. He needed to find somewhere else to stay. Perhaps Vijaya Palace? That would be the easiest solution, he could easily afford it, and would help him get close to Patil, but John thought it unlikely he could check into a reputable hotel like that without providing any identification.

Could he get a fake ID? John stepped over a low stone wall, then skirted a thicket of thorn bushes. Where would he do that? He could try another budget hotel and bribe the staff to get a room, but until he figured out how Rajiv had found him, that too was risky. Perhaps, all hotels were on the lookout for him? Maybe the hotel had CCTV, and Rajiv now had a photo of him, the way he currently looked? John kicked a stone from the path in frustration. He stopped in the shade of a tree and leaned against the trunk. Unable to think of a solution, he moved on to the next problem. The car was compromised. He had seen Rajiv take a photo of the registration. He would find out in no time the number plates were fake. John blew out a puff of air between pursed lips and shook his head. He was screwed. He needed transport. Mobility was important, and he didn't want to be dependent upon someone else. That was the whole reason he got the car in the first place. The hassle of getting another vehicle was something he really didn't need right now, but... That's it! A white Hyundai hatchback was a common sight on the roads of Bangalore. He would find another one and swap the plates. It would pass any cursory inspection. John allowed himself to smile for the first time since he left the hotel. That's what he would do. And while he solved that problem, his subconscious would no doubt come up with a solution about where he could stay.

An ant crawled over his hand, and he let go of the tree trunk and shook it off. He looked around, realizing for the first time how far he had walked from the road. Turning, he retraced his steps, following the path back to his parked car. As he stepped back onto the road, a tractor rumbled past, towing a trailer, filled with village women, dressed in brightly colored saris, their heads wrapped in cloth to protect them from the sun. A small girl in a school uniform sat on the back of the trailer, her dress torn and dirty, but her hair was tied in two immaculate plaits with red ribbons at the ends. Her bare feet swung back-and-forth over the back of the trailer as she stared at John with huge brown eyes. John gave her a wave and climbed into his car. As he reached forward to start the engine, he realized where he could stay.

## 52

It was John, it had to be. Why else would a westerner be hiding out in a hotel in Bangalore at the same time there was a threat to Surya Patil's safety?

Rajiv glanced in his rearview mirror and changed lanes as he drove slowly back to the station, deep in thought. It couldn't be a coincidence, surely. Granted, the hotel staff's description didn't match what John looked like, but it didn't take much to change one's appearance. Any man can grow a beard, and he could have dyed his hair.

If only the bloody hotel CCTV had been working. Rajiv shook his head in exasperation. What was the point in having a security system if you didn't maintain it? He had given the hotel receptionist a hard time, but it wasn't his fault. He was paid a meager salary, and decisions regarding the hotel had nothing to do with him. Hell, he couldn't even blame him for taking under-the-table money to check in a guest without registration. Everyone knew Bangalore had become an expensive city. It was enough of a struggle for Rajiv to make ends meet. He'd had enough arguments with Aarthi about earning more money, but there was no way he would compromise the law he was employed to uphold, just to make some extra money. Rajiv sighed as his eyes flicked to the mirror again. It wasn't the first time this sort of thing had happened. Truth be told, half of the police cameras didn't work, but it made his job so much more difficult. Yet these businesses were the first to complain about the police not doing their jobs. Fix the bloody cameras, and we'll catch the criminals much faster.

Rajiv pulled into the station carpark, switched off the engine, and stared unseeingly out the windshield. The big question was, what did he do now? He liked John, but he also had a duty to perform, and that duty was to protect the citizens of Bangalore, even if that included men like Surya Patil. Rajiv sighed, opened the door as his driver approached, and tossed the keys to him.

"Be ready to leave in fifteen minutes."

"Yes, Sir."

Rajiv strode across the parking lot, and just before entering the police station, he stopped and turned.

"Manjunath."

"Yes, Sir." His driver jogged toward him.

"Get me Surya Patil's security team on the radio."

## 53

John drove slowly along the row of modest and ramshackle homes, some simply comprising a concrete box with a tin or asbestos roof, many with additional blue plastic tarpaulins draped over them as extra protection against the monsoons. Pulling over next to a narrow lane, he peered through the windshield. He thought he had the correct place, but it seemed to have changed a lot since he was last here almost four years ago. Deciding, he indicated and pulled onto the dirt track, lined with gutters filled with stagnant black water. Some things hadn't changed. He crawled along, the car rocking and twisting on the rough track. There it was. He recognized the house, small and modest but notable as one of the cleaner ones in the slum, the bare ground outside swept clean, and a colorful design drawn with colored sand on the scrubbed front step. John stopped the car and looked for a space to park. The last time he had been there, he had found a vacant site opposite, but now, all the empty spaces were filled with huts. He put the car in reverse and backed out onto the road, leaving the car on the side. He picked up the box of sweets he had bought, locked the car, and walked back down the track. A woman sitting on the front step of her home eyed him curiously as she checked her child's hair for lice. John nodded, and she smiled, bobbing her head from side to side in the way only Indians can. John stopped outside the house and tapped on the front door with the back of his hand.

A girl's voice cried out from inside, and John waited as he heard a bolt being pulled back. The door cracked open a little, and he looked down to see a young girl looking back at him. He smiled to put her at ease.

"Geetanjali?"

The girl looked surprised and pushed the door closed. From inside, John could hear her calling out,

"Amma."

After a moment, the door opened again, and a tired-looking lady in an ankle-length, cotton nightdress looked out. She peered at John, a frown creasing her forehead as she wiped her hands on the front of her dress.

"Pournima?"

Pournima raised her eyebrows, then frowned even deeper.

"It's me, John. John Hayes."

Pournima's hand flew to her mouth as she gasped.

"Mr. John!" She gathered her wits and opened the door wider. "Come, come." She beckoned him inside.

John slipped off his boots at the doorstep and stepped in, watched by Geetanjali from the safety of the kitchen doorway.

The house was just as he remembered—small, clean, sparsely furnished, and smelling of flowers and incense. The only change was the large framed photo hanging on the wall, a garland of flowers hanging from the top corners. It was a photo of Sanjay, his former driver—the man killed by Surya Patil's son. John stood in front of it, and his eyes filled with tears. He reached for Pournima's hands and squeezed them. Although unused to holding another man's hands, she didn't flinch. Her eyes filled with tears, but she smiled bravely. She slipped her hands free and waved John toward a chair.

"Mr. John, please sit."

John sat down as Pournima disappeared into the kitchen. He wiped his eyes and smiled at Geetanjali, still peering at him from around the kitchen doorframe.

"Hello, Geetanjali. My name is John. I knew your father." Geetanjali said nothing. John held out the box of sweets. "Here, this is for you and Saumya."

He flipped up the lid, so she could see inside. Her eyes widening, she shyly stepped forward. Halfway, she hesitated.

"It's okay, you can take them."

She slowly came closer, then took the box and quickly retreated to the doorway.

Pournima came out with a plastic tray, holding a glass of water and a plate of biscuits. She placed them on the table beside John and stood back, tilting her head to one side.

"Is it really you? You look different... your hair." She raised one hand to her chin. "A beard."

John grinned. "Yes, it's a long story. Are you well?"

"Yes, thank you."

"And the girls?"

Pournima smiled and turned to look fondly at Geetanjali.

"I've never been able to thank you, Mr. John. The money you send, it..." She turned back to John, then looked down at the floor. "It makes things so much easier." She looked up, her eyes glistening again, "After Sanjay died... I couldn't manage. The school fees, the uniforms..."

"It's okay, Pournima. It's the very least I could do after everything Sanjay did for me." John looked at Sanjay's photo. "He was a good man." John looked back at Pournima. "And you don't have to worry. I'll pay for the girls' education until they graduate."

Pournima started crying silently, tears running down her cheeks.

"Amma?" A worried Geetanjali ran over and hugged her leg. Pournima smiled, wiping the tears from her cheeks with one hand as she stroked her daughter's hair with the other.

"Thank you, Mr. John, you are a good man," she replied, looking up at him.

John shrugged and half smiled. He didn't think so, not after the things he had done, but maybe paying for the education of Sanjay and Pournima's two daughters went some way to redressing the balance. Reaching for a biscuit, he popped it into his mouth to avoid answering.

Pournima went back into the kitchen and a minute later, came out with two glasses of steaming *chai*, passing one to John, and sat down in the chair opposite. They sat in silence for a while, sipping the hot sweet liquid, lost in their own memories.

"Where is Saumya?" he asked about Pournima's oldest daughter.

Pournima smiled. "She is at tuitions. She is very good at math." Pournima glanced at the small plastic alarm clock sitting on top of the television set. "She will be back soon."

"That's good." John nodded and took another sip of the *chai*. "How old is she now? Nine, ten?"

"She is nine and very bossy. She thinks she is my mother."

John chuckled and winked at Geetanjali, who had come forward and was sitting cross-legged on the floor in front of him. The family had suffered so much. He was happy to see the girls were growing up in a clean environment and getting an education, something difficult in a single-parent household. John was still racked with guilt at what had happened to their father. There was hardly a day that passed, even so many years later, he didn't blame himself for Sanjay's death. Which made it harder for him to ask what he had to ask.

He took another sip of his *chai*, then set it down on the table. Clearing his throat, he turned to look directly at Pournima.

"Pournima, I'm sorry, but I need your help."

## 54

The police Bolero pulled up outside Surya Patil's gates, and Rajiv stepped out. He straightened his uniform and donned his cap as the two armed police on either side of the gate stood to attention.

Rajiv nodded and smiled. "As you were."

The two men relaxed.

"Captain Sharma?"

One of the policemen jerked his head toward the gate. "He's inside, Sir."

"Thank you." Rajiv pushed open the gate and stepped inside. Four more policemen sat on plastic chairs, drinking tea in the shade of a tree while in another corner, Surya's driver and two large but overweight men, presumably Surya's own security, smoked and played cards.

The police looked up and jumped to their feet, seeing Rajiv walk in. He raised a hand, indicating they could sit. The private bodyguards ignored him, one clearing his throat noisily and spitting on the ground.

Rajiv walked to the house and stepped inside, glancing

through the open door to the left of the entrance hall. The furniture had been cleared to the side, and more policemen dozed on mattresses spread on the floor, but no sign of the commando captain.

A door at the back of the entrance hall opened, and a man stepped out, hesitating when he saw Rajiv. Rajiv recognized him as Surya Patil's servant from a previous visit.

"Captain Sharma?"

"Inside, Sir." The servant pointed to the room on Rajiv's right.

"Thank you."

Rajiv tapped on the closed door.

"Come in."

Pushing open the door, he saw Captain Sharma sitting at a table, his sleeves rolled up, a stripped-down weapon on the table in front of him. He smiled when Rajiv walked in.

"Inspector Sampath."

"Please, Rajiv."

"Take a seat, Rajiv." He held up a pair of oily hands. "Sorry, I can't shake your hand."

"Don't worry." Rajiv sat down in a chair as Ankit called out. "Constable."

The door opened, and one of the policemen popped his head inside.

"Ah, see if you can get the staff to rustle up some *chai* for us, please."

"Yes, Sir."

Rajiv watched as Ankit quickly and expertly reassembled the MP-5.

"I can see you've done that before," Rajiv quipped.

"I can do it with my eyes closed." Ankit winked. He slotted the last piece into place with a click, then wiped his hands on a rag.

"What brings you here, Rajiv? Any developments? Can we all go home?"

Before Rajiv could answer, the door opened, and the constable stepped in, holding the door wide as the servant entered with a tray and set it down on the table in front of Ankit.

"Thank you, that was quick."

"Venkatesh has a pot brewing all the time, Sir." the Constable responded from his position by the door.

"Good." Ankit smiled at the servant. "Thank you, Venkatesh."

He waited for the men to leave, then held out a glass for Rajiv. "There's sugar here, but it's probably sweet enough already."

Rajiv gave a wry grin. "My wife is always telling me to reduce my sugar."

"Ha, mine too." Ankit chuckled. "What would we do without them?"

Rajiv blew on the top of the tea, cooling it as he thought about what he would say. Still conflicted, he had to be careful.

"How's it going?"

Ankit wiped his lips with the back of his hand and set the glass down.

"It's okay. We've established a routine. The men have somewhere to rest." He shrugged. "Not much more we can do at the moment."

"Is he in?"

"Upstairs." Ankit raised his eyebrows toward the floor above. He picked up his glass again and lowered his voice. "Best place for him."

Rajiv gave a half smile and nodded slowly. He sipped his *chai* as Ankit watched, waiting for him to say something.

Rajiv frowned and looked down at the floor.

"Look, it may be nothing, and I don't want to waste your time."

"Waste my time?" Ankit raised an eyebrow, waving his hand around the house. "What do you think all this is? I have eleven men on permanent standby, protecting a single man from a vague unknown threat. If you know anything, at least give me something to work on. Otherwise, we should all go home."

"Yes." Rajiv stood up and walked over to the window, looking at the men sitting outside. Turning back, he said, "Captain..."

"Ankit."

"Ankit, there are... rumors on the grapevine that the man Patil is worried about is actually here in Bangalore."

"Rumors?"

Rajiv hesitated. "Some of my informants."

Ankit nodded slowly. "So, it's not just a figment of,"—he nodded toward the ceiling—"his imagination."

"It could still be, but it's better to be safe than sorry."

"Indeed." Ankit leaned his elbows on the table. "How reliable are these... informants?"

Rajiv walked back to the chair and sat down.

"As reliable as anyone who would sell out colleagues for money."

"Hmmm." Ankit frowned. "Any other information?"

Rajiv thought for a moment. "No."

Ankit leaned back in his chair and stared at Rajiv.

"Well, it shouldn't be too hard if he is, in fact, here. He's not Indian, so we just need to keep all foreigners away from Patil."

"In theory, yes."

"Good. Simple."

"If I hear anything else, I'll be in touch." Rajiv stood up.

"Thank you, Rajiv." Ankit stood and walked around the table. "I'll walk you out."

Rajiv walked toward the door but stopped as Ankit asked, "Why would a foreigner go to all the trouble of coming to India to harm Patil? In fact, having worked for,"—he again nodded toward the ceiling and lowered his voice—"him for a while, I'm surprised there isn't a queue of our own people lining up to get rid of him."

"Yes." Rajiv chuckled. "And many others like him. Our glorious leaders."

"Things will be different when we're running the country." Ankit put a hand on Rajiv's shoulder and winked.

"That's a job I'd never want." Rajiv grinned.

"No, maybe you're right. Come…" He opened the door and guided Rajiv out. They stepped out into the sunshine and walked toward the front gate. Rajiv looked toward Surya's bodyguards.

"What are they like?"

"Useless," Ankit scoffed. "They share a brain cell between them and just get in the way." He drew closer to Rajiv and muttered, "And we daren't leave any of our equipment near them."

"The one on the right is well known to us. A fine upstanding citizen." He winked at Ankit. "I wouldn't complain if you used him as a human shield."

Ankit burst into laughter, causing the men to turn and look. He clapped Rajiv on the back and held out his hand.

"Thank you for the advice."

Rajiv shook his hand, again marveling at the strength of Ankit's grip.

"Good luck, Ankit. Stay safe."

Rajiv stepped out the gate and waved to his driver. As the

car pulled up in front of him, he turned and looked back at the house. He hoped he had done the right thing.

## 55

Pournima hadn't hesitated in offering John a place to stay, even insisting he take the single bedroom. John had refused, telling her he would be happy to sleep on the floor in the living room. Besides, as he explained, he would come and go at odd hours, and the less he disturbed the girls, the better.

They had talked for a couple of hours, John explaining what he had been doing since leaving India the first time. He left out most of the gory details until he got to the story of what happened in Oman. There he told her why he was back, why he was hunting down Surya Patil. After hearing John's story, Pournima agreed he was doing the right thing.

"People like him think they can do anything to people like us, Mr. John. They have so much power, they think they are untouchable. There will never be any justice for men like him." She paused as she watched Geetanjali playing on the floor. "What happened to his son and his friends..." She turned to look at John. "I know that was you. It was right, Mr. John. It had to be done." Pournima turned to face her husband's photo. "I know Sanjay will have appreciated what you did." Turning back to John, she continued, "And now, you must finish the job. Otherwise, you will never be able to live in peace."

"Thank you, Pournima." John smiled sadly. He hadn't wanted to get her involved, but he was left with little choice.

"I will help you, Mr. John, however I can. My Sanjay would have wanted it."

John took his leave once Saumya returned home, and Pournima busied herself preparing dinner for the two girls.

Now, as he climbed back into his car, he thought about how, despite the horrible things that had happened to him —the deaths, the unnecessary pain—there were always good people around when he needed them most.

Starting the engine, he pulled out into the heavy evening traffic. Now, he needed to sort the car out.

Heading away from the Laxminagar Slum, he drove with no fixed direction. He was looking for a more middle-class area, somewhere with a higher ratio of private car ownership. He took a few random turns until he saw what looked like a housing sub-division built behind a public park. Turning off the main road onto the side street, he drove slowly, scanning the properties, ignoring the small apartment complexes, which usually had a night watchman and sometimes, even a security camera. An individual house might be easier, although he was worried about dogs. Ideally, what he needed was a car parked on the street, the same make and color. Simple. John grinned, feeling better after his chat with Pournima. He had got this far, no point in giving up yet.

He crisscrossed the streets of the sub-division but found nothing suitable, so he headed to the next suburb. It was two hours later, tired and fed up, when he finally found what he was looking for. Persistence always paid off. A white

Hyundai hatchback was parked on the street. The bonus, it was parked between streetlights. John drove to the end of the street and pulled over. He looked at his watch. It was still too early, too many people around. He would need to wait. Winding the windows down slightly, he reclined his seat and closed his eyes. Might as well get some rest while he could.

## 56

Waking with a start, John sat up and looked around, his heart racing, not sure where he was or what had woken him. Rubbing his eyes, he looked at the dimly lit suburban street as the sleep left him, remembering why he was there. He also remembered what had woken him. Shit! He had been dreaming—about Adriana.

They were sitting in a cafe in Lisbon, watching people stroll past on the cobblestone streets. Adriana sat close, resting her head on his shoulder as the sun filtered through the leaves of the jacaranda trees lining the footpath. Two young parents pushed their child past in a pushchair, and a lady with her hair tied in a scarf attempted to sell roses to the diners at each table. They heard the screech of tires as a black Mercedes van pulled up to the curb in front of them, and the side door slid open. Six men dressed in black, their faces hidden by balaclavas, jumped out and surrounded John and Adriana's table. John pulled Adriana behind him as one by one, they removed their balaclavas and grinned at him. He recognized them all—Surya, Fatty, Bones, Swami,

Hassan, and Bogdan—men he had killed. As one, they each drew a handgun and pointed it at John's head. It was Adriana's scream that had woken him.

In contrast, the street John was parked on was quiet, nothing moving, not a sound. He took a couple of breaths and got his breathing and heart rate under control, then checked his watch; just after one a.m. He had been asleep for hours. That explained his sweat-soaked shirt and raging thirst. He reached over to the passenger seat and picked up the plastic water bottle. Opening it, he took a long gulp, then checked his mirrors. The street was still empty, and most of the house lights were off. Now was as good a time as any. Draining the bottle, he tossed it into the passenger footwell, then made sure the interior light was set to off before opening the door. Stepping out, he eased the door closed and walked around to the front of his car, removing a pocketknife from his cargo pants before squatting down. He selected the screwdriver and unfastened the front plates, then did the same at the back. Taking one more look around, he stepped onto the footpath and slowly walked back down the street to the white Hyundai, the number plates held close to his body in case anyone saw him.

Reaching the other car, he squatted down and removed the plates replacing them with his own. He figured most people wouldn't even realize their plates had been changed, so he would be safe for a while. He did the same at the rear, then quickly walked back to his own car. He paused as a dog at the end of the street barked, but it quickly lost interest and went back to sleep. John squatted down and affixed the replacement plates to his vehicle, then climbed back into his car.

Starting the engine, he pulled quietly out onto the street, glancing in his mirror to see if anyone had seen him. The street remained quiet. He breathed a sigh of relief. If the police saw the car and ran the plates, the registration would match a white Hyundai.

John allowed himself to smile. He had a place to stay and, for now, his transport was sorted. For a day that had started badly, it had ended well.

## 57

The loudspeaker from the mosque in the slum woke John. He cursed and blinked his eyes open, turning his wrist to look at the luminous hands on his G-Shock; four thirty a.m. He had only been asleep for two hours. He cursed again and turned onto his side. Who in their right mind gets up at four thirty a.m. to pray? Yet another reason religion wasn't for John. He closed his eyes, and within minutes was fast asleep again.

At six, he was woken again by the call for the second prayer of the day. Giving up on sleep, he removed the single sheet that covered him and sat up. Rubbing the sleep from his eyes, he checked his watch. Pournima would be up in half an hour to get the girls ready for school. It would be better if the girls didn't see him sleeping on a mattress on the living room floor.

After scrubbing himself off with a bucket of water in the tiny bathroom, he got dressed and rolled up the bedding, stowing it in a corner beside the television. He heard sounds from the bedroom, and after a little while, Pournima emerged, her hair piled up in an untidy bun on top of her head. She seemed surprised to see him up already but smiled.

"Good morning, Mr. John. Would you like some coffee?"

"Good morning. Yes, thank you." He needed it.

John, Pournima, and two sleepy girls breakfasted on fresh steamed idlies and mint chutney, washed down with filter coffee served in small stainless-steel tumblers. It was simple, delicious food, served with love. John's heart melted when he thought how often people who have so little can be so generous, while those who have everything, people like Patil, were so evil.

Breakfast over, John watched the little girls head out the door to school, dwarfed by their huge backpacks filled with schoolbooks. Education was so valued in India. At that moment, he vowed, whatever happened to him, he would always ensure the girls' education would be taken care of.

Later, John drove for an hour to a shopping mall on the other side of Bangalore. He had a few things to get and wanted to ensure neither Rajiv nor any of his men would spot him.

John picked up some new clothes, his cargo pants needed a change, then purchased a new dress for each of the girls and a sari and matching blouse for Pournima. It was the least he could do, considering the kindness she had shown him. Finally, he purchased a box of samosas, something for the girls to snack on when they returned from school, then headed back to Pournima's home. He'd had little sleep and needed to rest before preparing for the evening.

## 58

This time, John didn't risk parking close to the hotel and hadn't wanted to take a taxi or rickshaw from the slum in case the driver remembered him later. Instead, he parked in a residential area three blocks away, then hailed a rickshaw to take him to the Vijaya Palace. He checked his watch; seven thirty—perfect.

Ramesh, the bartender, had let it slip that Maadhavi Rao habitually visited the bar at seven p.m. every evening. It sounded to John like she may have a drinking problem, but he wasn't one to judge. He just wanted access to Patil. He would arrive in five minutes, and by then, Maadhavi would be one or two drinks down and should be relaxed. John adjusted his shirt and brushed some dust off his pant leg. The new clothes he had bought earlier in the day—a smart shirt and pants and a pair of leather shoes—were more in keeping with the interior of a five-star hotel, rather than his hiking boots and cargo pants.

The rickshaw pulled up in the porte cochere of the hotel, and the tall mustachioed doorman made to shoo the driver away until he spotted John sitting in the back. A lot of hotels didn't like rickshaws entering their grounds, a vehicular snobbery, but John didn't want to use Uber or any other form of taxi, rickshaws the only form of public transport unlikely to have any GPS tracking. The less anyone knew of his movements, the better.

John paid the rickshaw wallah and stepped out. The doorman welcomed him like a long-lost friend, despite his transport, and guided him to the metal detector. John went through, retrieved his wallet and keys from the scanner, and entered the hotel lobby. The flower arrangement had changed, a three-tier display of white orchids filling the lobby with the sweet scent of vanilla.

John returned the greeting from the hotel reception staff and walked past them to the bar, pausing at the entrance and quickly scanning the room. Like most hotel bars, it wasn't exactly buzzing, but that suited John. A couple of tables were occupied, soft jazz was playing in the background, and two-thirds of the way along the bar, a woman sat alone, wearing an expensive sari, a thick cascade of glossy dark brown hair falling across her shoulders. As John approached the bar, he glimpsed long, manicured fingers and a fine gold watch on a slim wrist.

He sat three stools away from her and smiled at Ramesh.

"Good evening, Ramesh, how are you?"

"Welcome back, Sir. I'm fine, thank you." Ramesh smiled and rested both hands on the bar. "What can I get you, Sir?"

"A Botanist and tonic, please."

"Of course, Sir, lots of ice, a slice of orange, and a copa glass."

John grinned. "You remembered." John caught Maadhavi's eye, reflected in the mirror behind the bar, and turned to her, smiling.

"I'm very particular about my drinks."

Maadhavi smiled politely but said nothing, returning her attention to the half-full martini glass in front of her.

John made himself comfortable, reaching for a handful of nuts from the silver bowl, and popped them in his mouth —salted almonds today. Ramesh returned with his drink, and John took a sip.

"Perfect, thank you." He gave Ramesh a thumbs up, and the barman grinned with satisfaction.

John took out his phone and pretended to study it. He had no plan, his only goal for the evening to get closer to Maadhavi Rao, and hopefully, through her, get close to Patil, bypassing his security. He picked a news site and idly scrolled, pretending to read but all the while, thinking of his next move. He didn't want to frighten her off or appear as if he was trying to pick her up.

He took a long sip of his drink. He would probably need a few more before he relaxed. He was so out of the "chatting up women in a bar" scene, he didn't know what to say. It had been so long since he first met Charlotte, and with Adriana, things had happened so naturally, he hadn't had to think about it.

He risked a quick glance in the mirror. Maadhavi was still staring at her drink, tracing a pattern in the condensation on the glass with a long elegant finger, deep in thought. She was a very attractive woman—great bone structure, beautifully groomed—but she didn't look happy. She seemed filled with deep sadness as if something was really wrong with her world. Still, it wasn't his problem. She was a means to an end. His drink almost finished, he raised a hand to get Ramesh's attention.

"Same again, please, Ramesh. You made it perfectly." John smiled. "Oh, and please have one yourself."

John caught Maadhavi watching him in the mirror, and

she quickly looked away. Turning toward her, he said, "Excuse me."

She turned her head toward him.

"Would you like another one of those?" John pointed to her almost finished martini. She studied him for a moment, then nodded.

"Thank you, that's kind of you."

"My pleasure."

John nodded to Ramesh, who had been watching the exchange. He didn't say anymore to Maadhavi or even look in her direction. He didn't want her to think there were any strings attached to the drink. Instead, he went back to studying his phone while Ramesh prepared the drinks.

Ramesh slid a fresh gin and tonic in front of him, and John waited until he placed the martini before Maadhavi before picking up his glass. He nodded thanks to Ramesh, then turned toward Maadhavi. Raising the glass in front of him he gave what he thought to be a disarming smile.

"Cheers."

"Cheers. Thank you." She smiled but only with her mouth, her eyes still sad.

John took a sip and went back to looking at his phone. He sensed her watching him in the mirror.

"You're English?"

John looked up, pretending to be surprised, turning toward her.

"Yes." He smiled and added, "You're Indian?"

That got a chuckle.

"I've always been observant." He gave her another smile, then turned back to his phone, hoping he wasn't playing things too cool.

"Are you here for business?"

John turned back. "Of sorts, yes."

"Staying in the hotel?"

"No, I'm staying nearby." John tried to keep it vague without being evasive. "A serviced apartment."

"Ah, okay." Maadhavi nodded. "Is it your first time in Bangalore?"

"No, I've been here before." Suddenly, he knew a way to get the conversation flowing—bring up a subject everyone spoke about. "But the traffic is so much worse since I came last"

Maadhavi nodded and again, gave a half smile.

"I know." She sighed. "It's got to the stage, I think twice about going anywhere."

John nodded in sympathy. "The government needs to take some drastic action."

"Ha!" Maadhavi shook her head and went back to staring at her glass.

Shit. He had to keep the conversation going. John half stood and held out his hand.

"My name is ..." It was on the tip of his tongue to say John, but he stopped himself in time. "William."

Maadhavi turned, looked at his hand for a moment, then took it. "Maadhavi." Her handshake was confident, not hard like a man's, firm, yet still feminine.

"A pleasure to meet you, Maadhavi." John sat down and picked up his drink. "Where are you from, Maadhavi?"

"From here, Bangalore."

"Oh."

Maadhavi raised an eyebrow.

"Ah, no, I assumed you were from another part of India, given we're in a hotel," John explained.

Maadhavi smiled. "Actually, I live in the hotel."

"Really?" John took a sip of his drink, then put it down.

"I've never met anyone who lives in a hotel. I thought it only happened in the movies."

Maadhavi's forehead creased in a slight frown, which quickly disappeared. She picked up her drink and toyed with the olive.

"If you don't mind me asking, Maadhavi, what do you do?"

Maadhavi hesitated, still twirling the olive around in her drink. Picking up the glass, she took a sip, then turned to John.

"I'm an actress."

John feigned surprise. "Really? Plays or films?"

John could see Maadhavi visibly relax.

"Mainly films." She gave him a smile, a proper smile this time, one that included her eyes.

John leaned toward her conspiratorially and lowered his voice. "Are you... famous?"

Maadhavi chuckled, her eyes twinkling with amusement. "A little."

John raised his glass. "To Maadhavi, the famous actress. May you always be successful... and happy."

Maadhavi tilted her head to one side, watching him as he took a drink. "Thank you." She then picked up her glass and took a long drink, half emptying the glass.

John pretended not to notice.

Maadhavi turned to look at him again, studying him while John looked at his drink, pretending to be unaware.

"William, have you eaten?"

John looked up. "No," he lied, "in fact, I haven't."

"Then would you like to join me for dinner? It's the least I can do, and I hate to dine alone."

"I would be honored, Miss famous actress."

Maadhavi giggled, drained the rest of her drink, then slipped off her stool.

"There's a very good Indian restaurant upstairs. They do an excellent biryani. Have you tried biryani before, William?"

Again, John lied, "No, but if you say it's good, I'll be happy to try it."

"Good, that's settled then." Maadhavi turned toward Ramesh, who had been eavesdropping with interest, pretending to polish glasses. She gave a slight nod, which Ramesh returned.

John reached for his wallet, and Maadhavi placed a hand on his arm.

"It's taken care of, William."

John raised his eyebrows. "No, that's not right, I bought you a drink."

"Don't worry, someone else is paying for it, and that person can afford it."

"Oh." John pretended to look confused even as he realized Patil was footing the hotel bills. "Thank you." Damn, he should have ordered a round for the whole bar.

"Come. I'm starving."

## 59

The maitre d' seated them in a quiet corner, away from inquisitive eyes, although when they entered the restaurant, a polite but excited buzz was clear from the Indian diners.

Maadhavi sat with her back to the room, which suited John, who preferred to see who was coming and going. He didn't know what he would do if Patil walked in but guessed as Maadhavi was dining with him, she had made no plans with the man.

The staff fussed over her. Part of that could have been because she was a celebrity, but she treated them kindly and with respect, and it was obvious they all liked her. They ordered a bottle of red and agreed to share a mutton biryani between them.

Now that Maadhavi had let her guard down, she was easy to talk to—intelligent, witty, and well-informed. Not for the first time, John wondered what she was doing with a man like Patil. She asked John about his work and his background, but John avoided giving too much away while trying not to be evasive. He had heard somewhere, the best lies are based on the truth, so most of what he told her was based on fact—he just left out the controversial details. As far as Maadhavi was concerned, he was an expat in Bangalore to manage the back-office operations for a financial services company. She appeared satisfied with that.

The biryani was as good as promised—soft well-cooked mutton in moist, fragrant saffron-infused rice. It was delicious, and John needed it to soak up the alcohol. He thought he could handle his booze but was struggling to keep up with Maadhavi, who, despite her intake, remained lucid.

As John poured the rest of the second bottle of Argentinean Malbec into Maadhavi's glass, she dabbed her lips with her napkin, looked down at the mark left by her lipstick and the biryani spices as if surprised, then smiled at John.

"I've really enjoyed talking to you, William. It's rare I get to have normal conversations with normal people."

"I saw the reaction when you walked in." John gestured with his head toward the rest of the restaurant. "Then why live in a hotel?" He frowned. "Surely, that must affect your privacy?"

"It's a long story, William," Maadhavi replied and looked down at her plate. "Sometimes, you don't get to choose how you live your life." She looked up at John, suddenly, appearing very sad.

John raised an eyebrow. He agreed—his own life hadn't turned out the way he would have chosen—but he wanted to find out more.

"What do you mean? You are a young, successful, intelligent, and if you don't mind me saying, beautiful woman. The world is your oyster."

"Huh." She drained her glass and signaled for the waiter. Looking back at John, she asked, "A *digestif*?"

"Not yet, thank you." His wine glass was still two-thirds full.

Maadhavi ordered a Yamazaki.

"Nice whisky."

"Yes." Maadhavi gave a half smile. "It is, but I order it because it's expensive."

John raised an eyebrow.

"Don't worry." Maadhavi waved a dismissive hand. "It's a small revenge I take pleasure in."

"Are you not happy, Maadhavi?" Keeping the puzzled expression on his face, he waved his hand in a gesture meant to encompass the whole hotel. "You have a lifestyle millions of people in this country, in fact, the world can only dream of."

Maadhavi swirled her glass of whisky.

"Everything comes at a price," she said in a low voice, so low, John had to sit forward to hear her over the buzz of the restaurant. She looked up, fixing her gaze on John.

Were those tears in her eyes?

"Sometimes, that price is too much to bear." She picked up her glass and drained it in one go, banged the empty glass down on the table, and then stood. "I'm sorry, William, I have to go. It's been a pleasure talking to you."

John stood as well, his napkin in his hand, both eyebrows raised in surprise.

"Don't worry about all this." Maadhavi waved at the table. "It's all covered." Turning, she walked out the door as John sank slowly back into his chair, wondering what was going on in her life.

## 60

Rajiv drummed his fingers on the desk and stared at the phone amid the never-ending pile of paperwork.

He had tried to make inroads on the case files all morning but was having trouble concentrating. In fact, his mood had been off since he had paid the visit to Patil's house and briefed Captain Sharma.

Had he condemned John to life in prison... or even death? Was the westerner he thought he had seen even John? He exhaled loudly and stood. Walking over to the window, he looked out. A pair of squirrels ran circles around the trunk of the Peepal tree, their tails bobbing up and down in excitement, but Rajiv paid them no attention, his mind still on John. Where are you, John? What are you doing? He looked back at the phone on his desk, then looked at his watch; eleven thirty in the morning. He did a quick calculation; ten a.m. in Dubai. Giving John the benefit of the doubt, if he was still in Dubai, it was a reasonable time to call. Rajiv walked back to the desk and picked up the phone. Scrolling through the call history, he found the Dubai number John had called from and dialed.

It rang for a while, but when no one answered, Rajiv sighed and cut the call. Sitting down in his chair, he rested his head against the back of the seat while he twirled the phone in his hand. What had John said when he phoned last? He had hinted he was coming, that he needed to seek justice for what Surya Patil had done in Oman, for sending two hired killers after him.

"I really hope you aren't here yet," he said to no one in particular. Dropping the phone back on the desk, he picked up a file as the phone buzzed. Rajiv looked at the caller ID.

"Speak of the devil."

He picked up the phone but said nothing.

"You called?" said the familiar voice on the other end.

"I did. Where are you?"

"You called my number in Dubai."

Rajiv leaned back in his chair, running his fingers through his hair with his left hand. "Well, I hope you are in Dubai."

"I appreciate your concern."

"Look." Rajiv sighed. "I have a job to do. A duty I've sworn to perform..."

"I know."

"I wouldn't want any harm to come to you. You are a good man, but I can't do nothing."

"I understand, my friend. You are still a friend?"

What was he? What was the right thing to do?

"As much as a man in my position can be. It's... difficult."

"Yeah." There was a pause for a moment. "You must do what you have to do. And I must do what I have to do." Rajiv screwed up his face and rubbed his temple as John continued, "We are both men of honor."

"That's what worries me." Rajiv exhaled loudly. "Be careful."

"I'm always careful, but don't worry about me. Whatever I do, I'll try not to put you in a difficult position."

Rajiv nodded as if John could see him.

"I get the feeling from what you're saying, you aren't really in Dubai. You're already here." He heard John chuckle on the other end.

"One shouldn't always listen to one's feelings."

"No, but... I thought I saw you here in Bangalore, and a suspicious westerner with a stolen car disappeared from a hotel I investigated. So, putting two and two together..."

"You got five. That's bad math and not very good police work. I think you are losing your touch."

"I'm not so sure."

"Well, I hope you catch him, whoever he is, whatever he has done. I have to go now. Good luck, my friend."

The phone went dead, and Rajiv stared blankly at the wall in front of him. Unfortunately, he didn't feel any better than before the call. In fact, his mood was worse.

## 61

Surya Patil glanced at the caller display, then answered the call.

"What has she done now?" he growled. He glanced at the gold Rolex on his wrist. He needed to be in U.B. City soon for dinner, and he wouldn't get there if he was answering calls.

"Ah, S-S-Sir," a hesitant voice stuttered.

"Get on with it. I haven't got all day." Surya pushed back from his study desk, preparing to leave his house.

"Yes, Sir, it's just that last night, Madam had dinner with a man."

"What?" Surya stopped in his tracks, his grip tightening on the phone. "Do we know him? Is he a director, an actor?"

"A foreigner, Sir."

Surya felt a little knot of fear growing in the pit of his belly.

"Why did you wait until now to call me? I pay you to keep me informed."

"Yes, Sir, sorry, Sir. I was unwell, Sir. I just came back to work now for the evening shift."

"Idiot!" Surya shook his head. "I don't suppose you got a name, a description?"

"Ah, yes, Sir." The voice sounded happier. "Not a name, Sir, but my colleague described him."

"Well, go on, hurry up."

"Sir, he ah, had gray pants and a dark blue shirt—"

"Not his clothes, you bloody idiot, his face! What did he look like?"

"S-S-S-Sorry, Sir. Brown hair, a beard, taller than Ma'am."

"Dark brown or light brown?"

"Sir?"

"His hair, you fool!"

"Oh, light brown, Sir."

Surya frowned. That didn't sound like John Hayes. Then who the hell was she wining and dining on his account? He would have to teach her another lesson, stupid...

"Sir?"

"What is it?"

"My ah... payment."

Surya ended the call in disgust—the bloody idiots he had to deal with.

He stuffed the phone in his pocket, grabbed the door handle, wrenching it open, and stormed down the stairs.

"We go now," he roared as he reached the entrance lobby. The resting policemen scrambled to their feet and filed out the door, running to the vehicles. Captain Sharma walked out of his room.

"Sir?"

"Are you deaf? I'm going out. Now, you idiot!"

The commando blinked, hesitated a moment, then jumped into action.

"Yes, Sir."

Surya pushed his way out the door as his driver jumped up from his seat under the tree and ran to start the Mercedes. Behind him, Captain Sharma ran out, his MP-5 gripped in his left hand and began issuing commands to the men lined up beside the escort SUVs.

Surya strode across the driveway, spotting his two private guards standing under the tree.

"You two. Come with me," he shouted,

The men looked at each other, then flicked their cigarettes away and walked over to the Mercedes.

"Not in my fucking car!" Surya pointed toward the SUVs. "Ride with them and hurry up, you useless buggers."

Surya opened the rear door of the Mercedes and sat down, slamming the door behind him.

His driver turned back to look at him. "Where to, Sir?"

"Vijaya Palace."

The driver bobbed his head. "Yes, Sir."

The car started to move toward the gate when there was a tap on Surya's window. He powered down the window an inch and glared through the gap at Captain Sharma.

"Sir, where are we going?"

Surya turned to his driver and growled, "You tell him."

## 62

John pulled over, turned off the engine, and stared out the windscreen, tapping his fingers on the steering wheel. He had been thinking all the while about staking out Patil's house, but the more he thought about it, the more he realized it was too risky. Security was too tight, and if Rajiv had been to his old hotel, he might have given Patil's guards his description. Even though he had changed the plates, if he, a westerner, was spotted on the same street, in a white Hyundai hatchback, it wouldn't bode well for him. He sighed. So, he had to go with his second option, but he didn't really like that one either. It was too soon, but he couldn't sit around and do nothing. He was nearing the end of his second week away from Adriana and didn't want the situation to drag out. The longer he was in Bangalore, the riskier it was, so he had to bring things to a head... safely.

He made his decision. He would go back to the hotel and see if he could see Maadhavi again. Hopefully, she wouldn't think he was stalking her and perhaps, open up more, give him something he could use against Patil.

He locked the car, walked to the end of the street where it joined the main road, and waved down a rickshaw. He told the rickshaw wallah where to go, hiding his exasperation as he went through the painful rigmarole of agreeing on a price, despite the rickshaw having a meter, then sat back in the seat as the three-wheeler moved off. It took fifteen minutes to near the turn for the hotel. John was lost in thought until the rickshaw stopped. He looked up and saw the lanes blocked in front.

"What's the matter?"

"*Jam hogaya*, Saar," the rickshaw wallah stated the obvious. "Traffic jam." He turned his head and grinned at John, exposing a row of rotten brown teeth. "Don't worry, Saar! I can go around." He bobbed his head, revved the engine, and pulled out onto the opposite lane into the oncoming traffic.

"Bloody hell," John winced and closed his eyes, gripping the seat with both hands. The rickshaw accelerated past the line of stalled traffic, bumping and swerving around potholes and wider oncoming vehicles as the air filled with angry horns. Suddenly, John was thrown forward as the rickshaw braked heavily. He opened his eyes, expecting an imminent accident. Just at the turn for the hotel, a white Land Cruiser, headlights on full beam, red flashing lights on the roof, turned across in front of them and headed toward the hotel, followed by a white S Class Mercedes, its windows blacked out, and two more white SUVs with flashing red lights. John couldn't see who was in the Mercedes, the window tint too dark, but he knew in his gut who it was.

"Shit."

The rickshaw wallah looked back, "Saar?"

"Nothing, keep going."

The rickshaw waited for a gap, then took the turn for the

hotel, and John reached forward and tapped the rickshaw wallah on the shoulder.

"Go slowly."

The rickshaw slowed down, and John peered out the side toward the hotel. The Mercedes had pulled up in the porte cochere and between the bodies of the security surrounding him, he could see the unmistakable figure of Surya Patil.

The rickshaw swerved across the road to turn into the entrance of the hotel.

"No, no, go straight."

The driver shook his head, and John saw him give him a questioning look in the mirror.

"I've changed my mind. Keep going. Don't worry, I'll pay you extra."

The rickshaw wallah's head bobbed, his frown changing to a smile in the mirror.

John sat back in his seat. Bugger. Now, what did he do? He didn't want to go home. It felt like wasting an evening. How was he ever going to get close to Patil with three vehicles filled with armed policemen, accompanying him wherever he went?

The rickshaw pulled up at the end of the road, and the rickshaw wallah looked in the mirror.

"Saar, which way?"

John looked left, then right. He didn't know where to go... then it hit him.

## 63

John directed the rickshaw wallah for the next ten minutes until they pulled up in Shivnagar, near the turn for Surya Patil's street. John handed over double the previously agreed fare and waited as the thrilled rickshaw wallah sped off down the street, waiting until he turned the corner. If all the security was with Patil at the hotel, the house would be unprotected. He walked down the footpath on the opposite side to Patil's house, keeping to the shadows, his eyes on the house.

Lights were on inside, but from the street, there seemed to be little activity. John waited while a car drove past, then stepped off the curb and crossed the road toward the main gate. Just as he was about to step onto the curb between two parked cars, the gate opened. Shit. He froze, bent down and peered through the windows of the car at the gate, ready to run if necessary. An elderly man, in an ill-fitting guard's uniform and rubber flip-flops, stepped outside with a plastic chair, placed it on the path in front of the gate, and sat down. Crossing one leg onto his other knee, he started picking at his toenails. John slowly straightened up, turned around, and casually stepped out from between the cars, heading back in the direction he came from.

He remembered a few years ago when he had been staking out the house, Patil's son, Sunil, had somehow left the house and sneaked up on him. There must be a back way in.

He turned right at the end of the street, then right again at the end of the block. Walking down the street, he counted the houses until he estimated he was behind Patil's house. The house on this street was of a similar size, though all the windows were dark, suggesting it was unoccupied. It had a high wall and a locked gate. John frowned as he walked past, sneaking glances at the property in case he was being observed. He reached the end of the street and turned around. Apart from a few passing cars and two wheelers, the street was empty, the residents locked away in their air-conditioned castles behind high walls.

John walked past again and this time, stopped at the gate. He checked the padlock, but it was too strong to break, and besides, that would make too much noise. But the service door next to it, near the end of the front wall? Maybe that was worth a try? Walking over after glancing up and down the street again, he pushed on the door—locked. Bugger it. John puffed out air and frowned, then looked again at the handle.

There was a gap between the door and the frame, and as he looked closely, he could see the end of the slide bolt where it fitted into the receiver on the frame. Inserting his index finger and thumb into the gap, they just fit, and he wiggled the bolt. It moved. He tried sliding it back; it moved a fraction, then stopped. Shit. He shook his fingers out and glanced around again. A dog wandered past in the middle of the street, paused to look at him, then carried on.

John visualized the door bolts he had seen, realizing the handle of the bolt must be down, preventing it from sliding. He inserted his fingers again and gripping the bolt, rotated it toward him, hoping it wasn't padlocked from the inside. Sure enough, it moved. He kept twisting until he lost his grip, and the bolt slid back to its original position. He shook his cramping finger and this time, adjusted his grip. He twisted again until he felt it loosen, then slipped it to the right, so it wouldn't clip shut again. Still a little way to go. He gripped it again, sliding it a little more. He did this a couple more times until the end of the bolt slipped out of the receiver, and the door creaked open on protesting hinges. John winced at the noise and looked around, but he was clear.

Stepping inside, he pushed the door shut, just snicking the bolt to keep the door from swinging open, then looked around. He was standing in a paved parking area in front of a palatial three-story home. The windows were dark, the blinds and curtains closed. In the dull glow from the streetlamps, he could see the flower beds lining the parking area were unkempt, the plants dead from lack of water and maintenance. The area was strewn with leaves, weeds growing through the cracks in the paving stones. The house obviously hadn't been occupied for some time. That suited John. Pulling out his phone, covering the light with his hand, he turned on the torch, adjusting the brightness until it was very dim, then walked toward the house. The house took up most of the plot, the boundary walls as high as the front, but on closer examination, he saw on each side of the house, there was a gap of around a meter, allowing access to the rear. Shielding the light, John walked toward the right side and headed to the back.

## 64

Surya climbed out of the car and marched toward the entrance. Again, ignoring the metal detector and pushing the doorman aside, he stepped into the lobby, then stopped and turned, pointing at Captain Sharma.

"Tell your men to stay outside," Surya growled.

The commando captain stopped and raised a hand, signaling his men to stay back.

Surya turned to his two bodyguards who were hanging around near the vehicles.

"You two, come here."

The men grinned and swaggered past the armed police and two commandos. As one of them unsuccessfully attempted to shoulder his way past the captain, Surya impatiently commanded, "Hurry up!"

The grins disappeared, and the two men sheepishly increased their pace and joined Surya in the lobby as the door swung closed behind them. Surya glanced toward the reception desk where three staff were manning the desk, two young women and a young man. The young man nodded toward the bar entrance.

Surya glared at his men.

"She's in there. Bring her up to the suite. Twenty third floor, Suite 2301."

The two men stared at him vacantly, then one asked, "Who, Sir?"

Surya closed his eyes and took a deep breath. Who were these morons? He opened them again.

"Maadhavi Rao!"

The men looked at each other in surprise. "The actress?"

Surya stepped up to the questioner until his nose was almost touching.

"Yes, the actress, you bloody idiot. Bring her upstairs, and don't fuck it up." He raised a finger and jabbed the man in his chest. "If you fuck this up, that's the end of your days in the party."

The man gulped, grabbed his colleague by the sleeve, and headed to the bar.

Surya turned on his heel, ignoring the hesitant wave from the staff member, and strode toward the lifts.

Outside, Captain Ankit Sharma finished counting to fifty, then, his anger under control, turned to his number two.

"Rahul, leave one vehicle and three men with me. Take the rest of the boys back to the house."

"Yes, Sir."

"There's no point all of us hanging out here all night again."

"Are you sure, Sir? It feels different tonight. He seems pretty angry."

Ankit turned to look back at the hotel and adjusted his MP-5 on its sling.

"He's always angry." Turning back, he placed a reassuring hand on Rahul's shoulder. "Don't worry, I'll handle it. If anything, I'll radio you."

His second-in-command nodded, gave a half salute, and instructed the men. Ankit walked over to the side of the entrance and watched as two of the vehicles pulled out of the porte cochere.

"Can't be easy, working for a man like him."

Ankit turned toward the voice and saw the doorman standing next to him, watching the vehicles.

Ankit just smiled.

"We see a lot like him. They think they own the world, pushing us around and treating us like dirt." The doorman turned to face Ankit. "These politicians are destroying the country."

"We can't change the world in one day, brother." Ankit patted him on the shoulder. With a shake of his head, he walked over to his remaining vehicle.

## 65

John reached the end of the alley next to the house and turned off his phone light, slipping the phone into his pocket. There was plenty of light coming over the wall from Patil's house.

Strangely, the wall between the house and Surya Patil's house was lower, just over five feet high. The owners obviously didn't feel the need to have high security on Patil's side. Ironic, considering how dirty his hands were.

John approached slowly until he could see over into what appeared to be the service area of the house. The back of the house was dirty and unmaintained, in complete contrast to the glossy front facade. To the far left, at right angles to the house and abutting the boundary wall, was a small, ramshackle, single-story room, John assumed to be staff quarters. Next to it, a door hung open, exposing a squat toilet, lit by a single bare-light bulb hanging from an electric cable. Next to that, in the rear wall of the house was a row of windows, opening onto a darkened room. A door in the middle of the house stood open, light streaming out, and next to it were the windows into the kitchen. John could see a woman, Patil's cook, moving around inside, preparing food. The smell of spices and the hissing of a pressure cooker carried easily through a half-open window. John watched for a while from the shadows, waiting to see if anyone else came in. After a couple of minutes, a thin man, perhaps in his thirties, appeared. John guessed by his clothing, he was also a servant.

John thought for a while about what to do. He had found a weak spot, but it was only feasible when Surya wasn't home and had taken his security with him. John assumed they would station a guard at the rear when Surya was home. He was sure they wouldn't be stupid enough to leave the rear unguarded... although there was no one there now. He could always come back and check, but that would be risky. If a guard was in place when he came back, John would be spotted coming down the side of the house. Unless he waited now for them to return.

John looked around, his eyes adjusted to the poor light. There was nowhere at the rear of this house where he could hide. Perhaps, he could get inside. John walked over to the rear door and wiggled the handle—locked, of course. He retrieved his phone and shone the light on the lock and the handle. It looked strong, and John had no idea how to pick a lock. He couldn't bash the door in because of the noise. Moving over to the windows, he pushed and wiggled them, but they were strong, double-glazed glass, set in aluminum frames. Damn. He headed back around to the front of the house and tried the front door. If anything, it seemed more secure than the rear door. The front windows were strong as well with the additional protection of wrought iron grills. There was no way he could get in there. He stepped back and looked up at the house. The roof? He quickly dismissed the idea. The house was three stories high with no obvious way of getting up there. His earlier positive mood about finding a weak spot was rapidly disappearing.

What if he got into Surya's house and hid? It was risky, potentially trapping him, but did he have any other options? John stood in the darkness, his hands on his hips, chewing his lip. What was the sensible thing to do? He paced in circles. If he wanted sensible, he would have gone to Lisbon with Adriana. Fuck it.

He headed back down the side of the house. Nearing the back, he slowed and peered over the wall into the kitchen. The male servant was saying something to the cook as she kneaded dough on the bench top. She giggled and threw a piece of dough at him. He pretended to duck but caught the dough and tossed it back at her, sending her into another fit of giggles. Good, they were busy. John moved to the other end of the wall, next to the staff quarters. Jumping up, he got his right hand and left forearm on top of the wall, and using the toes of his new leather shoes for purchase, scrambled up the wall until he could push down with his right hand and lever himself up, so his chest was on the top of the wall. He swung his right leg up and over the wall, then pushed himself up, so he was sitting astride. Swinging the other leg over, looking for a clear place to land, he jumped off the wall.

## 66

Landing, his left leg slipped out from beneath him, and he fell back on the ground with a thud, knocking the air out of him. Gasping for breath, he forced himself up to watch the rear door in case the staff had heard him. He waited as he regained his breath, but no one came, the noise from the pressure cooker and exhaust fan enough to drown out any noise he had made. Sitting up, he climbed to his feet, cursing the new shoes, wishing he was wearing his hiking boots.

Bending double, John crept toward the kitchen window and cautiously peeked in. The two staff were still busy flirting. Good.

John moved back to the rear door and peered into the narrow hallway—a dirty rag served as a doormat and next to it were two battered gas cylinders. John stepped inside, slipped around the cylinders, and moved to the half-open kitchen door. Pausing at the door, he listened for any break in their conversation, but they were still unaware he was there.

John eased past the door, keeping his back to the wall,

and headed toward the end of the hallway. Putting his ear to the door, there was no sound from the other side, so he gently pushed down on the handle, opening the door just a little, and looked into the empty entrance lobby. He opened the door wider and looked around. An ostentatious chandelier hung down from the double height ceiling. Fortunately, it was turned off, or John would have been blinded. The light came from a pair of table lamps on a console table along the back wall. In contrast to the grimy service area, the floor gleamed in shiny white marble, and gilt-edged cornices crowned the walls and the top of the doors. To his left, a closed door stood at the foot of a curved staircase that wound its way up to the next floor. To his right, light filtered from the gap in a half-open door. Through the windows at the front of the lobby, John could see the front garden and parking area, now empty, apart from a pair of motorbikes parked near the side wall.

John walked to the door on his right, listened, then poked his head inside. Bedrolls covered the floor, and backpacks were piled against the wall. John stepped inside and had a quick look around. He needed a weapon, and perhaps, one had been left behind. There was nothing to be seen on the furniture, so he took a cursory look at a couple of backpacks, but they were only filled with dirty clothing and toiletry kits.

John went back to the lobby and crossed over to the other door. He put his ear to the door, then satisfied no one was inside, cracked it open. The room appeared to be a waiting room. Piles of chairs were stacked against one wall, a trestle table was set up at the rear, another backpack sat on the floor beside it, and a neatly rolled bedroll stood on its end in the corner. John walked over and took a quick look in the bag which held a black uniform. This must be where the commando was sleeping. Again, no sign of any weapons, so John moved back to the lobby. He stood at the bottom of the stairs and looked up. He couldn't hide downstairs, so he would have to go up.

He put his foot on the bottom step and froze as a red flashing light filled the lobby. He ducked down and spun around to look through the front window, seeing the gate swing open and two white SUVs pulling up to the curb. Fuck!

John heard a noise behind him and turned to see the door to the service area open and the thin male servant step out. Their eyes met, and the servant opened his mouth to shout. John sprang to his feet and rushed toward him. The servant was rooted to the spot, his mouth open, his eyes wide. John balled his fist and punched him straight in the stomach. The man bent double as a swoosh of air escaped his open mouth, then collapsed to the floor, winded.

John jumped over him and ran for the back door. He jumped out onto the rear step, then spun around and tipped the two gas cylinders over, blocking the hallway in a clatter of steel on tile. He heard a scream from the kitchen but didn't wait. Leaping at the wall, scrabbling for grip, he levered himself over, dropped to the other side, and sprinted for the front gate. He had to get out of there... fast!

## 67

Surya let himself into the suite with his personal key card. Maadhavi didn't know he had one. Why would he tell her? He could have a key to any room, the perks of being the owner of the hotel, but he wouldn't tell her that, either. Some things needed to remain secret, hence the need for offshore trusts and nominee shareholders.

He left the door partially open and walked over to the bar, pouring himself a large whisky. He drank half, then turned to look around the room. It looked the same as it usually did—the L-shaped sofa facing full-height windows with a view over the Bangalore cityscape, the flat screen TV on the wall, a white orchid on the side table beside a row of silver-framed photos of Maadhavi with her parents. She kept it tidy, he'd give her that. He wandered around slowly, looking for signs anyone other than Maadhavi had been in the suite, but the place was spotless. He turned and looked into the bedroom. The bed was made, a book on one bedside table, a copper tray with a small brass idol of Ganesha, and the remains of an incense stick on the other.

He took another sip of his drink and walked into the

dressing room. Racks of designer dresses and expensive saris hung above stacks of shoe boxes. Stepping through, into the en suite, his eyes quickly scanned the vanity unit, looking for an extra toothbrush, razor, anything that would point to another man having stayed over—nothing. He drained his glass, the drink calming him, the anger ebbing away. He stared at himself in the mirror, not liking the man looking back. He looked tired, old... and unhappy. Putting the empty glass down on the counter, he leaned on the marble top with both hands.

Was it all worth it? He had power, he had money, he could snap his fingers and get anything done, but his wife had left him, his son was dead, and now, he was flying off-the-handle in jealousy. He had men staying in his house, following him everywhere, expecting an attack around every corner. Maybe he was paranoid? All this stuff with John Hayes had set him on edge. Closing his eyes, he tried to remember happier times—when he first got married, the birth of his son—times when things were so much simpler.

Was it worth driving Maadhavi away? He had no one else now. Perhaps, just perhaps, there was a reasonable explanation.

He sighed, straightening up, and took his empty glass back to the bar. Refilling it, he put the bottle back just as he heard the door swing open.

"Oh, so now you send your goons to fetch me?" Maadhavi stormed in and stood with her hands on her hips, glaring at him. Her eyes blazed, and her chest rose and fell visibly with her breath. The two men followed her and stood in the doorway, one with a stupid grin on his face, the other staring around the suite with undisguised awe.

"Get out, both of you," Surya snapped and waited as the men backed out the door. "Close it!" he growled.

Maadhavi hadn't moved, staring at him with murder in her eyes. She looked beautiful, like an angry goddess. Surya gestured toward the sofa.

"Sit down."

"No."

"I said, sit down."

Maadhavi flinched at the force of his command and reluctantly moved and sat on the sofa, as far from him as she could. She crossed one leg over the other, smoothed the folds from her sari, crossed her arms, and stared out the window, across the city.

Surya took a sip of his drink, then glass in hand, walked around the sofa, and stood, facing her, blocking her line of sight, his back to the view. She moved her head slightly, so she could continue to look past him.

"Who did you have dinner with last night?"

Maadhavi looked up and sneered. "So, you're spying on me now."

Surya could feel his temper rising again. He took a breath. "Answer the question."

Maadhavi narrowed her eyes and stuck her chin out.

"None of your business."

"It is my business. I'm paying for everything here."

"Oh, so that gives you the right to know everything I'm doing?"

Surya closed his eyes and counted to three.

"Answer the question. I know it wasn't someone from the film industry."

"How do you know?"

"He was a foreigner."

"So what? You don't own me."

Surya's grip tightened on his glass, and he looked at it before tossing half the contents back, gulping it down, then wiped his mouth with the back of his hand. He'd had enough with being polite.

"Actually, I do. Do you really think you will get any work in this town without me? Do you?" Surya stepped closer until she had to bend her head back to look at him. He raised a finger and pointed it at her. "I control this town. I control you, so I'll ask you one more time. Who was that man?"

Maadhavi stood, her face inches away from Surya, her shoulders rising up and down, her face red with anger.

"None of your business, old man. Now, get out."

"Get out?" Surya couldn't control himself anymore. This bitch was getting too big for her boots. "This suite is mine. I pay for it. I pay for everything. Even last night's meal while you were whoring around with some foreign guy. I've had enough. You get out."

"I'll make sure everyone knows about us. About how you raped me, how you've been cheating on your wife. Surya Patil, the strongman of Karnataka. Ha! You can't even be a man without those little blue pills."

"You bitch." He swung his right hand and slapped her across the face with an open palm, knocking her backward across the sofa. She raised her hand to her face and pulled her knees into her chest as he stepped closer, bending down over her.

"Out of respect, I'm giving you two days to clear your stuff and get out of here. I don't expect to see you again." Straightening, he finished his drink, dropped the empty glass on the sofa next to her, then walked toward the door. Before leaving, he stopped and looked back. "And don't go thinking you can talk to the press. I know where your parents live."

He opened the door quickly, one of his men almost

falling in. Surya glared at him as he stepped back, a guilty look on his face. Surya stepped closer and looked straight into his eyes. He said nothing, just glared at him until the man broke eye contact and looked down at his feet.

"Get the car ready. I'm leaving."

"Yes, Boss."

Surya strode over to the lift and stared at his reflection in the steel of the door.

Now, he really was alone.

## 68

John pulled the bolt open and wrenched open the door, looking left and right in a panic, not knowing which way to go. He decided left. The security vehicles would come from his right. He sprinted down the street as he heard shouts from Surya's house. They would be on him in seconds. He whipped his head left to right, looking for somewhere to hide. High walls surrounded all the houses, affording no way in. He was trapped. John increased his pace, again cursing his new footwear. He reached the end of the street, indecision hitting him once more. They would expect him to go right, but left was back toward Patil's house.

He went left just as a white SUV screeched around the corner into the street behind him. John ducked low, crossed the road, and ran. He could hear the vehicle getting closer, but again he had nowhere to go, high walls lining both sides of the street. The red flashing lights got brighter, and there was no way he could get away, so he threw himself to the footpath beside a car, rolled off the curb, then pulled himself under the vehicle, the rough road surface scratching his stomach and knees. Lying there, gasping for breath, he prayed he hadn't been spotted as the vehicle skidded to a stop at the junction. He heard doors open and slam shut and shouted commands while the red lights flashed. He couldn't make out what they were saying, and all he could see were the vehicle's tires and the brown shoes of the armed police as they fanned out across the street. John counted four pairs of brown shoes and a pair of black boots, which he assumed belonged to the commando. John watched as two pairs of shoes headed away from him while two came closer. Holding his breath, he tried to make himself smaller, his heart pounding away as one pair stopped near his car. John closed his eyes. Was this where it was all going to end? Lying under a car in the street, never to see Adriana again?

John pictured Adriana by the pool in Oman, her skin kissed by the sun, her hair piled high on her head, a bead of sweat trickling down her elegant neck. Even behind her Ray-Bans, he knew she was smiling at him.

"Adriana," he whispered.

He tensed as he heard a foot scuff on the ground. Opening his eyes, he watched the shoes move away, further up the street. Hearing the engine rev, he turned his head to see the SUV roll forward as radios squawked and buzzed. Another shouted command and the two pairs of shoes closest to John turned and jogged back to the SUV. The vehicle rolled slowly away from John, the men spread out around it. John breathed out in relief as the flashing red light lessened in intensity.

He seemed to have survived to fight another day.

## 69

"Rajiv, your phone."

Rajiv muttered under his breath and toweled his face dry. Hanging the towel on the rack, he ran his fingers through his hair, then stepped out of the bathroom. One of these days, he would just turn his phone off, pretend he had lost it. He had only been home ten minutes, and it was already ringing. Jogging down the stairs, ducking his head in the kitchen, he gave Aarthi a quick kiss on the cheek. She smiled and pointed to the phone, lying on the dining table.

"It's rung twice already."

Rajiv shook his head and sighed. "It must be the station, probably lost something or too scared to make a decision for themselves."

He picked up the phone and glanced at the call log—two missed calls from the commando captain.

"Shit," he muttered and pressed redial.

"Ankit, sorry, I was tied up."

"We've had an intruder."

. . .

Despite the lights and the siren, it still took thirty minutes for Rajiv to reach Patil's house, the roads so jammed, the vehicles couldn't move out of his way. He used the time to make calls, mobilizing his men, arranging for them to question the neighbors. He didn't expect them to turn up much, most people hidden away in their luxury cocoons, but he had to try.

Rajiv alternately cursed and thumped the horn, forcing his way through the traffic. By the time he pulled up and double-parked outside Patil's gate, he wasn't in the best of moods. Jumping out, he tossed his keys to one of the armed police manning the gate.

"See if you can get someone to park it." He muttered almost to himself, "Can't upset the neighbors."

Hearing raised voices, he pushed through the gate. Surya Patil was waving his arms around as he ranted and raved at the two commandos while his two hired thugs smirked in the corner.

Rajiv cursed. His boss Muniappa had arrived before him and was glaring at Rajiv as he approached. Rajiv nodded a greeting as Surya Patil noticed him and turned to Muniappa.

"This is your man?"

"Yes, Sir."

Patil stepped forward and raised a finger, pointing it at Rajiv's chest.

"Why haven't you caught him yet?" His lip curled in a snarl. "You are useless, all of you."

Rajiv glanced over his shoulder at Ankit, who rolled his eyes and gave his head an imperceptible shake.

Patil stepped even closer until Rajiv could feel his breath on his face. The smell of whisky was strong.

"I. Will. Have. You. Transferred." He punctuated each word with a jab of his finger in Rajiv's chest.

Rajiv's jaw tightened, and he ground his teeth together. It never paid to argue with these people. Better to let them vent.

Patil turned and glared at Muniappa.

"I'll have you transferred too!"

Muniappa's eyes widened in panic as the attention switched to him, his eyes darting from Rajiv to Ankit and back again.

"Sir, let's not be too hasty." He gestured toward Rajiv. "Detective Inspector Sampath is my best man. If anyone can catch this man, it will be him."

"Why haven't you done it already? You've had plenty of time!"

"S-S-Sir, these things take time, but we will catch him."

Patil stared at him, then turned slowly and fixed Rajiv with his beady eyes. Raising a finger again, he opened his mouth as if to say something, then changed his mind. He turned and walked toward the house, pushing Ankit out of the way, and went inside, slamming the door behind him.

Rajiv exhaled as Muniappa approached him. He too poked Rajiv in the chest with his forefinger.

"Make sure you get results fast, or I'll bloody well have you sent back to the village. I'm not taking the blame for this."

Rajiv kept eye contact with his boss while he imagined grabbing the finger with his right hand and twisting it back until it snapped. Instead, he nodded.

"Yes, Sir."

Muniappa stared at him for a moment longer. "I want a report first thing in the morning."

"Sir."

"And I will request more security,"—he turned and pointed at the two commandos—"because you obviously can't handle it." With that, he turned and marched off to the gate.

Rajiv watched him leave and realized his jaw was still clenched. Willing himself to relax, he turned to Ankit, and they shared a grim smile. They had both been here before.

"I should have listened to my father," Ankit joked. "Stayed on the farm."

Rajiv shook his head and sighed.

"What happened?"

"We escorted Mr. Patil to the Vijaya Palace Hotel. While we were out, someone got in through the back door. When our team returned, he assaulted one of the staff and escaped though the property at the back. We searched the streets for thirty minutes, but there's no sign of him."

Rajiv exhaled sharply. "Did anyone see the man? Do we have a description?"

"Venkatesh, Patil's servant, said it was a foreigner."

"He's sure?" Rajiv narrowed his eyes. "It wasn't just a burglary gone wrong?"

"I think it's our man." He gestured toward the house. "But ask him yourself. He's in the kitchen. He's pretty shook up."

"I will. Thanks, Ankit. What's your plan now?"

Ankit looked around the front garden.

"We're doubling patrols, increasing the men on watch each shift. The house behind is unoccupied. I'll put a couple of men there, so he can't get back in that way. There's not much more we can do. We can't leave the house unattended anymore, but I'll work it out." He nodded toward the upper floor.

"I'm sure he'll also put in a request for more manpower."

He jerked his head toward the two thugs, who were smoking. "He'll probably get more of them." Ankit shrugged. "But this guy can't be too hard to track down. He's a foreigner, he'll stick out."

"Yeah, I hope you're right." Rajiv grimaced. "I've got my boys conducting door-to-door inquiries as we speak. He'll pop up somewhere. If it was the foreigner, he won't be able to hide. I'll go in now and see if I can get a decent description."

Stepping past Ankit, he entered the house, crossed the lobby, and walked down the corridor into the kitchen. The servant sat on a stool, sipping *chai* while a lady, Rajiv assumed to be the cook, fussed over him. He jumped up when he saw Rajiv enter, almost spilling the *chai*.

"It's okay." Rajiv waved toward the chair. "Please sit down."

The man nodded, sat back on the edge of the seat, and looked down at the floor, avoiding eye contact.

"What's your name?"

"Venkatesh, Sir."

"Okay, Venkatesh, why don't you tell me what happened."

Venkatesh stuttered. "S-S-Sir, I went out to open the front door. I heard the cars coming back. When I walked out, I saw a man by the stairs. He hit me and knocked me over."

The cook handed Rajiv a cup of *chai*, and he sipped on it gratefully. It was much better than the stuff at the station. He smiled at the cook, then looked back at Venkatesh.

"Then what happened?"

"Sir, he ran out the back door... but I didn't see anything after that."

"Okay." Rajiv took another sip. "Are you okay, are you hurt?"

Venkatesh shook his head.

"That's good, Venkatesh. Now, I need you to concentrate and tell me what he looked like."

Venkatesh nodded eagerly. "He was huge, Sir, very strong." He made a fist with his hand. "He had a fist as big as a cannonball, and teeth, sharp teeth like a demon." The cook took a sharp intake of breath and covered her mouth. Venkatesh, enjoying the attention, continued, "He was pale, white like a ghost, and..."

"Venkatesh," Rajiv interrupted, his tone of voice putting a stop to Venkatesh's tale. "What color was his hair?"

"Ah... yellow, Sir. No, lightish like ah... corn... I think."

Rajiv nodded. "Good. And was he clean shaven?"

"Yes, Sir." Venkatesh nodded eagerly. "I mean, no."

Rajiv took a deep breath and counted to five.

"Venkatesh, drink your tea and think very carefully. I need to find out what he looked like."

"Yes, Sir." Venkatesh took a sip of his tea and stared at the floor. After a moment, he looked up. "Sir, he had a beard." He motioned to his own face. "Full beard, Sir."

"Good. And how tall was he?"

"Very tall..."

"Venkatesh."

"Ah, Sir." Venkatesh glanced toward the cook. "Same as you, Sir."

Rajiv nodded, finished his tea, and handed the empty glass to the cook.

"What was he wearing?"

"Pants, Sir."

Rajiv closed his eyes and counted to five again.

"Venkatesh, what color pants?"

Venkatesh swallowed, "I-I don't remember, Sir." He hung his head.

Rajiv moved closer and squatted down in front of him.

"You have been very brave, Venkatesh. Thank you. Is there anything else you can remember? Anything I should know?"

Venkatesh shook his head, still looking down at the floor.

Rajiv patted him on the knee and stood.

"If you think of anything, you tell the captain. Okay?"

Venkatesh nodded.

Rajiv stepped back and turned to the cook. "Thank you for the *chai*. It was very good."

The cook blushed as Rajiv turned and walked out the door. He didn't have much to work on, but he could guess who it was.

## 70

John heard a squeak and turned his head slowly to the right. A rat scurried down the gutter and stopped to stare at him through beady black eyes, its nose twitching as it smelled him. When it took a few steps closer, John reached for a pebble and with difficulty in the cramped space under the car, tossed it in the rat's direction. He hated rats. He could bear most things, but rats gave him the creeps. The rat scampered away, and John shifted his body slightly to ease the pressure on his hips and chest.

Turning his wrist, he checked the time. It was almost midnight. He had been under the car for over three hours. He was tired and thirsty, but it hadn't been safe to leave. Police vehicles had been patrolling the streets, and from the sounds and activity, it had appeared police had also been going door-to-door. For the last hour, the street had been silent, but still, John had waited. Having successfully escaped, he didn't want to be captured, walking down the street.

Something was crawling down his neck, but he couldn't

reach it. He tried not to think about it as a cockroach ran across his hand. Actually, he hated cockroaches almost as much as rats. He shook it away and decided—time to get out of there. Dragging himself along the ground until he was out from under the car, he sat up. Looking around, he saw the street was clear, so he stood and stretched out the aches and kinks, then looked down at his new clothes, now covered in dirt, a hole torn in the right knee of his pants. John brushed himself down, then with another quick glance up and down the street, headed off.

Keeping to the shadows and the smaller streets, he put as much distance as he could between him and Patil's house. He remembered reading somewhere, one shouldn't flee in a straight line, one should put as many right angles between him and his pursuers as possible, so he took random turns, left, right, further and further until he didn't know where he was.

After thirty minutes, he came to a larger road with a group of men gathered around a late-night *chai* stand. John needed a drink and some sugar. He paid for a *chai* and waited while the man filled a small paper cup from the steel urn lashed to the side of a battered motor scooter. The other customers talked quietly among themselves as they smoked and sipped their tea on the side of the road, occasionally throwing curious glances in John's direction. Taking the tea, he took a sip. Just what he needed—hot and sweet... very sweet. He felt the rush of warmth revitalize him and knocked the tea back quickly before tossing the cup into the pile of used cups by the curb. Walking over to a man dozing in his rickshaw nearby, he shook him awake. Giving him a destination a block away from his car, he climbed in as his phone buzzed in his pocket. The rickshaw wallah pulled on the starter handle, and the rickshaw coughed and spluttered to life as John sat back in the seat, then glanced down at the caller I.D. on the phone.

Rajiv.

John dropped the phone on the seat beside him. He was in no mood to speak to him right now.

## 71

John watched the two girls on the floor. Geetanjali played with a rag doll, talking to it while she stroked its woolen hair. Saumya was lying on her stomach, writing lines of sums with a pencil in a dog-eared notebook. The small scene of domesticity made him feel a little more at peace as if he was living a normal life, even though the girls weren't his, and he was hiding in a house in India, but he felt better than he had all day. The talk with Pournima earlier in the day had helped too.

John had risen early before the girls woke up, showered, and dressed in clean clothes, but after they left for school, he had rolled out his bedding and slept again, fully clothed. The stress of the previous night had drained him. He was depressed and had needed to recharge before he could face the day. He slept for another four hours and woke to find his clothes had been washed and were already dry after hanging in the strong midday sun. Pournima sat in one corner with a needle and thread, repairing the rip in the knee of his pants. She smiled as he sat up, rubbed his face, then looked at his watch.

"Oh, I'm sorry, Pournima."

"It's okay, Mr. John." Her smile turned to a frown. "I heard you come back last night. It was late."

"Yes." John stood, rolled his bedding, and stowed it in the corner. Pulling out a plastic chair, he sat down and watched Pournima stitch the tear in his pants.

She tied off the thread, biting the excess off with her teeth, then turned the pants the right way out again. She inspected her work, then held them out to John. He took them and looked down at the nearly invisible repair.

"Thank you, Pournima." He gave her a sad smile.

"What happened, Mr. John?"

John shrugged and looked back at the pants. "It's nothing, I tripped."

"I mean, what happened to you? You are unhappy today."

John looked up in surprise, nodded thoughtfully, and sighed.

Pournima stood up. "Wait. I will make coffee. Then you tell me."

John waited while Pournima busied herself in the kitchen. Last night had been horrible. He had almost blown it and was very lucky to have made his escape. If he had been caught, he would never have seen Adriana again, instead, spending the rest of his life in an Indian prison... if Patil didn't have him disappeared.

Perhaps, he should just give up? Get out of India and get on a flight to Portugal and spend his life in peace with Adriana. He glanced up at the framed picture of Sanjay. A garland of fresh flowers hung from the frame, and someone had put a dot of sandalwood paste on the glass in the space between his eyes. At that moment, Pournima walked out with a tray, catching him staring at the photo.

"He loved working for you, Mr. John. He always used to tell me you are a good man."

"I don't think so, Pournima." John grimaced. "I've done a lot of bad things."

Pournima placed the tray on the table between them and passed John a stainless-steel tumbler of filter coffee.

"I don't think so, Mr. John." She took a sip of her drink. "When I was a young girl in my village, there was a wise man, Mr. Ramanathan. He was the schoolteacher. He was a great man, Mr. John. He had so many books. English books, Hindi books." Pournima shook her head and smiled at the memory. "He knew so much and taught us so many things."

John smiled and sipped his coffee quietly, wondering where she was headed.

"One thing he told me, Mr. John, I've never forgotten. It's not the deed that is important. It's the thought behind the deed that matters. Do you understand, Mr. John?"

"I think so."

"So, Mr. John, those things you say you have done. Why did you do them? That makes it good or bad."

"Thank you, Pournima." John smiled and reached over to touch her arm with his fingers.

They sat in silence, sipping coffee, both looking at Sanjay's photo. John placed his empty tumbler down on the table beside him.

"Pournima?"

She looked at him, waiting for the question to follow. John leaned forward, his forearms on his knees, staring at the floor, thinking of the words.

"Do you ever wish Sanjay had never worked for me? Had never got involved after they killed Charlotte?" he asked without looking up.

"Mr. John, he loved working for you and Ma'am. Those

were the happiest times of his life. He was always talking about you. He would tell the girls stories about England Ma'am had told him."

John nodded slowly.

"But after? When he shared the information about Sunil Patil?"

Pournima put her tumbler down and sat forward.

"Mr. John, it wasn't your fault. Sanjay did what he felt was right, and I am proud of him. I miss him every day, but it was his duty to tell you what he knew." She leaned even closer. "As it's your duty to do what you have to, to make sure your loved one is safe."

John leaned back and studied her face, and she looked away shyly, the confidence and forcefulness that showed in her voice disappearing as quickly as it had come. This simple, unworldly, widowed, single mother with barely a rupee to her name, in her modest home in one of Bangalore's largest slums, was more astute than she appeared. He was already feeling better. It was a wonder how wisdom often appeared in the unlikeliest of forms but always at the right time.

"Thank you, Pournima."

## 72

"Bom dia."

John heard a chuckle on the other end of the line.

"You've started learning Portuguese?"

"Of course, I'll need to communicate when I'm there." John walked slowly away from Pournima's house, up the track toward the main road.

"When are you coming?"

John paused and ran his fingers through his hair.

"Soon, my baby. Soon." He smiled and looked up at the cloudless, deep blue sky.

"Good. I miss you."

"Yeah, me too. It's been too long."

John's eyes followed a pair of eagles as they circled freely high above him. No effort, just gliding around and around in circles, slowly getting higher and higher as they rode the updrafts. That sight and the sound of Adriana's voice filled him with a renewed determination, one that had been lacking since the previous night.

"Adriana, baby, it won't be long now. I have a good plan, and before you know it, I will be on a plane back to you."

"What plan? Tell me about it? Is it dangerous?"

John chewed his lip and kicked at a stone with his hiking boot.

"I won't tell you about the plan. I don't want you to worry, but..." He glanced back toward Pournima's little house. "I have people helping me."

He spent the next five minutes telling Adriana about Pournima and the girls, about Sanjay and his death, and about the advice Pournima had given him.

"John, please thank her from me, too."

"I will."

"And John?"

"Yes?"

"When this is all over, can we do something for the girls?"

John smiled. "Of course. Pournima will be very happy."

"Thank you."

The phone went silent, and John glanced at his watch,

"Adriana, baby, I need to go now. I love you."

"I love you too. Be careful."

"I'm always careful," John laughed. "I'll call you soon. Bye."

"Bye."

John disconnected the call and stared thoughtfully up the track. He had lied to Adriana. He didn't have a plan, but he was now more determined than ever to finish this and get back to her.

A loudspeaker sounded as the afternoon call to prayer carried across the slum from the mosque. John stared in the direction of the sound, the seed of an idea germinating deep in his subconscious, but he couldn't grab it, couldn't pull it to the surface. Shrugging it off, he slipped the phone back in his pocket and headed up to the main road. He had some thinking and planning to do, and he always did that better when he was moving.

# 73

"Shit!" John cursed. He tightened the focus on the binoculars and scanned the street.

The street was almost blocked, SUVs parked on both sides of the road, double the number that had been there before. Armed police guarded Patil's gate while large men in white *kurtas* and jeans milled around under the streetlights. The security was double what it had been. There was no way he would get past that.

John cursed again and ducked back behind the wall at the corner of the street. He stared down at the small bird-watching binoculars he had picked up earlier in the day at a camping shop, realizing his hands were shaking. Closing his eyes, he breathed in. He couldn't lose it now. Hearing a car engine, he opened his eyes. A car was approaching down the street. John ducked his head and started walking, keeping as much to the shadows as possible. The car passed, and John relaxed. He slipped the binoculars into the side pocket of his cargos and kept walking. What were his options? The house was out now. You couldn't get in there without an army. John clenched his fists and screwed up his face, letting out a silent scream of anguish. Fuck, fuck, fuck! When was he going to catch a break?

He kept walking, putting distance between him and the house. He was left with the hotel. He had to concentrate all his efforts there. It was the only place he knew Patil let his guard down. As long as John didn't stuff that up too.

Hearing the distinctive buzz of a rickshaw, he stepped off the curb and raised his hand.

Twenty minutes later, the rickshaw pulled up outside the Vijaya Palace Hotel. John paid and went through the metal detector. He had tossed the binoculars on the side of the road after getting into the rickshaw. He regretted getting rid of a useful piece of equipment but didn't want to have to explain to the hotel security why he had a pair of binoculars in his pocket. The less attention, the better. Angling his face away from the reception desk, he headed for the toilets. He needed to make himself look a little more respectable. He had dressed for a stakeout, not a night in a five-star hotel.

## 74

John was sitting at the corner of the bar, staring at his drink when he felt her walk in, a presence that seemed to fill the room. The heads of the few men in the bar turned to watch her. It wasn't just her looks. She was a beautiful woman for sure, but there was something about the way she carried herself, an aura that enchanted. John could see why she had been destined for the big screen.

But when you looked closer, past the glamor, the grooming, and the expensive saris, you could sense she was filled with sadness, a sadness she hid with her personality and the way she interacted with the staff. He watched her as she sat down at her usual seat at the bar and gave the barman, Ramesh, a smile. She hadn't spotted John yet, and he was content to observe her. Placing a small clutch on the counter, she stared into the mirror behind the bar, her fingers drumming a gentle tattoo on the bartop while Ramesh fixed her drink.

Ramesh placed a martini in front of her, and she accepted it with another smile, stirred the olive around in the drink, then raised her glass. As she took a sip, she glanced along the bar, spotting John for the first time. John smiled and raised his glass in salute.

Maadhavi broke into a smile and raised her glass again. Looking over her shoulder, she gave a quick glance in Ramesh's direction, then tapped on the bar beside her.

Understanding the unspoken message, John pushed back his chair, picked up his drink, and walked over to join her.

"William, how lovely to see you." She gestured to the stool beside her. "Please, join me."

John sat down beside her and, for the first time, noticed the slight discoloration on her cheek. Noticing the direction of his gaze, her hand went involuntarily to her face before she quickly removed it.

"How are you?" She glanced down at his hiking boots and cargos. "Have you been hiking?"

"I had a day off, Maadhavi." John gave her a broad smile. "I didn't expect to see you so soon," he lied.

"Ha." Maadhavi touched his forearm with her fingers and leaned closer. "Are you sure you weren't waiting for me?" She winked.

John grinned. "You caught me. I'm a stalker."

"Not my first, William, trust me." Maadhavi turned away and took a sip of her drink. The smile had disappeared, and she stared morosely into her glass. John sat quietly beside her, waiting for her to say something. She looked up, hesitated, glanced over at Ramesh, who was polishing glasses at the end of the bar, then turned to John.

"Would you like to have dinner with me again, William? I enjoyed our chat last time, and... I need cheering up."

"I would love to."

Maadhavi nodded and glanced again toward Ramesh.

"Let's eat in my suite. We'll get room service."

"Okay."

"Don't get any ideas. There's a reason for it, which I will explain later."

John frowned and nodded.

Maadhavi drained her glass and placed it back on the counter.

"Follow me after ten minutes. I'm in Room 2301."

John frowned again, wondering about the reason for the subterfuge.

"Sure."

Ramesh saw Maadhavi getting up and rushed over.

"Another drink, Ma'am?"

Maadhavi put on a dazzling smile. "No, thank you, Ramesh. I've got a bit of a headache tonight."

"Okay, Ma'am." Ramesh looked concerned. "Please get well soon."

"Thank you, Ramesh." Maadhavi reached over and touched his forearm, turning Ramesh's face bright red. "You are always so good to me."

John watched her leave in the bar mirror, then ordered another Botanist and tonic. He may as well. He had ten minutes to fill.

## 75

Ten minutes later, John exited the lift and walked along the corridor. It was easy to find the room, only four suites occupied the floor. He tapped on the door and waited. After a brief moment, the door opened, and Maadhavi stood there with a welcoming smile. She had changed out of the sari she had worn in the bar and was dressed in a long, flowing, silk blouse and wide-legged pants, her hair loose and tumbling over her shoulders. She seemed more relaxed, now that she was in her own space.

"Welcome." She opened the door wide as John walked in, gesturing toward the sofa. "Make yourself comfortable, I'll grab us some drinks."

John walked over, but before he sat down, his eye went to the floor-to-ceiling windows. The door to the balcony was open, and a cool breeze blew gently through the suite.

"What an incredible view," John said over his shoulder as he stepped onto the balcony. As far as he could see in every direction, the massive city spread out before him in a carpet of millions of lights, twinkling and sparkling in white, yellow, and orange. Stepping to the edge, he looked over the railing. Far below, he could make out the well-lit hotel forecourt and the street beyond. The street was still filled with movement, but the ever-present noise and dust were muted by the height of the building. Feeling Maadhavi join him, he turned as she held out a drink. He took it and grinned.

"You know my drink."

"You were so particular when you ordered it, how could I forget?" She held up her own glass. "I even made one for myself."

"You won't drink anything else after this. Trust me." John raised his glass. "Thank you. Cheers."

Maadhavi raised hers in salute and took a sip. She raised her eyebrows and nodded in appreciation, then leaned her forearms on the balcony rail and stared out across the city.

"It looks so peaceful when you see it like this."

"It does." John leaned on the rail next to her.

"Don't let it deceive you, though. It's not peaceful at all."

"I know."

"I don't mean the traffic."

John sighed. "I know."

John sensed Maadhavi looking at him.

"Why all the secrecy tonight, Maadhavi?" He didn't look at her when he asked, keeping his gaze on the cityscape. "Does the bruise on your cheek have something to do with it?"

"It's a long story."

John turned to face her. "I have all evening."

"I don't know you well enough." Maadhavi shook her head and took a big sip of her drink.

"Maadhavi, whether or not you know me well is irrelevant. Maybe I can help you. No one has the right to hit you."

"Oh, so we have dinner and a few drinks together, and

you think you're my protector?" Even in the dim light on the balcony, her eyes blazed. She turned and walked back inside, draining her glass as she did. John followed her in and watched her as she fixed herself a fresh drink. She glanced over at him, and he shook his head. He still had half a glass and wanted to keep his head clear. Taking her drink, she sat down on the sofa and stared at the floor. John moved over and took a seat in the armchair opposite. Leaning forward, his elbows on his knees, he fixed her in his gaze.

"You are a beautiful, intelligent, successful woman with her own career. You don't have to allow someone to have power over you, to abuse you. Why?" He gestured around the suite. "For this?"

"Don't you dare judge me. You don't even know me." Maadhavi looked up, her eyes on fire, her face flushed.

John held up a hand. "No, no, I will never judge you." He sighed and sat back in the chair, staring at his drink as he swirled the ice in the glass. "You're right, I don't know you." He looked up. "I'm just trying to understand."

"You'll never understand, William. You come here from another country, spend a little time here, and think you know how everything works. Life here is not that simple."

"You're right." John stood and moved to the bar. His drink wasn't finished, he just needed space and time to think, to think about how far to push the conversation. At the end of the day, he wasn't here to counsel her. He was here to get close to Patil. But at the same time, he needed to treat her right, or he was no better than men like Patil. He added more ice to his glass and topped it up with tonic. Glancing over at Maadhavi, who was staring out the open balcony door, John moved back to the chair and sat down.

"Maadhavi, people only have power over us if we give them that power."

Maadhavi snorted. "Ha, nonsense. You're a man. You'll never understand. Have you any idea what it's like to be a woman in this industry?"

"No."

"Exactly, so don't go spouting your wisdom at me."

John held up both hands. "I'm sorry." He paused, "Should I go?"

Maadhavi took a deep breath and exhaled slowly.

"No, it's okay. I'm sorry. I've had a rough couple of days, and..." She raised her head. "To be honest, I feel comfortable talking to you. You're not from here. You're not in the industry. I don't believe you will judge me... which is why I got angry before."

John smoothed an imaginary crease from his trouser leg, took a sip from his glass, then looked at her again.

"The reason for the secrecy tonight is the staff here report everything I do to a very powerful man. A jealous man." She waved her hand at the suite. "He pays for all of this."

John raised an eyebrow but said nothing, letting her continue.

"He found out I had dinner with you and confronted me. We had an argument." She pointed at her cheek. "He hit me."

John thought fast. The staff would have given his description to Patil, who may or may not have passed it on to Rajiv and the police. He would have to be even more careful.

"Is he your boyfriend?"

"No," Maadhavi sneered. "But I *am* his mistress." She looked up, challenging him. "Are you disgusted? Is the glamorous movie actress you met just a whore now?"

John sat forward in his seat.

"Maadhavi, I said I wouldn't judge you. We all have to make decisions in life... to survive."

"My decisions were taken from me." A single tear trickled from the corner of her left eye. "And now, I have to suffer for the rest of my life."

John frowned. "What do you mean?"

Maadhavi took another drink and studied her hand. When she looked up, the tear had been joined by another.

"I was raped by this man..."

"Fuck." John's fingers clenched.

"Yes, fuck. And since then, he has claimed me as his own. He controls everything I do,"—again, she gestured around the suite—"where I live, and what work I get. He controls it all."

"Surya Patil?"

Her gasp was audible as she looked up in shock.

"How do you know? Has the hotel staff said something?"

John took a deep breath of his own. It was time to come clean.

"Maadhavi, I can help you."

She looked at him, confused.

"I know all about Patil. He's an evil bastard."

"How do you know him?"

John sighed and reached out for her glass.

"It's a long story, and you'll need another drink."

# 76

"I'm not who I said I was."

"What?" Her eyes raised in alarm. "Who are you?"

"It's better you don't know... not everything." John raised a placatory hand as he saw the worry on her face. "But don't worry, I'm not here to harm you. I'll explain."

Sipping his drink, he wondered the best way to start. He had to maintain his anonymity but also gain her trust. Taking a deep breath, he put the glass down on the table in front of him.

"Four years ago, my wife was kidnapped, gang raped, murdered, her body left to rot in a ditch."

Maadhavi's hand went to her mouth. "Oh my god!" She leaned forward and reached for John's hand. "Oh, I'm so sorry."

John looked down at the table as the memories came bubbling up. He swallowed and stared at his hand held in Maadhavi's.

"Surya Patil's son, Sunil, and three of his friends did it."

"Oh, William, I don't know what to say. I'm so sorry."

John slipped his hand free and sat back in his chair. His

jaw clenching, he willed himself to relax. Maadhavi still sat forward, studying his face. Her eyes narrowed.

"Wait, I think I remember that. I remember seeing it in the news, but... they never caught the people who did it."

"No, and they never will. Because people like Patil control the police and the media."

Maadhavi sat back in her chair and stared at the table between them.

"The bastard," she muttered. Then she frowned and looked up. "Didn't Sunil Patil commit suicide?"

John said nothing, watching her, waiting for her to connect the dots. He saw her expression change, from a frown to slow realization.

"It wasn't suicide?"

John still didn't say anything. He leaned forward, picked up his drink, swirled it around, listening to the ice tinkle against the glass. Taking a sip, he held the liquid in his mouth for a moment, savoring the taste before swallowing.

"The world can be very unfair. Some people have all the power, all the money. They could do so much good with it, but instead, they use it for their own means—to control others, to skirt the law, to do whatever suits them. People like Surya Patil." He took another drink while he gathered his thoughts.

"There is a legal system in place, a police force, but when they fail to deliver because of powerful influence, what do people like us do? Do we accept it and try to gather up what's left of our lives, move on, knowing we will never get justice for our loved ones?" John shook his head. "No. That's not right. I say it doesn't have to be that way."

"But, William, you say this as if it's easy. As if you are a crusader for justice..."

"No." John shook his head. "I'm not. I'm just an ordinary

person. But if I can do it, anyone can. Or at least try. Why give up? Why continue to let these people have power over us?"

Maadhavi shook her head, not convinced.

"Surya Patil raped me, destroyed my innocence, my dreams. That... bastard... has since controlled every aspect of my life. If I had fought back, if I had gone public, I would have no life, no career. I wouldn't get work anywhere." She waved her hands as she became more animated. "I have two elderly parents I support. What could I do? It's not as easy as you make out."

"It's not easy, I agree, but I couldn't imagine living a life where I had sat back and done nothing." He waved his hand around the suite. "How long have you lived like this? As a prisoner in a gilded cage?"

Maadhavi's eyes widened in indignation. She began to protest but realized he was right. Slumping in her chair, her shoulders folding in on herself, she looked down at her hands in her lap.

"Three years," she whispered.

John sat forward and leaned his arms on his legs, lowering his head, so his gaze met hers.

"That's three years of your life he has taken from you."

Maadhavi nodded slowly, her eyes tearing up.

"I hate him."

"I hate him too, Maadhavi. I hate all people like him who play with other's lives."

She looked up and regarded him with misty eyes,

"But why do you hate him so much? It was his son who did it."

John gave a grim smile.

"I've only told you half the story."

John explained how he had met someone. Someone he

loved dearly and wanted to spend the rest of his life with. How Surya Patil had hired mercenaries to hunt him down, how they had taken Adriana hostage. He explained, leaving out the gory details, how he had dealt with the men, how he had discovered who was behind it all.

Maadhavi listened with rapt attention, not moving, concentrating on every detail. When John finished and sat back in the chair, she just stared at him with a mixture of disbelief and admiration.

"I'm sorry you've had to go through so much, William. He's an evil man. But why are you telling me all this?"

"Because I can help you, Maadhavi. I can help you be free. Do you want to be free?"

"Yes, William, I do." Maadhavi nodded slowly at first, then faster. "I really do. I can't go on like this. I'm living a lie."

"Good. But first, I need you to help me."

## 77

Maadhavi ordered room service, and John hid in the bedroom when it was delivered.

She had brightened up significantly after the conversation, and as they sat down to eat, John started to plan.

"Do you have somewhere you can go for a while? Somewhere you can lie low?"

Maadhavi thought for a moment, her mouth full of food. She swallowed.

"I suppose so... but Surya has eyes everywhere. I'm well known in Karnataka. Someone will see me wherever I go."

"Hmmm, in that case, you will need to go further afield."

"In fact, I was already planning to leave. I've been putting money away. I've paid off my parents' house, but it would mean giving up my career..." She trailed off, looking down at her plate.

John reached for another piece of Tandoori chicken. He was starving.

"Maybe you don't have to?"

Maadhavi looked up in surprise. "What do you mean? What's your plan?"

John smiled and took a bite of chicken, chewed for a while, then swallowed.

"I'm still working on it, but let's see."

"He's threatened to harm my parents."

"Prick."

Maadhavi raised an eyebrow.

"Sorry."

"He is, though." She grinned shyly. "A small one."

John almost choked on his chicken, and they both burst out laughing, the tension of the previous hours dissipating with humor.

They continued with their meal, avoiding the topic of Surya Patil, discussing travel and Maadhavi's work, but John's mind was only half on the conversation. An idea was forming, an idea that would help both of them.

At the end of the meal, John pushed aside his plate and dabbed his mouth with his napkin.

"Do you have a passport?"

"Of course." Maadhavi looked surprised and a little indignant at the apparently random question. "Why?"

"Good." John smiled. "An Indian passport?"

"Obviously." Maadhavi looked more confused than ever. "I am Indian, in case it escaped your attention."

"I had noticed." John grinned. "But nowadays, people have passports from all over the place." He frowned. "Unfortunately, an Indian passport makes things a little more difficult. There aren't as many options for a visa on arrival."

"Can you please explain where you're going with this?"

John nodded, only half listening to what she was saying.

"How about visas? Any valid visas?"

"I have a Schengen and a U.S. visa."

"Hmmm..."

"John?"

John looked up, noticing her expression.

"I'm sorry, just thinking. You will need an alibi, and the best one is to be out of the country. I'm just thinking where you can go."

"Go? I can't just jump on a plane. I have commitments."

John fixed her in his gaze.

"Do you want to be free of this man? It's your choice."

Maadhavi exhaled, the fight quickly going out of her.

"Yes, yes, I do."

"Then you will have to make some decisions quickly. Make some sacrifices. Freedom isn't free."

"No," she sighed. "Okay. What do I have to do?"

"Think where plausibly you can go by yourself, so if you are questioned later, people will believe it."

"Hmmm..." Maadhavi stared out the window as she considered her options. "Europe is too far and a little hard to explain." After a moment, her face lit up. "Dubai! I go there often. I have a U.S. Visa, so they grant me a visa on arrival."

"Great." John thought for a moment. "In fact, excellent. I have a contact there who will look after you."

"I don't need looking after."

John sighed. "I know you don't. It's just for safety. Just in case. Patil hired the mercenaries from there. He has contacts there. If he has you followed, I need to know."

"Okay."

John stood and paced around the room, thinking as he walked. Maadhavi bit her lip as she watched him. John stopped and spun around.

"Do you have your own credit card? One that doesn't go to Patil?"

"Yes."

"Good. Use that and book yourself a ticket on a flight tomorrow to Dubai. The earlier, the better."

"I think there's one around ten in the morning." Maadhavi sat up.

"Perfect." John walked over to the armchair and leaned on the back of it. "Book a hotel, and... a spa treatment, anything like that, so you can document where you have been."

Maadhavi frowned. "Why do I need that?"

"Because Maadhavi, whatever happens here, it must never track back to you. You need a cast-iron alibi."

"What are you going to do?" Maadhavi looked worried.

"It's better you don't know the details. That way, you can always deny everything. But I plan to put a stop to him."

Maadhavi screwed up her face, opened her mouth as if to say something, then closed it. She fidgeted with her hands, then looked up again.

"Are you going to... hurt him? Or...?"

John stared at her sternly.

She looked away. "Okay," she sighed. "I'll get my laptop."

John nodded, his expression firm.

"And book a hotel car to take you to the airport."

# 78

John stepped onto the balcony, slid the glass door closed behind him, then pulled out his phone, removed a business card from his wallet, and dialed.

"Hello?"

"Steve, it's John."

"John, mate. You're back in Dubai?"

John smiled at the familiar Australian accent.

"No, Steve, just using a Dubai SIM. It's a long story, I'll explain later." John turned to look back inside. Maadhavi sat on the sofa, typing away on her laptop, giving no sign she could hear him. She must have sensed him looking because she looked up and smiled. John turned away, facing out over the balcony rail again.

"I need some help, Steve. I'll pay your usual rate."

"Hey, don't worry about all that. What do you need?"

"I need you to keep a discreet eye on someone. Make sure she's not followed, protect her if necessary."

"For sure, mate."

"Thank you, Steve. I appreciate it. I'll explain everything

later. She will arrive tomorrow on the Emirates flight from Bangalore."

"Bangalore?"

John could sense the raised eyebrows.

"Yeah."

"Say no more, mate. You be careful."

"I will. I'll text you the flight and hotel details and her photo. I owe you, my friend."

Steve chuckled on the other end. "The tab's running mate. You still owe me the beers from Oman."

"I haven't forgotten, my friend. I'll be in touch."

John ended the call and stared out over the city. Once Maadhavi was on the plane, he wouldn't have to worry about her. Steve was a good man. He'd had John's back in Oman, had done more than anyone could ask. John owed him much more than a beer. John turned around and caught Maadhavi watching him.

It was time for her to put on her acting shoes.

## 79

Maadhavi stared at the man outside on the balcony. Who was he, this man with strange blue eyes and hair that didn't match the color of his beard? None of it seemed to match, the parts put together without thought to aesthetics. Despite that, she found him incredibly attractive. He was tall and lean, had a deep tan, and carried himself with quiet confidence as if he could handle whatever the world threw at him. He had a power, an inner steeliness she found very sexy. But she sensed a deep sorrow too. It was there when he thought she wasn't looking, as if he had seen and done things that had removed his innocence. She could relate to that, her life had been the same. Perhaps that's why she found him attractive.

She watched as he ended the call and turned to face her. She sighed. Perhaps if things had been different... but she was damaged goods. No man would be interested in her, at least not long term, not a relationship. Most men were the same, only interested in one thing. She needed to find someone like William or whatever his real name was. A man who loved so intensely, he thought nothing of traveling to the ends of the earth to seek revenge on the man who had wronged him and his lover.

Breaking eye contact, she looked down at her laptop as he slid the door open and stepped back inside.

"It's all sorted. Someone will be watching you. He's a good man. He'll make sure you are safe, but you won't know he's there. He's very discreet."

Maadhavi looked up and nodded. "Thank you." She looked down at her laptop again. "I've made the bookings. Hotel and flights."

"Good. Show me."

Maadhavi swiveled the laptop around and watched as he took photos of the bookings with his phone, then looked at his watch.

"It's after ten. Is it too late to phone him?"

"Who?"

"Patil."

"Oh... no, it's not, but..." She could feel her heartbeat increasing, just thinking about it. "He said he doesn't want to hear from me again. He said I have to leave this suite."

John moved over and squatted in front of her, so his head was at the same level.

"Maadhavi, I know it's difficult, but I need you to do this. I need you to call him, say you're sorry, that you want to make amends. Say anything, but convince him to come over tomorrow night. Can you do that?"

"I... I..." She looked away, suddenly nervous, unsure of herself.

"Maadhavi, look at me."

She raised her eyes and looked into his, once again thinking about the unusual color. He fixed her in his gaze as if he was looking right into her.

"Think of it as a movie role. You are playing the role of a

lifetime." He grinned, the white of his teeth glinting amid his dark beard. "I've Googled you. I know you can do it."

Despite herself, she blushed. "So, you were stalking me."

"Guilty as charged," he admitted, grinning.

She liked it when he looked happy.

She took a deep breath, held it for a second, then exhaled.

"Okay. I'll do it."

"Good. I know you can." He stood. "I'll leave you alone. I'll be in the next room."

Leaning forward, she picked up her phone from the coffee table. Despite his assurances, her heart was racing. She stared at the phone, composing herself.

"Break a leg," he said from the bedroom door.

Maadhavi turned around to look at him, but he was already gone, the bedroom door closed behind him.

## 80

Surya sat alone, slumped in the leather armchair in his study, a half empty bottle of Black Label on the table beside him. There were rumors the young guns in the party were pushing for his replacement. He'd spent the day wheeling and dealing, making promises, alliances, and threats, all the things necessary for the alpha male to keep control of his pack. In times past, he had reveled in it, taken pleasure in the cut-throat world of party politics, but now, it drained him, weakened him. Was he losing his touch? He had been sitting there for two hours, wallowing in a pit of self-pity. The drinking was doing nothing to cheer him up.

His house was empty... empty apart from all the men downstairs. He couldn't go out alone, couldn't even roam his own house freely. His wife had gone, and he had no idea where. The only sign she still existed was the letter from a lawyer, initiating divorce proceedings. He had fought with his mistress. There was no one left in his personal life, and he had lost his freedom because of some mother-fucking Englishman. Draining the glass, he slid it onto the table, pushing it away from the edge with his fingertips. He thought back to the fight with Maadhavi. Perhaps he shouldn't have been so harsh. She was bound to meet people. He couldn't watch her all the time. His life was better with her in it. She was his lucky charm.

Leaning forward, he poured himself another three fingers of whisky. As he picked up the glass, the phone vibrated and shifted across the table. He glanced at the screen—speak of the devil. Canceling the call, he picked up his glass and sat back in his chair. Hmmm. Should he give her a second chance? He started to feel a little better. He still had his power. He smiled when the phone rang again. Sooner or later, everyone came running back to Surya Patil. He was still the King of the Jungle. He picked up the phone and took the call.

## 81

John kept his ear to the door. He had told her he would give her space, but he wanted to hear what she said, didn't want any surprises. The conversation started slowly, hesitantly. John could only guess at half the conversation, but as Maadhavi got into a flow, found her role, he had to admit, she was very good. It was an Oscar-winning performance. If John hadn't known better, he would have truly believed Surya Patil was her long-lost love, and she couldn't live without him. She balanced it perfectly—a submissive pleading with enough subtle flattery to boost his ego. If Patil didn't fall for it, no one would.

The conversation ended, and John moved away from the door and sat on the bed, not moving until there was a gentle knock on the bedroom door. He opened it to see Maadhavi looking drained and fragile, the confident shell she surrounded herself with in public nowhere to be seen.

"It's done." Turning, she walked over to the bar, grabbed a fresh glass and the whisky bottle, and poured herself a shot of whisky. She tossed it back in one, the drink restoring some of her vigor. "He'll be here at eight tomorrow night."

"Well done." Smiling, he walked over to her and put a comforting hand on her upper arm. "I knew you could do it."

"He sounded... happy." She reached for his hand. "Am I doing the right thing, William?"

"Maadhavi, he's happy because he thinks you have gone running back to him. It's not love or affection. It's power." John reached up and touched her cheek. "No man has the right to do that. No man has the right to do what he did to you... has continued to do to you. Remember that."

Maadhavi studied John's face for a moment, then nodded. "Yes, you're right. What do I do now?"

John smiled. "You'd better pack."

## 82

John checked his watch—three thirty p.m. She should have landed by now. He pulled out his phone and dialed.

"Gidday," Steve's laconic voice came on the line.

"Hi, Steve. Did you find her?"

"Yeah, mate. Easy peasy. She's clear. Couldn't see anyone following her."

"Good." John breathed a sigh of relief. He could move on to the next phase.

"I'm just following her to the hotel." He heard a honk and a curse. "Bloody camel jockeys."

"Try not to crash, Steve. I need you for a few more days."

"No worries, mate. It will be my pleasure. She's easy on the eyes. Not like some of the ugly mugs I've had to follow."

"I bet, but avoid temptation, my friend. I want you to be discreet, stay in the background."

"Got it."

"Thanks, Steve. Oh, hey, one more thing."

"Yeah?"

"If you do have to speak to her, my name is William."

"William? Like the prince?"

"Yes, Steve, like the prince."

"Okay, your highness, keep me posted."

John chuckled and ended the call.

He looked down at the items laid out on Pournima's plastic dining table. He had made the purchases earlier but was still waiting for two more items only Pournima could get for him. It was time for him to get ready. He wanted to be back in the hotel in plenty of time before Patil arrived.

Picking up the latex surgical gloves, he put them in the side pocket of his cargos, along with a packet of cable ties and a car polishing cloth. He wanted a weapon, just in case, but there had been little time, and he had no contacts who could provide him with anything. If everything went to plan, he wouldn't need one. Still, it was a niggling doubt that wouldn't go away. A handgun of some sort would give him so much more confidence.

He heard the door open behind him and turned as Pournima returned.

"Did you get them?"

"Yes," Pournima replied, a little out of breath.

John pulled out a chair for her and went to the kitchen to fetch her a glass of water. He came back and passed it to Pournima, who took a couple of sips, then placed it back on the table and dabbed the perspiration from her forehead with the end of her *duppata*.

She handed a small cardboard box to John, the lid held shut with a rubber band.

"You didn't need a prescription?"

Pournima shook her head, her mouth full of water as she drank from the glass. "No, I paid a little extra. You know how it works, Mr. John."

"Yes, but I'm still surprised."

John slipped the box into his other pocket, then took the larger bag from Pournima and looked inside.

"Great, but I might need your help to wear it."

Pournima giggled.

John pulled the black cloth out of the bag and shook it out. There were, in fact, two items. Taking the larger of the two, he found the opening and pulled it over his head, then slipped his arms through the sleeves.

Pournima covered her mouth with her hand, but there was no mistaking the amusement in her eyes. Standing, she adjusted the fit until it covered John properly, then stood back.

"This is the large size?" John asked as he swung his arms around and twisted his body.

"Yes."

"Hmmm, okay" It was a little tight under his arms, but it would have to do. He reached for the other piece of black cloth but was at a loss as to what to do with it. Pournima saved him. Taking it, she unfolded it, then reached up to place it over John's head. John ducked his head down to make it easier. She secured it under his neck, pulling the cloth over his head, so he was completely covered.

"Okay, Mr. John, it's done."

John straightened up and adjusted his gaze, so he could see her through the narrow mesh slit.

"What do you think?"

Pournima giggled again. "You look like a *begum* now. A very tall *begum*!"

"Good." John lifted the veil back over his head until it was hanging behind him. "It's so hot under this. How do they do it?"

Pournima shrugged, still highly amused at the sight of John dressed in a full *burqa*.

"Do you think it will work, Pournima? Will I pass as a Muslim woman?"

"Yes, Mr. John." Pournima bobbed her head in agreement. "No one can see who you are. They might think you are very big, but no one will pay you too much attention."

John nodded and looked down at the black dress that reached the floor. The idea for the disguise had come when he'd heard the call to prayer from the mosque in the slum. Just as he'd wanted Maadhavi to have a watertight alibi, he wanted no trace of him on the CCTV camera footage for tonight.

"Can you cut a slit in the side?" he showed her where. "I want to reach my pocket without taking this off."

"Yes, Mr. John. I'll get my scissors."

"Oh, and one more thing. Can you write the hotel name and address for me in *Kannada*? I don't want the rickshaw wallah to hear my voice."

## 83

The rickshaw ride had gone without a hitch, the driver glancing curiously at the large Muslim woman climbing into his rickshaw, but as soon as John handed him the address, he was all business and headed to the hotel without a second thought.

After paying him, John stepped out in front of the hotel, stooping a little to hide his height, and moved to the entrance in as ladylike a fashion as he could, given he was wearing a long black cloak and his field of vision was severely limited by the head covering. Sweltering under the extra layer, he blinked away the sweat running down his forehead into his eyes. He could smell his breath as he breathed in and out, the air trapped under the cloth. Looking left to right, he scanned his surroundings as much as he could to see if anyone had seen through his disguise, but the doorman and a security guard barely paid him any attention as John shuffled over to the metal detector and stepped through the detector without setting off any alarms —he had made sure he had nothing metallic in his possession. The doorman held open the door, making no eye contact. The simple act of donning a *burqa* had made John invisible.

Walking inside, he felt more confident with every step. He turned his head slightly to look toward the reception counter. A staff member glanced briefly in his direction but paid little notice, returning their attention to whatever work they were doing behind the counter. The other two staff members ignored him completely. Shuffling over to the lifts, he took little steps to ensure the floor length *burqa* didn't ride up and expose his trekking boots. He pressed the button for the twenty-third floor and waited. Three men walked over and joined him by the lift. John tensed, waiting for them to say something. When the lift to the left of him chimed its arrival, John stepped inside. He looked at the men, but they hadn't moved. He waited for them to join him, but one smiled and said, "It's okay Madam, you go first."

John nodded and allowed the doors to close. Under the cloth, he allowed himself to smile, relieved he was inside safely and amused that donning a piece of clothing could change drastically how one was perceived.

On the twenty-third floor, John stepped out and looked up and down the empty corridor. Walking down to the door to Maadhavi's suite, he reached through the slit Pournima had cut in the *burqa* to retrieve the spare key card Maadhavi had given him. Swiping it on the lock, then covering his fingers with his sleeve, he pushed down on the handle and entered the suite, the door clicking shut behind him. Lifting the veil from his face, he flipped it over his head, took a deep breath of fresh air, then reached up and used the ends of the veil to wipe the sweat from his face.

The suite was immaculate, housekeeping having visited earlier in the day. John checked his watch. He still had three hours before he expected Patil to arrive for his meeting with Maadhavi. Reaching into his pocket, he removed the latex gloves, pulled them on, flexed his fingers, then removed the polishing cloth from his other pocket. Housekeeping had been through the suite, but he wanted to make sure there would be no trace of his visit the previous evening. He set to wiping down anything he might have touched—door handles, furniture, the glasses and bottles on the bar counter. He was thorough; he had plenty of time. As he wiped, he mentally rehearsed everything he had planned, considering other options, alternative scenarios. By the time he had finished, thirty minutes later, he was confident whatever happened, he would have it covered.

The only thing missing was a weapon, something that had been nagging at him for days. There were a couple of knives in the kitchenette, but John was reluctant to use them. They would be okay as a threat, but a threat was only effective if he was prepared to carry through with it, and he wasn't with what he had planned. He stood, his hands on his hips and looked around the suite once more, making sure he hadn't missed anything. His eyes fell on a bowl on an occasional table beside the door, holding keys and a pile of loose change. It held his attention for a moment, but he couldn't think why until a light bulb went off in his brain. Turning, he walked back to Maadhavi's bedroom, then into the dressing room. He looked around, spotted a set of drawers to one side, and slid them open. Rifling through the lingerie and underwear, he felt a little guilty but couldn't find what he needed. Damn. He straightened and chewed his lip, his mind whirring away. Sighing, he walked back into the living room and sat down.

Unlacing his boot, he removed it, then pulled off his sock before replacing his boot. He stood, walked over to the door, and tipped the bowl of loose change into the sock, shook the sock until all the coins were at the bottom, then tied a knot around the change to hold it in place. Satisfied, he hefted the sock in his hand, holding it at the top, the end with the coins swinging like a pendulum. He swung it behind him, then over his head, bringing his hand down in a striking action. The coin weighted sock flew down in an arc, striking an imaginary foe in front of him—perfect. The sock gave him an extra thirty centimeters of reach, and the centrifugal force of the coins made it a very effective club. Good. John checked his watch—nothing to do now but wait.

## 84

Surya Patil checked his reflection in the mirror again. Pouring a drop of coconut oil into his palm from a small plastic bottle on the vanity top, he rubbed his hands together before smoothing the stray strands of hair on the side of his head. Picking up a bottle of Old Spice he hesitated, then put it back and picked up the fancy foreign cologne he had bought in Dubai Duty Free, liberally splashing it on both cheeks before standing back.

He had to admit, he was excited to see Maadhavi again. He missed her, despite the arguments and her disloyalty. Now that she knew her place again, things could go back to normal. Knowing one of the most beautiful women on the silver screen was at his beck-and-call, that he could have his way with her whenever he wanted, gave him immense satisfaction. In fact, since the call the day before, his mood had improved tremendously. Today, he had dealt with one of his more irritating opponents with ease and cut a deal on a major infrastructure project that promised to enrich him for years to come. It was like the old days. She was his lucky charm, his Lakshmi, the goddess of wealth.

Squaring his shoulders, he straightened his back and raised his chin to reduce the effect of the fleshy jowls around his neck. His reflection stared back at him proudly. He was Surya Patil, King of the Jungle, The Lion of Karnataka.

## 85

The time passed slowly. As it got closer to eight p.m., John's nerves were increasingly on edge, an uneasy feeling in his chest. Sweating under the *burqa*, he had already adjusted the air-con twice until finally, it was on the lowest setting, but beads of sweat still formed on his brow. He had contemplated removing it, but it would give him the element of surprise when needed. He stood up for the hundredth time and paced around the suite, ostensibly checking if there was anything he might have missed, but in reality, using the movement to burn off the excess adrenaline and calm his nerves.

Walking into the bedroom, he tried to remember where he had sat and what he had touched while Maadhavi had made her call, but he had wiped every surface already. His eyes fell on the little brass statue of Ganesha sitting on the bedside table. The elephant-headed Hindu God was said to be the remover of obstacles, the deity all Hindus prayed to first before starting anything. Despite himself, he closed his eyes. He didn't pray, what was the point? He didn't believe in God... as such. The world was too shitty to believe a supreme being watched over him, but he remembered what that man had told him, the wandering ascetic at the filling station—breathe.

John took a deep, slow breath, in through his nostrils, and exhaled slowly through his mouth. He did it again, holding the breath for a moment this time before exhaling. Slowly, he blinked his eyes open. It hadn't helped. He shook his head. The only one who would fix this was him. He glanced at his watch again—almost time.

John walked back into the living room, moved the armchair so he could face the door, pulled the veil over his face, and sat down.

## 86

Surya stepped out of the house and walked to the Mercedes, now secretly enjoying the bustle of activity his appearance created. His driver rushed to the car, pressing the key fob, the lights flashed, and he opened the passenger door and stood at attention.

Two armed police pulled the gates open while the others rushed outside and climbed into the waiting SUVs. The black-clad commando captain strode toward him and snapped to attention.

"Where to, Sir?"

Surya avoided looking at him and growled, "Vijaya Palace," before climbing into his car.

"Sir."

The door closed behind Surya, and he watched through the tinted glass as the captain shouted commands and ran toward the lead SUV. Surya now had four Black Cats looking after him, and his security detail had grown to eighteen armed police. With his own private security, the convoy had increased to eight vehicles, not including his Mercedes.

Finally, he had the Z level of security that befitted a man of his stature. All it had taken was a petty thief to break into his house. He settled back into his seat with satisfaction as the Mercedes pulled out onto the street behind the two lead Land Cruisers. Engines revved, doors slammed, and lights flashed on the vehicle roofs, filling the street with strobing red light as the convoy pulled out. The Lion of Karnataka was on the move.

A mere twenty minutes later, having bullied and forced their way through the evening traffic, the convoy pulled into the forecourt of the Vijaya Palace. Surya waited as the men fanned out, surrounding his car, blocking the entrances and exits, preventing access to the hotel from the street, and forcing the staff to stand back. A polite tap on the window, then the door opened, and Surya climbed out. Adjusting his belt, he smoothed his shirt down over his belly with the palm of his hand, then headed to the entrance, surrounded by a cordon of armed men. The doorman pulled the door open wide and stood to attention as he approached. Surya stopped in the doorway and turned to look at the commando captain. He saw the question in the captain's eyes, despite his face being covered by the balaclava and shook his head. Surya stepped into the lobby, and the door closed behind him, leaving his security detail outside.

Pausing, he looked around the lobby, making sure everyone had noticed him, then swaggered across the lobby to the lift. From the corner of his eye, he noticed the general manager heading in his direction.

"Sir."

Surya waved him away. He couldn't be bothered speaking to that obsequious shit right now.

"But, Sir..."

Surya glared at him and snarled, "Not now," stopping the general manager in his tracks. "Bloody idiot," Surya muttered. He had better things to do.

It was time for the Lion to vanquish his lioness.

## 87

Swiping the key card on the lock, the lock whirred and clicked inside the door, and a green light flashed above the handle. He pushed down on the handle and stepped inside, allowing the auto-closer to shut the door behind him.

"Maadhavi?"

She wasn't in the living room. He looked toward the bedroom door. It was slightly open. She must be in there.

"Maadhavi?" he called again. No response. Frowning, he stepped forward and heard a noise behind him. He turned his head and noticed the Muslim woman for the first time.

"Who are you? Where's Maadhavi?"

The woman said nothing and didn't move. Surya frowned. She was tall for a woman and seemed stocky under the black *burqa* which reached to the floor. Why wasn't she speaking?

"Maadhavi, is that you? Is this a joke?" No, it couldn't be her. The woman was too tall and broad to be her. "Who are you?"

Again, no response. Maybe she didn't speak English.

Most Muslims spoke Hindi, so he switched languages and asked again, "*Aap kaun hai? Maadhavi kahan hai?* Who are you? Where is Maadhavi?"

Again, no response or movement. What was wrong with her? Surya turned his head back to the bedroom.

"Maadhavi, where are you? Who is this here?"

Silence. He clenched his jaw. This was getting irritating. She had called him last night and pleaded for him to come, and the dumb bitch wasn't even here. As for this stupid Muslim woman, standing there like a black statue... Surya shook his head and glanced back at the woman. He hated the bloody Muslims. They were causing all the problems in the country. They should have all gone to Pakistan in 1947 when they had the chance.

"I don't know who you are, but this is my suite. You need to get out."

The woman just stood unmoving, unresponsive.

"Are you deaf?" He shook his head and muttered, "Mental case." He turned away and walked to the telephone. Raising his voice, he said over his shoulder. "I'm calling security."

Picking up the handset and reaching his other hand forward to punch the keypad, he felt a stinging pain in his right cheek, which knocked his head sideways. His vision starred, and he brought his hand back, touching his fingers to his cheek. What the fuck was that? His fingertips warm and sticky, he looked down to see them covered in blood. Then everything went black.

## 88

Shit! The bloody veil restricted his vision. Quickly flipping it up over his head, he swung again, adjusting the arc of the coin-laden sock, this time, hitting his target. The ball of coins struck Patil on his right temple, his knees shook, and he collapsed to the floor, out cold. John exhaled the breath he had been holding and stepped forward to look at the body lying at his feet. He was still breathing, and a trickle of blood seeped from a split in Patil's cheek.

John had hesitated, seeing the man before him—the man he hated. He was pathetic in person—overweight, balding, his physical presence, in reality, nothing to be afraid of. He'd had doubts, hadn't been sure if he was doing the right thing. It was the threat of security that had spurred him into action. Now, he had to carry through with it. John took a couple of breaths, calming his nerves, then reached over and grabbed the handset swinging on its cord and replaced it back on the phone.

Stepping over the body, he moved to the kitchen and tore off a strip of paper towel. In a drawer, he found a plastic bag and dropped the sock weapon into the bag. He walked back to the body and dabbed at the blood on Patil's cheek and cleaned the blood off his fingertips before adding the used paper towel to the plastic bag. He wanted to avoid contamination of the scene he was setting. So far, everything was going as he had planned.

John picked up the chair from in front of the writing desk and carried it closer to the body, then took a deep breath, grabbed Patil under the arms, and heaved the body off the floor. Fuck, he was heavy. Dragging Surya toward the chair, he pulled him onto it before letting go of his arms. He stood there panting, regaining his breath. John had never met him in person, just knew him by reputation and deed. He was a man people feared, but the arrogance so clear in the video call he had made from Oman was gone. Now, he was just a fat old man, slumped in a chair.

Removing the cable ties from his pocket, he secured Patil's wrists to the arms of the chair, then did the same with his legs. He double checked Patil couldn't move, then stepped back. Now onto stage two. John grabbed a bottle of Black Label and a glass from the bar and walked back to Patil. He placed the fingers of Patil's right hand onto the bottle and the glass, ensuring his fingerprints were all over them, then placed them on the coffee table.

Taking out the box Pournima had given him, he knelt beside the table, scanning the label. He didn't recognize the brand, but it was a strong opiate-based pain killer, and as Pournima had shown, easily available over the counter—exactly what he needed. Removing a strip, he popped out all twelve tablets onto the table. Using the base of the glass, he crushed them into a powder, then using his hand, swept the powder off the table surface into the glass. He twisted the top off the bottle of Black Label and filled the glass to three-quarters. Dipping his index finger into the glass, he stirred it around, making sure the powdered pain killer mixed in with the whisky. Now to get it into Patil.

John sat back on his heels and looked up at him. He was still unconscious, his head lolling sideways, a string of spittle hanging from the corner of his mouth. John wrinkled his brow. Patil would probably need to be conscious to swallow the liquid. Standing, he pulled the veil down over his face, stepped toward Patil, and shook him. No response. He slapped him on the face, but he still didn't respond. Shit. John raised the sleeve of the *burqa* and looked at his watch. Only ten minutes had passed since Patil had entered the room. John still had time; no one would expect him to leave a visit to his mistress quickly. In fact, Maadhavi had told him, Patil usually stayed most of the night, not leaving until the early morning. But the longer he was here, the more risk John was taking, and he needed Patil to drink the liquid. He had to wait until he came around. John walked to the door and put his ear to it. He couldn't hear anyone outside. He peered out through the peephole, but again the corridor seemed empty. Slowly, he opened the door and looked out —empty. He slipped the 'Do Not Disturb' sign over the door handle, then closed the door, latching it with the security bolt. For good measure, he dragged over a dining chair and wedged it under the handle.

Now, all he could do was wait.

## 89

"Take a left up here," Rajiv instructed his driver.

"Sir."

Rajiv had half an hour before he planned to call it a day. He was trying to have a few earlier nights this week. He had been neglecting Aarthi and was making a conscious effort to spend a little more time with her. Early was relative, though. It was almost nine in the evening, but at least he would be home before she went to bed. Being married to a policeman often meant you hardly saw him.

The police Bolero took the left turn, and Rajiv pointed up the street toward the Vijaya Palace.

"Stop in there."

"Yes, Sir."

Earlier, Rajiv had taken a drive past Surya Patil's house. The street had been clear, Surya's convoy missing, and the two armed police manning the gate had told Rajiv where Surya had gone. Rajiv's inquiries had thrown up nothing about the mystery intruder, but Muniappa still demanded daily progress reports. Despite nothing more coming of the investigation, Rajiv thought a friendly visit to Captain Ankit and his team wouldn't do any harm. He always believed in keeping relations cordial. One never knew when you might need to call on someone for help.

As they neared the turning for the hotel, Rajiv could see the line of white SUVs filling the forecourt. The entrance barriers were down, and armed police were standing on the footpath, eyeing passing traffic.

"Lights."

Rajiv's driver reached forward and flipped a switch on the dashboard, the street filling with the blue and red strobe of the police lights. The Bolero pulled up in front of the barrier, and Rajiv wound down his window, smiling at the police guard approaching his side of the vehicle. The police constable snapped to attention and called out to the hotel security to open the gate.

"All okay?"

"Yes, Sir."

"Good." Rajiv nodded. "Thank you."

Rajiv turned to his driver. "Take it inside."

The Bolero rolled forward, up the sloping drive, and pulled into the porte cochere. Rajiv opened the door and stepped out, telling the driver to switch off the lights. Looking around, he spotted Ankit walking toward him.

"Ankit." He held out his hand.

Ankit took it in his customary firm grip. "Rajiv. How's it going?"

"Good." Rajiv glanced around at the extensive security detail. "Your team has expanded, I see."

"Yes." Ankit gave a half smile. "He got what he wanted in the end. Any luck with finding our intruder?"

"No, nothing. He's like a ghost." Rajiv shook his head slowly, his eyes on two black-clad commandos, standing beside one of the Land Cruisers. "Are you still in charge?"

"Yes, for what it's worth. Although,"—Ankit jerked his head toward the hotel entrance—"he calls all the shots."

Rajiv pursed his lips. "What's he doing here?"

Ankit guided Rajiv out of earshot of his men and lowered his voice. "Apparently, he has a mistress here. We come here twice a week. Always at night."

Rajiv raised his eyebrows. "Really?"

"Yeah. No wonder his wife left him. She's an actress, apparently."

"His wife?"

"No, his mistress. Someone big in Kannada movies. I don't remember her name. I prefer Hindi films." Ankit sighed and looked toward the convoy of vehicles. "Not that I get time to watch them."

"Hmmm..." Rajiv half listened, his mind on the information Ankit had shared. Information was always useful. Snapping back to the present, he placed his hand on Ankit's arm.

"Thank you, my friend. I'll just go in and look around. Never been inside this hotel before."

"Ha, enjoy yourself. I've never been inside, either." Ankit shrugged. "He doesn't allow it."

"I'll take some photos for you." Rajiv grinned, turning to walk to the entrance.

## 90

Surya jerked and snorted, a deep intake of breath sucking the string of spittle back into his mouth, causing him to choke and cough. John pulled the veil back down over his face. He wanted to keep Patil guessing, keep a psychological advantage.

Surya blinked his eyes open and went to move his arms. Realizing he was restrained, he looked down and struggled to free his arms and legs.

"What...?" He looked up in alarm at the *burqa*-clad figure sitting in front of him. "Who...? Do you know who I am?" He struggled again to get free. "What's going on?"

John said nothing, just watched him struggle for a moment, then reached for the glass of whisky and pain killers and stood. Surya frowned, his head following John as he stepped behind him.

Grabbing a handful of the hair on the back of Surya's head, he pulled his head back. Surya's eyes widened with alarm, his arms and legs twitching in protest.

"Stop, stop..."

Raising the glass, he poured the liquid slowly into

Surya's open mouth. Surya spluttered and choked, whisky splashing out over his face and down his neck onto his clothes. He clamped his mouth shut and twisted his head side to side. John yanked on his hair again. Surya cried out, and John poured more liquid in. Surya tried closing his mouth again, but John kept pulling his head back by the hair. Every time Surya closed his mouth, John yanked on his hair, pouring more liquid each time. He got most of it into Surya's throat, the balance spilling down his face and body.

The glass empty, John let go of Surya's head and stepped back, leaving him gasping and coughing.

John walked around in front of Patil and put the glass on the table, then picked up the bottle, again walking behind him.

"No, no, stop... please," Surya cried out, realizing what John was about to do.

John ignored him, pulled his head back by the hair, and started pouring Black Label into Surya's mouth. Surya struggled, but the more he twisted his head, the harder John pulled on his hair, causing Surya to keep his mouth open. Emptying half the bottle into Surya, his fingers cramping from pulling Surya's hair, he let him go and walked in front of him again.

Putting the bottle down, he sat in front of Surya, who was now whimpering, his chest rising and falling as he tried to regain his breath.

John waited until Surya had calmed down, watching him through the mesh of the *burqa* veil. Surya's chin hung on his chest, the top of his shirt damp with spittle and whisky, two streams of mucus running from his nose.

John sat forward, leaning his elbows on his legs, causing Surya to raise his head and look at him.

"Who... who are you? What do you want?" He sniffed. "Do you know who I am? You can't do this to me."

John reached up and lifted the veil over his head.

Surya peered at him, not registering at first, but suddenly, his eyebrows rose, his eyes widening in shock.

"You!"

John sat back in the chair and stared at him.

"Bastard! I'll have you killed!"

"Really?" John curled one side of his mouth in a half smile. "And how do you propose to do that?"

"I'll hunt you down. My people will hunt you down, you fucking English bastard."

John nodded calmly.

"What makes you think you are getting out of that chair?"

"Someone will come. I have security downstairs. They will come." Surya sniffed, cleared his throat, and spat at him, the globule of phlegm landing on the front of John's *burqa*. John looked down at it and shook his head, then grabbed the bottle and stood up.

Surya started struggling and kicking at the cable ties holding him to the chair.

John walked around behind him, grabbed his hair, pulled his head back, and started pouring again. As Surya coughed and choked, he hissed, "No one is coming, Surya. No one knows I'm here."

After a moment, he stopped pouring and moved back to the chair. He placed the now two-thirds empty bottle of Black Label back on the table and sat, waiting for Surya to get his breath back.

"You see, Surya," he said once Surya's breathing was back to somewhere near normal. "You hired two men to kill me." John looked down at his gloved hands, turning them over as if examining them, then looked up at Surya and shrugged. "I can sort of understand that. You were upset." He leaned forward and narrowed his eyes. "But what I will not accept is you coming after someone I love."

Surya shook his head. "That wasn't my instruction."

John pointed his finger at Surya. "You paid them. You are responsible."

"You killed my son."

John jumped to his feet and leaned over the table, grabbing Surya by the throat.

"Your mother-fucking, shit-bag of a son raped and killed my wife. He and his friends deserved everything they got," John snarled, squeezing harder and harder. Surya's face darkened as the blood flow reduced. He struggled to free himself, but filled with rage, John tightened his grip, digging his fingers into the fat flesh of Surya's neck. He wanted to squeeze the life out of this man, this man who had caused so much harm and destroyed the happiness in John's life. John squeezed and squeezed until somewhere from the back of his mind a note of reason sprang forth. This wasn't the plan.

John released his grip and straightened, shaking out his hands and fingers. Taking a deep breath, he exhaled slowly, calming himself as Surya panted. John stepped away and paced across the room. He needed to remain calm, not let anger get the better of him. Returning to his chair, he sat down and looked at Surya. The fight seemed to have gone out of him. Silent tears streamed down the side of his face as his lips quivered.

"He was my son..."

"He was an evil spoiled little shit."

"My son..." Surya trailed off into sobs.

John studied him. He had no sympathy. Men like Patil

dealt pain whenever they wanted their own way, but when it came back to them, they couldn't handle it.

Surya raised his head slowly, "Maadhavi? Did you...?"

John snorted. "I'm not like you. She's alive and well, but you'll never see her again."

Surya started sobbing again

John tilted his head to one side.

"Why are you sad? You raped her, took away her dreams, then kept her under your thumb, imprisoned in this ivory tower of yours."

"No, no..." Surya shook his head. "She was free."

"Really? If she didn't do what you wanted, you would cut off the purse strings, make sure she wouldn't get any work. Yes or no?"

Surya hung his head.

"Exactly. You are scum."

Surya raised his head, a look of hope on his face. His words, when they came out, were a little slurred.

"I'll give you money. How... much do you want?"

"It's not about the money."

Surya's eyes rolled, and he blinked as if having trouble focusing.

"Then... what do you... want?" His chin dropped to his chest, and his eyes closed for a few seconds. He blinked them open again and shook his head, trying to clear the fog.

John watched him, waiting for the mixture he had fed him to take effect.

"Listen to me, Patil." He lowered his head, so his eyes were on the same level as Surya's. "Look at me."

Surya looked up, but his eyes were unfocused.

"I could take your money and walk out of here with your promises to leave me alone." John moved his head, keeping eye contact with Patil as his head lolled. "Listen to me." Patil's eyes closed. John reached forward and slapped him. "Look at me. But what about the others? What about women like Maadhavi? What about the people who would get in the way of your deals? The poor, the people with no power? No." John shook his head. "The world will be better off without you."

Surya's eyes rolled back into his head, and his head fell backward.

John watched him for a moment, then stood and walked closer.

"Patil." He slapped him on the cheek. "Surya." No response. He was out cold. John exhaled, closed his eyes, took another deep breath, and exhaled slowly. Almost done. He knelt down, and taking out his pocketknife, began to remove the cable ties.

## 91

Rajiv paused in the entranceway and gazed around the beautiful space surrounding him. A glistening white marble floor spread out before him and a flower display three times his height took up the center of the lobby, orchids and lilies sending soft fragrance through the air. A chandelier sparkled from the ceiling three floors above. He had been to a few fancy hotels before, mainly for work, once on his wedding anniversary when he had treated Aarthi to dinner, but this was special. Walking to the reception counter, which stretched the length of the wall on the left side, the three staff members avoided eye contact and pretended to be busy, studiously shuffling papers under the counter. Rajiv chose one, a young man in his twenties, and stood in front of him. The young man looked up nervously.

"Can I help you, Sir?"

Rajiv looked down at his name tag. "Shashank." He gave the young man a big smile. "I need some help."

Shashank glanced at his colleagues, but realizing he wouldn't get any help from them, nodded.

"Surya Patil. Where does he go when he is here?"

"Sir..." Shashank shook his head. "Sir, I am not allowed to give that information."

Rajiv sighed. "Do you see my uniform?"

Shashank gulped. "Yes, Sir."

"Good." Rajiv leaned closer and lowered his voice. "I suggest you answer my questions. If you don't, you will have a lot more to worry about than your boss." Rajiv smiled again. "Do you understand me?"

Shashank nodded unhappily.

"Good. Now, where does he go?"

Shashank lowered his voice, dropping his head. "The twenty third floor. Suite 2301."

"He stays there?"

Shashank looked around, making sure his colleagues were out of earshot. He lowered his voice even more, so Rajiv had to lean forward to hear him.

"Maadhavi Rao."

Rajiv frowned. "The actress?"

Shashank nodded eagerly, warming to the subject.

"What about her?"

"Sir, she is his mistress. She stays there."

Rajiv pursed his lips and nodded slowly. He had heard some unusual things in his time, but this was up there with the strangest. He didn't get much time to watch films, but he knew who she was. He couldn't understand what a beautiful, successful actress like her was doing with a fat old toad like Patil. He was old enough to be her father.

"Thank you." Rajiv turned away, still puzzled.

Money and power—it had to be. A thought struck him, and he turned back to Shashank, whose look of relief at the end of the questioning quickly vanished. Rajiv pulled out his phone and scrolled to the photo app. He found the photo of John Hayes and held it up in front of Shashank.

"Have you seen this man?"

"No, Sir."

"Look properly. His appearance may have been altered."

Shashank peered at the screen again and shook his head. "No, Sir."

Rajiv looked toward the other staff. "Call them. We'll ask them too."

Shashank's colleagues came over, but they didn't recognize John either.

"What has he done, Sir?" Shashank's colleague, a young lady with a Bengali accent, asked. "He doesn't look like a bad person."

"None of your business." Rajiv scrolled through the photos and pulled up the artist's sketch of the intruder at Surya Patil's house. He looked at it doubtfully. Based on the servant's description, he wasn't confident they would ever find the right person. Anyway, it was worth asking.

"How about this one?"

The three staff peered at the phone, their brows wrinkled, but all three shook their heads. "Sorry, Sir."

"He looks like that cricketer," added the Bengali girl. "The Australian one."

Rajiv stifled a groan. "Thank you, you've—"

A loud crash followed by a scream and men shouting, cut him off. Spinning around, he saw people running outside the entrance. He stuffed his phone into his pocket and ran for the door.

## 92

Rajiv pushed his way through the silent crowd of armed police and hotel staff until he got to the front. Shit.

Where the windscreen of Surya Patil's Mercedes used to be was a body, half inside the car, the legs splayed across the crushed hood. The driver sat inside, his face white with shock, his body covered in white powder from the airbags, and blood streaming from what looked like a broken nose.

"Everyone, stand back." He raised his hands and stepped forward to get a better look at the body. Leaning forward, he angled his head so he could see inside the car.

"Shit, shit, shit," he cursed. He straightened up and looked around, catching Ankit's eye, nodding.

Ankit closed his eyes and shook his head. Rajiv looked at the body again, then turned and looked up at the hotel towering above them.

"No one touch the body," he commanded. "Ankit, come with me. Quickly!"

Rajiv ran back into the lobby, Ankit hot on his heels.

Spotting the reception staff by the door, Rajiv grabbed Shashank by the arm.

"Do you have a master key?"

Shashank nodded.

"Come with me." Rajiv pulled him by the arm to the lifts. He stabbed at the button and waited impatiently for it to arrive.

"Which floor? I'll take the stairs," Ankit asked, adjusting his MP-5, so it hung behind him.

"Twenty-Three. The lift will be quicker."

A chime announced the arrival of one of the lifts, and Rajiv pushed forward, pulling Shashank after them. They rode up in silence, and when the doors opened on the twenty-third floor, Ankit held up his hand, readied his MP-5, and poked his head out into the corridor. Rajiv waited until he gave the all clear, then followed him out. They walked down the corridor to the suite, then Rajiv, holding his finger to his lips, beckoned Shashank forward and pointed to the lock. Ankit shook his head and held out his hand for the passkey. Shashank handed it over, and Ankit motioned for him to step back out of the way. Passing the keycard to Rajiv, he raised his weapon and stood ready.

Rajiv stood to the side of the door, reached forward, and swiped the passkey in the lock. The lock whirred and clicked, the light turning green, and he pushed down on the handle. Ankit shouldered the door open, his MP-5 held ready, finger curled around the trigger and scanned the room. The door swung behind him, and Rajiv stuck his foot in the gap to prevent it closing. A moment later, Ankit called out, "Clear."

Rajiv glanced toward Shashank. "Stay outside. No one comes in."

Shashank nodded, happy not to get more involved.

Rajiv stepped inside the room and allowed the door to close behind him. Ankit stood, his weapon hanging by its sling, staring at the open balcony door, the evening breeze blowing the curtains toward him. He looked back at Rajiv and shrugged.

Rajiv turned his attention to the room.

"Have you touched anything?"

"No."

"Good. Don't." He walked over to the coffee table and noted the whisky glass and the almost empty bottle of Black Label. Beside it, among a faint dusting of white powder, was an empty foil strip of pills. He knelt down and peered at the label.

"What is it?"

"I don't know." Rajiv looked up. "I can't read the label and don't want to touch anything yet." Standing, he looked around—no sign of foul play. The suite was tidy, no sign of a struggle. He walked over to the balcony and stepped outside. Looking over the edge, he could see the crowd around the Mercedes far below. He turned and stepped back inside.

Ankit was watching him. "I didn't think he was the type."

"Type?"

"Suicide."

Rajiv shrugged and let his eyes scan the room again, looking for something out of place. He walked over to the kitchenette and the bar—an unopened bottle of vodka, a half empty bottle of Botanist, and no other used glasses. Taking out a pen, he lifted the lid of the rubbish bin—empty. He switched his attention to the bedroom. Walking in, he noticed the unused bed, the little brass Ganesha on the bedside table, and a copy of the book *Eat, Pray, Love* beside it with a bookmark showing it was half read.

He moved to the en suite. It hadn't been used that day. Below the mirror were a couple of women's perfume bottles and on a shelf in the shower cubicle, numerous shampoos and conditioners. He stepped into the dressing room, filled with women's clothing and shoes. There were a few empty hangers and spaces where shoes had been removed. A woman stayed here, which corroborated Shashank's story, but it looked like she hadn't been there today. Rajiv walked back out into the living room.

"I've seen enough. Let's go."

They stepped out into the corridor where Shashank was waiting.

"No one is allowed in this room. No one. Understand me?"

"Yes, Sir."

"Good. Stay here until one of my men comes up."

Rajiv turned to Ankit.

"Let's deal with the body."

## 93

Back downstairs, while Ankit set up a cordon around the Mercedes, Rajiv sent one of the uniformed constables up to guard the suite, made some calls, then went to inspect the body. He stood with his hands on his hips, wondering what would drive someone to throw themselves out of a twenty-three-story window, especially a man who seemed to have it made—one of the most powerful men in the state with untold wealth. It made little sense. Why would he do it?

He felt a presence at his side and turned to see Ankit beside him.

"Why would he do this?"

"Who knows?" Ankit shrugged. "His wife left him, maybe that's why?" He wrinkled his nose. "You can smell the booze on him. Maybe he just fell over?"

"No. The balcony rail is too high." Rajiv shook his head. "It doesn't make sense. If he was suicidal, then why go to all the trouble getting security to protect him."

Ankit turned to Rajiv.

"I've given up trying to understand these people a long

time ago. I just do what I'm trained for, ignore their insults, their strange habits, and every couple of months, I get to go home and see my wife and kids." He turned back to look at the body. "Can't say I'm sad to see him go, to be honest." He shrugged. "I'm glad he landed on his own car and not one of mine. Imagine the paperwork."

One of Ankit's commandos walked over and murmured something to Ankit.

"Where is he?"

The commando pointed toward a middle-aged man in a suit, hovering at the edge of the cordon.

"Let him through." Ankit turned back to Rajiv. "The G.M."

Both men turned and watched the man approach. His eyes darted toward the body, and he grimaced.

"Are you the hotel manager?" Rajiv asked.

"Yes, Anil Kripalani." He held out his hand, his eyes flicking from the body to Rajiv and back again.

"Detective Inspector Rajiv Sampath." Rajiv gestured to Ankit. "Captain Ankit Sharma, Special Ranger Group." He waited for Ankit to shake hands before continuing.

"We'll have this cleared away soon, but no one is to enter his suite until I say so."

"Yes, Sir." The G.M. looked at the body again. "This is terrible. That's Surya Patil."

"Yes. Tell me, who is staying in his suite?"

"Ah..." The G.M. cleared his throat. "Miss Maadhavi Rao, the actress."

"And where is she now?"

"Well, that's what I tried to tell Sir." His eyes went to the body again. "Earlier. She left this morning. She went to the airport."

"Are you sure?"

"Yes. She went in the hotel car."

"Do you know where she was going?"

"Yes, she told the driver she was going to Dubai for a few days."

Rajiv pursed his lips and nodded. "Okay. We'll be out of your hair as soon as we can. Please, don't speak to the press until we make an official statement. I'm sure your hotel won't want publicity of this nature."

The G.M. shook his head unhappily. "No."

"Here's my number." Rajiv handed over a card. "Give me your card. I'll be in touch if I need anything."

"Ruined his night," quipped Ankit as they watched the unhappy G.M. head back into the hotel. Ankit glanced over Rajiv's shoulder. "Now, it's your turn."

Puzzled, Rajiv turned his head and groaned inwardly as S.P.I. Muniappa approached through the crowd. He stopped and stared at the body of Surya Patil lying on the car. Ankit stepped a respectable distance away while Rajiv waited for the recrimination that was sure to follow.

"How could you let this happen?"

"Sir?"

Muniappa turned to face him and gestured toward the car. "This. He was in your protection!"

"Sir," Rajiv said through clenched teeth. "My job was to make sure we found whoever threatened him. If he throws himself out of a window, it's not the fault of my team or me."

Muniappa scowled and turned to look back at the body.

Rajiv couldn't help himself.

"I expect you'll need to pack your bags, Sir?"

Muniappa's head whipped around.

"What do you mean?"

Rajiv kept his face expressionless as if just stating the facts.

"Well, Sir, your benefactor is gone. We all know there's no one in the Progressive People's Alliance who can fill his shoes. Without Surya Patil, the party has no strength. He was the party. The opposition will take over." Rajiv shrugged, his tone level. "It definitely won't be pretty for anyone who benefited under Patil."

Muniappa scowled, drawing himself up to his full five-foot-seven height. Raising his hand, he pointed his finger at Rajiv. Rajiv braced himself. Muniappa opened his mouth as if to say something, hesitated, then his shoulders slumped. Rajiv watched as he turned on his heel and walked away.

Rajiv caught Ankit's eye and winked.

"That felt good."

Ankit grinned and reached out a hand.

"I'll leave you to it." He nodded toward the road where a line of police vehicles approached. "Looks like your guys are arriving. I'll stand my team down."

"Thank you, Ankit." Rajiv took Ankit's hand in both of his. "It's been an honor and a privilege. Despite the end result."

"For me too. Stay safe."

Rajiv smiled as Ankit walked away to gather his men.

Neither of them noticed the tall Muslim woman in a black *burqa* slip out the front entrance.

## 94

Rajiv sent half his team up to the suite to photograph the scene, take fingerprints, and bag the whisky bottle, glass, and pill strip. It was all a formality since everything pointed to suicide. As to why, that was anybody's guess. Rajiv had been on the job long enough to give up trying to understand the workings of people's minds. People never did anything that made sense.

Once the photographer finished photographing the body, Rajiv waved the staff from the morgue forward to take it away. The sooner it was out of there, the better. Someone had already tipped off the media, and they were crowding around the entrance, clamoring to be let in. Rajiv watched as the two men in dirty white coats pulled and tugged on the body, freeing it from the car's clutches. Patil's shirt rode up as they dragged him across the hood, exposing a bloated hairy belly.

There was no dignity in death.

His left arm flopped over the side of the car, and something about it caught Rajiv's eye.

"Wait."

He stepped forward and pulled out his phone. Turning on the flashlight, he shone it at the arm. Something had caught his eye, but he wasn't sure what. He ran the light down the arm from the shoulder to the wrist.

There.

Reaching forward, he slid Patil's shirt cuff higher. He frowned, peering closer at the red welts around the wrist. Leaning over the body, he grabbed the other wrist and slipped the cuff up, exposing a matching set of red marks. Rajiv stepped back and frowned. Strange.

"Sir?"

"Yes?"

The morgue staff looked at him expectantly.

"Yes, sorry. Take it away."

Rajiv watched them load the body into the ambulance, then turned and walked to the hotel entrance, deep in thought. Inside the lobby, he looked for Shashank and beckoned him over.

"Yes, Sir?"

Rajiv put a hand on his shoulder and drew him closer.

"Where is the control room for the CCTV?"

"I'll show you, Sir."

Rajiv followed him behind the reception desk, and through a door to the back office. Shashank opened another door at the rear of the office to reveal a security guard, watching a movie on his phone while sitting in front of a bank of black-and-white monitors. Shashank cleared his throat, and the guard glanced over his shoulder, then sprang to his feet, noticing Rajiv in his uniform.

"I want you to show me the feeds from today for the twenty-third floor."

The guard glanced at Shashank.

"Ah, Sir," Shashank stepped forward. "There are no

cameras on the twenty-third floor. Sir, that is, Mr. Patil didn't allow it."

Rajiv cursed inwardly. "What about the lifts?"

"Yes, Sir." Shashank nodded at the guard. "Show him."

Rajiv moved closer to the monitors. "Show me from... midday today."

"Yes, Sir." The guard entered a few commands on the keyboard, then pointed to three screens. "These three, Sir."

"Good, fast forward. I can't watch them in real time, it will take too long."

The guard fast forwarded the footage, and they watched as guests rode the lifts up and down.

"I'm looking for the man whose photo I showed you earlier."

Shashank nodded and stepped closer, concentrating on the scenes unfolding before them.

The three of them peered at the screens, pausing the feed now and then to double check a face before resuming the playback. The feed caught up to the present, but there was no sign of John. Rajiv closed his eyes and pinched the bridge of his nose. His instincts were usually good, but it looked like they had let him down today.

"Play it again."

"Yes, Sir."

Again, they watched, the footage racing past in a black-and-white blur. Rajiv sighed, nothing.

"Wait." He pointed at the screen on the right. "Go back. Slowly."

The guard rewound the footage frame by frame.

"There. Stop."

Rajiv leaned forward and stared at the screen. Despite himself, he felt his mouth twitch.

"You clever..."

"Sir?" Shashank leaned forward too and stared at the image of the guest in the lift, a woman in a *burqa*.

"I don't suppose you know who this guest is?"

"No, Sir. I've no idea."

"No, I didn't think so." Rajiv patted the guard on the shoulder. "Thank you." He nodded to Shashank and turned toward the door. "I've seen enough."

## 95

John flashed his lights as he slowed for the barrier. The security guard stepped out of his cabin and raised the boom. John drove through, smiling, and waving as he did so. The security should have stopped him, asked for identification and who he was visiting, but John knew from experience, they were often flustered when seeing a westerner, assuming they lived inside the gated community. Driving from memory, although it had been years since he and Charlotte had lived there, he took a left, then a right until he pulled up outside the familiar house. Pulling over, he wound down the window and switched off the engine. A light was on inside and a late model BMW 3 Series was parked in the carport. The bougainvillea climbing the pillars of the carport had grown a lot since John's time, and branches of red flowers cascaded over the roof, but the small patch of lawn was brown and in dire need of water—some things didn't change.

John felt strange sitting there, looking at the house where he had such happy times with Charlotte. He hadn't known what to expect but needed to see it, get some closure.

At first, he felt nothing, but then slowly, the longer he sat there, the memories came flooding back—mornings having coffee at the table on the back lawn, Charlotte's studio upstairs where he would find her when he returned from the office in her paint smeared jeans. An overwhelming sadness filled his body, tears welling. He gripped the steering wheel and closed his eyes. A clear vision of Charlotte appeared before him, the clearest for years. She was smiling, a lock of golden hair hanging down on one side of her face. She wore the blue shirt she always wore while painting, and her cheeks were smudged with color. She looked happy. She raised a hand to him, and John broke down as the stress and tension of the past few weeks gave way. He sobbed, banging the steering wheel until finally, the flood wave of emotion was spent, and he started smiling. Charlotte smiled with him, and he felt her reach to touch the tears on his cheek. John opened his eyes, wiped his face, and glanced toward the house.

"It's over, Charlotte. It's over."

Reaching forward, he twisted the key in the ignition. He had a long drive ahead of him.

## 96

John woke with a start, disoriented. Sitting up, he looked around. His shirt was stuck to him, his throat dry. It took a moment to realize where he was.

He had driven hard from Bangalore, taking National Highway 75 east toward Chennai before heading northeast at Chittoor, stopping only to bury the *burqa* in a hole on the side of the road. He had already thrown the cable ties and latex gloves out the window at various points on the journey. He skirted the famous temple town of Tirupati in the early hours of the morning before sleep finally got the better of him near the city of Nellore in Andhra Pradesh. Barely able to keep his eyes open, he had pulled off the highway onto a village road, then parked on the edge of a field. He had wound the windows down slightly, locked the doors from the inside, and reclined the seat. Within minutes, he was fast asleep.

Something had woken him. He raised his seat back and looked around. The sun was up, and he glanced at his watch. He had been asleep for just over three hours. There it was again, the sound that had woken him. In his fatigued state, it took a moment for him to realize his phone was buzzing. He removed it from his pocket and glanced at the screen. Damn it—Rajiv.

John thought for a moment. Should he take the call? His thumb hovered over the screen, indecisive. What were the risks? He was four hundred kilometers away from Bangalore. No one knew where he was, of that, he was certain. He wasn't a hundred percent sure himself where he was.

He answered the call.

"Good morning, Rajiv."

"Where are you?"

John forced a smile, hoping it would reflect in his voice.

"Rajiv, you keep phoning me in Dubai and asking where I am? Perhaps, you need to think about a change in career?"

"Did you kill Surya Patil?"

"I'm in Dubai. Why would you ask me that?"

"I'm serious, John. Did you kill him?"

John unlocked the door and climbed out of the car, stretching the kinks out of his back, then leaned against the front wing.

"How did he die?"

John heard a sigh.

"He appears to have fallen off a hotel balcony."

"Really? That was careless of him, but I have to say it couldn't have happened to a nicer person." John stared across the fields as he waited for Rajiv to respond. He could hear Rajiv breathing, but he didn't speak.

"Perhaps, he jumped? Maybe he finally felt guilty for all the shit he's caused?"

"John..."

John heard Rajiv sigh again.

"John, you can't keep taking the law into your own hands."

John watched a farmer guide his bullock cart down the track which led between the field John was parked in and the next one.

"Rajiv, did you hear the rumor about his affair with an actress?"

"Yes. Very recently."

"Well, I guess you won't have heard he raped her three years ago." John heard what sounded like a curse on the other end of the phone. "After raping her, he took control of her life, using threats and blackmail. Controlled what she did, who she met, what films she got."

"No, I wasn't aware of all this."

"I didn't think so. But now you know what I mean when I said it couldn't have happened to a nicer person."

John waited for a response. It was a while in coming.

"John, you know I have a duty. I have to do my job."

"I know, Rajiv. You are one of the few honest ones left."

"I don't think so anymore, John. I really don't think so."

John could hear the conflict in Rajiv's voice. He felt for the man who had become a friend of sorts. If only it wasn't death that had brought them together. John pushed himself off the car and scuffed at the ground with the toe of his boot.

"Don't worry, my friend. I won't trouble you anymore. Keep doing what you believe in. The world needs men like you."

Rajiv remained silent. John looked at his watch.

"I have to go. Take care, my friend."

He still had a long way to go before he was safe.

# 97

Feeling a hand on his shoulder, John opened his eyes and looked up at the smiling crew member.

"Sir, we are preparing for landing."

"Yes, yes, thank you."

John straightened his seat, folded the blanket, and stuffed it in the cubicle in front of him.

He had made the overland journey back to Kathmandu in two-thirds the time it took him on the way out, but it had taken its toll, and he had slept most of the six-hour flight from Kathmandu to Doha, then again on the eight-hour leg from Doha to Lisbon. He hadn't realized how exhausted he was until the flight had left Nepalese airspace, and he could finally relax.

John was looking forward to a long hot shower and a shave—his beard itched like crazy—but most of all, he was looking forward to seeing Adriana again. At least now, he was confident they could live the rest of their lives without having to look over their shoulders.

In the business class lounge in Doha, he had scanned

the internet for news of Surya Patil's death. All the reports spoke of his suicide and speculated about the reasons, most putting the blame on lasting depression since his son's suicide years ago, compounded by his wife leaving him. John was relieved his plan had worked, and no one suspected foul play. He ignored the adulations and lists of Patil's achievements—it was all bullshit.

Thirty minutes later, he was on the ground. Immigration was swift and efficient, and since he had no luggage, he headed straight for the arrivals hall. His stomach churned a little, and he could feel his heart rate increasing. He felt like he was on a teenage date again. John saw her before she saw him, and he stopped and stared. She was more beautiful than he remembered—tall and slim with her raven colored hair tumbling loosely over her shoulders. She scanned the arriving passengers until her eyes passed over him. Frowning, she looked at him again, then her eyes widened, and she jumped up and down. John grinned and walked toward her. She threw her arms around him as he lifted her off her feet, spinning around and holding her tight.

Burying her face in his neck, she hugged him as if afraid to let go. Pulling away, he looked into her eyes, eyes filled with tears. He leaned forward, kissed her lips, her eyes and forehead, then pulled his head back again and gently placed her back on the ground.

"It's done."

Adriana grinned and wiped the tears from her cheeks.

"Good." She grabbed both his hands. "Now, I'm not letting you out of my sight."

"I'm not planning on going anywhere."

"You look so different." Adriana raised an eyebrow as her gaze went to his hair. "I'm not sure about that. Your roots need doing." She let go of his hand and touched his beard. "But maybe this can stay."

John laughed, happy again for the first time in weeks.

## 98

SIX MONTHS LATER

John scanned his email inbox, mentally deciding what to read and what to ignore. An email from Steve with the subject line "Watch this" caught his eye. Intrigued, he opened the email. He hadn't spoken to Steve for months, not since he had settled his bill for keeping a watchful eye on Maadhavi Rao.

Clicking on the link in the email, his web browser opened, and the webpage of an Indian movie news site filled the screen. The video in the center of the page started autoplaying.

"At the Sudarshan Film Awards this evening, Maadhavi Rao accepted the award for best actress for her role in the movie *Hridaya Humbalisu Tade* - The Heart Yearns. Despite Maadhavi now being based in Dubai, her career has really taken off in the last few months, showing the promise that was seen earlier in her career. The persistent rumors of her alleged involvement with a senior politician who took his own life earlier in the year do not seem to be holding her back."

The video switched to Maadhavi standing on a stage, an

unusually shaped crystal award in her hand. The camera zoomed in as she made her acceptance speech. She was looking well, the dark circles gone from under her eyes, her face less puffy, her cheekbones now defined. She looked happy. John increased the volume.

"I'm grateful to all of you for the support you have given me. For a while, my career seemed to be stalling, and I am so grateful you had the confidence to stick with me, to keep coming to see my films. Thank you. There is a lot more to come." She looked down at the award, pausing for a moment, then held the award up in front of her and looked directly into the camera.

"Most of all, this award is for you, William." She winked. "Thank you."

# GLOSSARY

**Begum** - colloquially used to denote a married muslim woman

**Bhai** - literally brother, but also added to the end of names

**Burqa** - a long, loose garment covering the whole body from head to feet, worn in public by women in many Muslim countries

**Chai** - Indian tea

**Duppata** - a length of material worn arranged in two folds over the chest and thrown back around the shoulders, typically with a salwar kameez

**Jaanu/jaan** - my love

**Jai Gurudev** - Hail to the Guru

**Ji** - used with names to denote respect. Sometimes used as a respectful "yes"

**Kannada** - local language of the state of Karnataka

**Kurta** - a loose and long collarless shirt

**Paisa** - money

**Sadhu** - a holy man or ascetic

**Subedar** - In the National Security Guard (NSG Commandos), otherwise known as the "Black Cats" the rank of Subedar is a Junior Commissioned Officer

## ALSO BY MARK DAVID ABBOTT

### Vengeance - John Hayes #1

**When a loved one is taken from you, and the system lets you down, what would you do?**

John Hayes' life is perfect. He has a dream job in an exotic land, his career path is on an upward trajectory and at home he has a beautiful wife whom he loves with all his heart.

But one horrible day a brutal incident tears this all away from him and his life is destroyed.

He doesn't know who is to blame, he doesn't know what to do, and the police fail to help.

What should he do? Accept things and move on with his life or take action and do what the authorities won't do for him?

### What would you do?

Vengeance is the first novel in the John Hayes series.

**Available now on Amazon**

## A Million Reasons: John Hayes #2

### John Hayes is trying to move on but it's not easy.

Haunted by nightmares after the death of his wife he attempts to start a new life in Hong Kong, but the excitement and glamour of the city soon wears off and he finds himself deep in a rut. A mental state bordering on depression, a job he hates, and a salary that fails to last til the end of the month.

Until one day he finds a million dollars in his bank account!

It could change his life forever, but…..it comes with dangerous strings attached. Once again he is tested. Should he keep the money, break the law and potentially turn his life around, or should he give it all up and continue with his unhappy depressing existence?

Just how far is he willing to go?

What would you do?

### What people are saying about "A Million Reasons"

"A great read, definitely worthy of 5 Stars. Written by a true wordsmith who knows how to draw his readers in to an exciting story with a number of unexpected twists."

"The second book in the John Hayes series is even better than the first!!"

### Available now on Amazon.

## A New Beginning: John Hayes #3

A chance meeting with a fascinating woman has the potential to change John's life. Could she be the one to bring him the happiness he lost after his wife was brutally murdered?........ Will it be that easy?

Newly wealthy John Hayes is living an idyllic life in the exotic city of Bangkok. He spends his days keeping fit, exploring the city and enjoying the wonderful food but he is lonely,........and when a beautiful woman walks into his life he thinks he has a chance to start afresh.

But with John life is never simple.

A penniless young girl desperate to start a new life..........a high flying foreign businessman with a murky past.......an alluring woman....... all come together to test John once again. Should he get involved and potentially risk his life and the lives of others? Or should he walk away and lose the woman he is growing to love?

*"Great Book. Captivating. Well written and with enough suspense along with a bit of romance that keeps you turning the pages."*

**Available now on Amazon.**

# ALSO BY MARK DAVID ABBOTT

## No Escape: John Hayes #4

After a chance encounter in the lobby of a Dubai hotel, someone from the dark corners of John's past comes back to haunt him, threatening to sabotage an idyllic holiday and to annihilate everything John Hayes holds dear.

**No Escape,** another fast-moving page-turning thriller in the **John Hayes Thriller Series,** takes you from the glitzy hotels of Dubai to the vast desert sands of Oman, where once again John has to dig deep and call upon all his wits to fight evil and save the woman he loves.

*"These books are very difficult to put down! Like any truly good book, this thriller feels very realistic and I ride the suspenseful roller-coaster of emotions with every page turn. I look forward to seeing what's next for John Hayes..."*

Available now on Amazon

## READY FOR THE NEXT ADVENTURE?

The next book is currently being written, but if you sign up for my VIP newsletter I will let you know as soon as it is released.

Your email will be kept 100% private and you can unsubscribe at any time.

If you are interested, please join here:

**www.markdavidabbott.com**
(No Spam. Ever.)

## ENJOYED THIS BOOK? YOU CAN MAKE A BIG DIFFERENCE.

First of all thank you so much for taking the time to read my work. If you enjoyed it, then I would be extremely grateful if you would consider leaving a short review for me on the store where you purchased the book. A good review means so much to every writer but especially to self-published writers like myself. It helps new readers discover my books and allows me more time to create stories for you to enjoy.

## ABOUT THE AUTHOR

Mark can be found online at:
www.markdavidabbott.com

on Facebook
www.facebook.com/markdavidabbottauthor

on Instagram
instagram.com/thekiwigypsy

or on email at:
www.markdavidabbott.com/contact

- facebook.com/markdavidabbottauthor
- instagram.com/thekiwigypsy

Printed in Great Britain
by Amazon